I0523776

MAGGIE CHRISTENSEN

Secrets in Pelican Crossing

Copyright © 2024 Maggie Christensen

Published by Cala Publishing 2024
Sunshine Coast, Qld, Australia

This publication is written in British English. Spellings and grammatical conventions are conversant with the UK.

The moral right of the author has been asserted.

All rights reserved. No part of this book may be reproduced, stored in a retrieval system, or transmitted by any means, electronic, mechanical, photocopying or otherwise, without the prior written permission of the author.

This is a work of fiction. The locations in this book and the characters are totally fictitious. Any resemblance to real persons, living or dead, is purely coincidental.

Cover and interior design: J D Smith Design
Editing: John Hudspith Editing Services

Dedication

To my loyal early reader, Maggie,
who suggested the title for this book.

Also by Maggie Christensen

Oregon Coast Series
The Sand Dollar
The Dreamcatcher
Madeline House

Sunshine Coast books
A Brahminy Sunrise
Champagne for Breakfast

Sydney Collection
Band of Gold
Broken Threads
Isobel's Promise
A Model Wife

Scottish Collection
The Good Sister
Isobel's Promise
A Single Woman

Granite Springs
The Life She Deserves
The Life She Chooses
The Life She Wants
The Life She Finds
The Life She Imagines
A Granite Springs Christmas
The Life She Creates
The Life She Regrets
The Life She Dreams

A Mother's Story

Bellbird Bay
Summer in Bellbird Bay
Coming Home to Bellbird Bay
Starting Over in Bellbird Bay
Christmas in Bellbird Bay
Finding Refuge in Bellbird Bay
Escape to Bellbird Bay
Second Chances in Bellbird Bay
Celebrations in Bellbird Bay
Happy Ever After in Bellbird Bay

Pelican Crossing
The Restaurant in Pelican Crossing

One

Liz Phillips was enjoying a mid-morning cup of coffee on her balcony. From here she had a perfect view of the Pelican Crossing marina and across the bay to where her friend Poppy's house stood on the clifftop. She'd bought the apartment six years ago, after her divorce, and always felt at peace here among the pots of vegetables and herbs she'd established after reading the book by Indira Naidoo which described how to grow your own vegetables in a small space.

But this morning, peace was hard to find. Her mind was in a turmoil. It was her birthday, her fiftieth birthday. Where had the years gone? It seemed only yesterday she'd been a young girl eager for what life had to offer. These days, when she looked in the mirror, she could see the wrinkles and laugh lines around her eyes and mouth, and the black hair she'd been so proud of was now showing a few streaks of grey. The only things that hadn't changed were her eyes, that unique shade of green Tommy had told her had captivated him.

Tommy! It was six years since the divorce, since he'd left her. Her mind went back to those halcyon days when they'd first met.

Liz had had the reputation of being a bit of a wild child and a flirt until Tommy Phillips came to town and bowled her over. A Scotsman who was backpacking his way around Australia, he had found bar work at *The Grand Hotel* in Pelican Crossing. He'd only been there for a week when Liz walked in with a group of friends. They were there to celebrate her eighteenth birthday when it was legal for her to drink alcohol. Their eyes met and the rest, as they say, was history. She had sponsored him to obtain his resident's visa when Tara was on the way, and after they married, he'd taken out citizenship.

Tara's birth had taken them by surprise, but they'd both fallen in love with their little girl and had planned a large family. It was only after a few years of disappointment and several miscarriages that Mandy had arrived.

Tommy had continued to work at *The Grand*, progressing from barman, to manager, to owning the hotel. It was when Mandy was seventeen and just after Tara's marriage, a new barmaid had caught his eye. The news the girl was pregnant was the last straw for Liz who had turned a blind eye to his various affairs over the years. Tommy and his new love left town, the hotel was sold, and Liz started work at the medical centre vowing never to let another man into her life... until Mandy started to bug her about online dating, and Liz realised how lonely her life had become with Tara married and Mandy sharing a house with an old schoolfriend.

But the passing years weren't the only things disturbing her this morning. In the collection of cards she'd picked up from the mailbox when she returned from her early morning walk, there had been an envelope with unfamiliar writing, one which made her gut churn and sent her heart rate spiralling. It was one she'd been both hoping for and dreading for the past sixteen years. She'd read it and slid it into the drawer in her bedside table. She'd decide what to about it later.

She drained her coffee and rose. Tara and Mandy would be arriving soon. They were taking her out to lunch at *Crossings*, the restaurant owned and managed by her friend, Poppy, and she had to shower and change before then.

When she heard their voices at the door, Liz was ready, dressed in a pair of tailored navy pants and a blue and white striped shirt, her short hair a mass of curls which, to her surprise, showed the grey streaks to advantage and suited her heart-shaped face. A small, slim woman, she'd always worn her hair long until a few weeks ago when she'd decided to have it cut. She was still getting used to it.

'Happy birthday, Mum!'

First, Mandy, then Tara, hugged and kissed her.

'You're looking great,' Mandy said. 'Love the hair. I have to admit I wasn't sure when you said you planned to get it cut, but it suits you. Don't you agree?' She turned to her sister.

'I do. Despite the grey, I think it makes you look younger,' Tara said.

'Hmm.' Liz wasn't sure about that, but she was glad her daughters approved of her new look. 'Shall we go?'

The restaurant was a two-storey building situated across from the beach. Originally a fish shop, Poppy's parents had transformed it into a restaurant, then Poppy and her late husband had renovated the hundred-year-old building to create the prize-winning restaurant it was today. When they entered the restaurant, Poppy hurried to greet them. 'Happy birthday, Liz,' she said, hugging her. 'Let me show you to your table.'

Once they'd ordered the special of the day which was spanner crab lasagne with mango cheesecake to follow, they were surprised when Poppy sent over a complimentary bottle of Frogmore Creek chardonnay.

'Happy birthday again, Mum,' Tara and Mandy chorused as the three clinked their glasses.

'Thanks, girls. I'm feeling so spoiled. I can't believe I'm fifty.'

'A very young-looking fifty,' Mandy said with a grin. 'This is for you.' She handed Liz an envelope.

'Thanks.' Liz took a sip of wine before opening it. She didn't trust the gleam in her daughter's eyes. Inside the envelope was a card, and inside the card was a voucher for…

'A hot air balloon ride? You've got to be kidding!' Liz gazed at her daughter. Mandy had come up with a few weird ideas as birthday gifts over the years, but this was by far the strangest. Had she forgotten Liz's fear of heights?

'Come on, Mum. You'll love it. Just think, you'll be up above Pelican Crossing just as the sun is rising. What better way to celebrate turning fifty?'

Liz could think of plenty, one of which was to spend the day in bed. The previous few months had exhausted her, the work in the busy medical centre where she was practice manager taking its toll, not to mention the array of would-be partners from the online dating service – another of Mandy's *good* ideas.

She looked at her older daughter, hoping for support.

To her surprise, Tara said, 'Mandy may be right, Mum. Don't they say that fifty is the new thirty? You're not too old to try something new. It'll be an adventure, take you out of your comfort zone.'

'I think Mandy already helped me do that when she persuaded me to try online dating.' Liz couldn't forget the selection of no-hopers who had turned up, culminating in an email she'd rather forget.

'You didn't give that a chance either,' Mandy complained. 'As you've always told me, you have to kiss a few frogs before you find your prince.'

'They were certainly frogs.' But Liz laughed. 'Anyway, I won't be going down that route anytime soon. I'm quite happy being single.'

And she was, though she remembered telling her friends, the three women she met regularly for lunch, that she was still in her prime and sometimes it got lonely. But after her experiences with Happy Hearts, the online dating service Mandy had persuaded her to join, she knew she wouldn't find a new partner there.

It would be different, she thought, if she had grandchildren to fill her time, like her friend, Rachel. Even Poppy had become a grandmother recently, with two grandchildren and another two babies on the way. She gazed across the table at Tara. Her older daughter showed no sign of wanting to start a family.

'Don't look at me like that,' Tara said, as if she could read Liz's mind – which she often could; they had been very close since Tara was a child. 'You know Mark and I are in no rush to start a family. We want to do more travelling first. Just because Jess and Amber chose to have babies doesn't mean we have to,' she said referring to her two best friends who were thirty, the same age as she was.

'I'm only trying to help,' Mandy said, still talking about the hot-air balloon ride. 'Like I was with the online dating. I'm sorry you weren't prepared to give it a chance. But maybe a new experience will help. You have to admit you've been in a rut since Dad left.'

Liz was about to deny it, then she considered Mandy's words. Maybe she was right. After Tommy left and the hotel was sold, she knew her life had to change. The family home had been sold as part of the divorce settlement and she'd bought her apartment. She taken the job at the medical centre and her life had developed a new routine. Was she in a rut?

Their meals arrived, and the conversation moved to what they planned for Easter, which was only six weeks away, Tara surprising both Liz and Mandy by announcing she and Mark planned to travel to Paris for a couple of weeks and spend Easter there.

'What about you, Mandy?' Liz asked. Although she delighted in trying to arrange her mother's life, Mandy hadn't managed to find her own Mr Right. At twenty-four, she still had plenty of time, but Liz worried about how her younger daughter's relationships never seemed to last.

To her surprise, Mandy blushed. 'I'm going on a diving trip,' she said. 'Remember Gary Whittaker who I went to school with? His dad runs that fishing charter close to the marina.'

'Of course. I know who he is. Didn't he open a dive school alongside his dad's business last year?' Liz always managed to keep up with the local news, some gleaned through her work at the medical centre and some from Mandy herself. Among her friends it had earned her the reputation of being a gossip, but she just liked to keep informed and to share her news with others.

'Yes.' Mandy blushed again. 'We caught up again when a couple of my clients decided to learn to dive… and I joined them. He's organising this diving trip on Magnetic Island over Easter.'

'Sounds like fun.' Tara grinned at her sister.

Liz stared at her youngest daughter. Mandy had always been good at sport as a child, so it was no surprise when she decided to study to become a personal trainer rather than go to university. She wasn't normally secretive, usually sharing even the smallest details of her life with her mother, but this was the first Liz had heard of her learning to dive.

'I wasn't sure you'd approve,' she shrugged, clearly seeing Liz's stunned expression, 'and Gary and I… it may not last, but…'

'I don't have a problem with diving… or Gary. I agree with Tara. It sounds like fun.' But it meant Liz would be alone over the holiday weekend, a time they usually spent together as a family. Of course, she knew the time would come when her girls had other plans. She just hadn't expected it to arrive so soon… and so suddenly.

After lunch they all went for a walk along the beach before parting with more hugs and kisses, Mandy to get ready for her part-time job waitressing at the local yacht club, and Tara to return home to her husband.

Since she didn't feel very hungry, Liz decided to make do with cheese and biscuits for dinner, taking a plate through to eat in front of the television along with a glass of wine.

As she sat there sipping wine, she reflected on her day. It had been a good birthday with a few surprises. She loved the scented candle Tara had given her, but the voucher for the balloon ride… Would she take up the challenge Mandy had set her?

Then her mind went to the card she'd received that morning. There had only been a few words written there, but those words had the potential to change her life completely.

Two

Finn Hunter absentmindedly pushed his glasses onto the top of his head. He stared through the glass wall of his office to where his staff were busily composing stories for the next edition of *The Crossing Courier*, Pelican Crossing's local newspaper. They were a good bunch. He was lucky they'd accepted him so readily when he joined the paper as its editor only a year earlier.

It had been an upheaval to move from Bellbird Bay where he'd led the team at *The Bellbird Bugle* since moving to Queensland after his divorce. But it had been an easy decision to make when he received the call from his distraught daughter telling him her husband had perished in the ocean, swept out to sea when he was trying to save his five-year-old son.

It was a fluke Sandy had survived, rescued by another swimmer when his dad was caught in a rip and carried out to sea. His body was found several days later, by which time Finn had arrived to comfort his hysterical daughter. Sandy hadn't been aware what had happened at first and couldn't understand where his dad was. It was only a few days later it had sunk in that the father he loved was gone for good.

Finn had only left briefly to settle things temporarily back home in Bellbird Bay, hoping Adele would be able to cope. But she was so immured in her grief, Finn could see Sandy was suffering. For the little boy, it was as if he'd lost not one parent, but two. When Finn learned that the position of editor at *The Crossing Courier* was open, it was an easy decision to apply.

Now he was glad he had. Located several kilometres north of Bellbird Bay, Pelican Crossing was home to a large marina and a long stretch of white beach. It was the stopping off place to several of the islands for many visitors to the region and was a larger town than the one he'd left, the main street housing a string of old buildings, many of which had been renovated over the years.

In the short time he'd been here, Finn had joined several local organisations and liked to think his influence in these and with the newspaper had made a difference to the town. He had been flattered when he was invited to play a major part in a town meeting late the previous year. It was held in an attempt to prevent a Sydney developer from buying up property and spoiling the unique nature of the town. Fortunately, it had proven successful, though not for the developer who had been involved in an explosion leading to him suffering serious burns to a large proportion of his body.

But all of that was in the past, and while the story of the development and the explosion had filled the pages of *The Courier* for a time, it was now old news.

Adele was gradually improving, but was still in a state of grief, leaving much of Sandy's upbringing to her father. It was Finn who'd enrolled the little boy in school at the start of the school year and who dropped him off and picked him up every day, grateful his position as editor of the local paper allowed him the flexibility to do so.

Since his father's death, Sandy had become afraid of the ocean and while he still enjoyed playing in the sand, kept well away from the water. It worried Finn but he was unsure what he could do to help. He was also worried about the nightmares Sandy was having recently. In the past six months, the little boy had frequently wakened up screaming in the middle of the night, seemingly reliving his near-death experience.

Some days Finn felt burdened by worry about his daughter and grandson, and it was a welcome respite to get to the office where he could put them aside to concentrate on what was happening in the town and the world at large.

But perhaps things were going to change. He thought about his conversation with Adele over breakfast that morning, while Sandy was getting ready for school.

'I think I'm ready to look for work,' she said, twirling a strand of hair with her fingers. 'I feel I haven't been fair to you, Dad. You turned your life around for me and Sandy when…' She paused. She still couldn't talk about what had happened. 'But we can't lean on you for ever. It might even help Sandy if he could see me getting on with my life.'

'Are you sure?' While pleased to hear Adele was considering moving on with her life, Finn didn't want her to made decisions based on any feeling of obligation to him.

'Yes, I am,' she said, sounding more forceful than he'd heard her since he moved here. 'And I'm going to start by taking Sandy to school this morning.'

Finn had watched as a delighted Sandy took his mother's hand and the pair set off to walk to school. He hoped this would prove to be the beginning of Adele's return to a more normal life. Now, he was looking forward to returning home to discover if her new state of mind had lasted or if she'd sunk back into one of the bouts of depression that had plagued her over the past year.

*

'Grandy!' A small ball of energy barrelled into Finn as soon as he opened the door.

'Woah!' he said, picking Sandy up and twirling him around. 'Did you have a good day at school? Where's Mum?' Finn glanced around. The house was quiet.

'She took me to school and picked me up,' Sandy said, 'then she went to lie down.'

Finn's heart plummeted. This wasn't good.

'I'm hungry, Grandy.'

'Right. Let's get you some milk, and why don't I make you sandwich?'

'With Nutella?' Sandy asked hopefully.

'With Nutella,' Finn agreed, his eyes softening as he gazed at the little boy he loved so much.

Sandy was seated at the kitchen table with his milk and Nutella sandwich, his mouth rimmed with a mixture of milk and chocolate, and Finn was debating what they had to cook for dinner, when Adele appeared in the doorway.

'Sorry, Dad. I've had a busy day. I think I may have found a job, and I took a long walk along the beach thinking about Tim. He wouldn't want me to hide away, to leave everything to you, including Sandy.' She glanced across to where the little boy was happily munching on his snack. 'I just needed a rest. I'm fine now.'

'You sure?' She didn't look fine, her eyes still bleary from sleep. But Finn did detect a new sense of purpose about her, something he hadn't see in her since Tim died. 'A job? Where?'

'It was when I dropped Sandy off at school, I heard one of the teachers mention how one of the teacher's aides had suddenly left. Something just clicked with me.'

'You plan to apply?' Although she hadn't worked since before Sandy was born, Adele had trained as a teacher and worked in that role for several years before becoming pregnant. Being a teacher's aide was a bit of a comedown, but it was a start.

'I picked up an information pack. I spent the afternoon updating my CV before picking up Sandy. I think that's what tired me out. It was hard, remembering how my life used to be, before...' Her voice broke.

'Oh, sweetheart.' Finn pulled her into a warm hug. 'You'll be a great teacher's aide, and your hours will fit in with Sandy's.'

'If I get it.' Adele grimaced, but with the hint of a smile.

'You will. They'd be lucky to have you.'

'Maybe. Anyway, I'll give it a go. And I dropped into the medical centre and made an appointment with the counsellor. I know I need help.'

For a moment, Finn was too overcome to speak. Adele had been ignoring his suggestions she needed help since he came to live here. 'Well done,' he said, his voice hoarse with emotion. He cleared his throat. 'No need to worry about dinner. I've got it.' Finn had remembered there was some roast left over from the weekend and a pack of frozen chips in the freezer. 'Why don't you and Sandy go into the living room and you can hear his reading?'

Alone in the kitchen, Finn started to organise dinner. He had a smile on his face. He began to hum to himself. Maybe it was going to be all right.

Three

It was Wednesday and the day for Liz's lunch with her three friends, the gang of four as Poppy's husband had called them before he met his untimely death. The four women – Liz, Poppy, Rachel and Gill – had first met at a mother-baby group when they were new mothers and had immediately bonded. Their friendship had continued over the years and, even though their babies were now almost thirty, they continued to meet for lunch on a monthly basis. Liz was lucky her job at the medical centre allowed her one day off each month; this is how she preferred to spend it.

All the women, except Rachel who ran a B&B, took turns to host the lunch, and today it was Poppy's turn.

Liz loved going to Poppy's home. With its clifftop location, the house had views in both directions, towards the marina in one, and to the mouth of the Boodalang River in the other, boodalang being the aboriginal name for pelicans and where the town got its name. Poppy and her late husband had built the house, and their three children – all girls – had grown up there. All three were now married, two with children of their own and one pregnant with twins.

Liz felt the familiar twinge of envy when she thought of how her friend had become grandmother twice over only a few months earlier, as well as having a new man in her life. But the feeling didn't last. She was happy for Poppy who'd lost her husband in a freak accident just over five years earlier. Her friend had dealt with her grief by throwing herself into making the restaurant she and Jack had built together the success it was today; it had won several awards and been mentioned in a number of magazines. It was only fitting that she and Jack's best friend had finally got together.

'Liz, good to see you. How are you?' Poppy greeted her at the door, her little West Highland Terrier running around the two women and almost tripping Liz up in his excitement. 'Sorry about Angus,' she said, not waiting for Liz to reply. 'He's excited we have company.' She led Liz through to the large airy kitchen which led out onto a wide deck. 'Wine?'

'Thanks.' Liz was glad she was first to arrive. She knew once all four got together, the wine would flow as would the gossip. But whereas she was normally the one to provide the news about all the goings-on in Pelican Crossing, today she just wanted to sit quietly and listen. It had been three days. She still hadn't decided what to do about the card hidden in her bedside drawer. And it was weighing on her mind.

Poppy had barely poured two glasses of white wine when Angus began to bark, there was the sound of knocking at the front door, and suddenly the kitchen seemed to be filled with people.

'So, what's new?' Rachel asked looking around the group when they were all settled on Poppy's deck. 'I can see the new grandmother is glowing.' She nudged Poppy who grinned.

'Now Scarlett and Lachlan have moved back, and she and Megan are new mothers, I don't seem to have any time to myself,' she said.

I suppose it's nothing to do with the fact Cam Mitchell has moved in with you?' Rachel asked, winking.

Poppy blushed. 'That too,' she said. 'I'm just getting used to having a man around again.'

There was an awkward silence. Liz shifted uneasily in her seat and glanced at Rachel and Gill who appeared to feel equally uncomfortable. For the past few years, they'd all been single, Poppy and Rachel widowed, Liz divorced and Gill undergoing a divorce which seemed to be taking for ever to settle. Although they were all pleased for her, it was as if Poppy had left the club.

Liz decided to fill the silence. 'I have news,' she said. 'Tara and Mark are planning to spend Easter in Paris, and Mandy is going off on a diving trip with Gary Whittaker.'

Suddenly all eyes were on her.

Gill was the first to speak. 'Springtime in Paris,' she said. 'Max took me there once. It's a romantic city.'

The others stared at her in surprise. Gill rarely spoke of her husband other than to say how difficult he was being over their divorce. As a divorce lawyer herself she found it especially awkward that they didn't seem able to reach an agreement.

'Somewhere I always wanted to visit. Kirk and I planned to go there one day. There always seemed to be lots of time... then there wasn't,' Rachel said, referring to the fact her husband had died after a long illness.

'It's not too late,' Poppy said.

'For me, it is. I couldn't go on my own. I'd always been thinking how Kirk should be there with me.'

All four were silent, Liz thinking how different it would have been if Tommy had died instead of running off with a barmaid. Would it have been better? She wasn't sure. At least in her case, there were no more tears to shed.

'I didn't know Mandy had taken up diving,' Poppy said. 'When did she take lessons? I haven't seen her around the dive school.'

Liz suddenly remembered how, when Poppy and Cam got together, she had taken diving lessons and they had gone diving together. 'I don't know,' she said embarrassed. 'She only mentioned it at the weekend, and I think... her and Gary...'

'Oh, he's a great guy, a real chip off the old block. He reminds me of what his dad was like at his age. Jamie, Cam and Jack were all at school together and kept in touch. You must be pleased.'

'I think so, though she hasn't had much success with relationships in the past. I guess that's why she didn't tell me about him before now. I just hope...'

'It's all we can do.' Gill's eyes took on a faraway look, making Liz remember that her daughter, Freya was living overseas and was still unmarried.

'Do you hear from Freya?' she asked.

Gill sighed. 'She's not the world's best communicator. As you know she left Australia soon after Max and I separated. She was always her daddy's girl, and I suspect she's in touch with him. She doesn't answer my calls, but I continue to try, and I text her regularly too.'

'I'm sorry.' Rachel put a hand on Gill's arm. 'It must be difficult. I can't imagine what it's like not to know what's going on in her life. I often feel that way about Alexander, though he does call me regularly,' she said, referring to her son who also lived overseas.

'I'll just duck in and fetch lunch,' Poppy said rising, her words changing the atmosphere which was beginning to become melancholy.

'Can I help?' Liz rose too and joined Poppy in the kitchen.

During the delicious lunch of poached salmon served with a couple of salads, the conversation became more general, and Liz began to tune out. It was lovely sitting here on Poppy's deck, a gentle breeze wafting over them and the distant sound of the ocean. Now they were eating, Angus had settled under the table in the hope of some crumbs coming his way, and Liz could feel his soft furry coat at her feet. Although she wasn't fond of dogs and preferred cats, it was comforting to feel him there as her mind wandered.

She was brought back to the present by something Rachel said. She'd missed the earlier part of the story, but now she heard her friend say, 'It was so strange how they hadn't met since she was a baby, but they felt as if they knew each other right away.' Her ears pricked up, wishing she knew who or what Rachel was talking about, but she didn't want to ask, to admit she had been daydreaming.

When lunch was over, the women began to take their leave, Gill reminding them it was her turn to host next time. It would be almost Easter by then, and while Liz was resigned to spending Easter weekend on her own, she determined to have a family dinner before her girls left town.

On her way home, Liz's mind went back to Rachel's words, to the person who'd reconnected with someone they'd only known as a baby. Could it really be that easy?

When she arrived home, she went straight to her bedroom and opened the drawer. The envelope was still there where she'd placed it. She opened it and took out the note, her eyes blurring with tears as she read again the words she'd committed to memory.

I believe you are my mother. My name is Julie Barton and I was born in Brisbane on January 3rd 1990. I'd like to meet you. You can reach me at the above address, email or phone number. I hope to hear from you. Julie

Four

'Grandy!

Finn was awakened by Sandy pulling at his arm. He blinked, realising he'd fallen asleep on the sofa when he was supposed to be minding the small boy.

'Hey, little man. Did I go to sleep?' Finn rubbed his eyes and blinked again. 'Mum not back yet?'

Sandy shook his head, his eyes clouding.

Finn frowned checking his watch. He could only have been asleep for a few moments but had no excuse. He'd picked Sandy up again today because Adele had her first appointment with the counsellor. He'd set the little boy up with his milk and biscuit and dropped into an armchair intending to check the emails on his phone. He must have closed his eyes. 'Okay, champ. Just give me a minute.'

Sandy chuckled, his eyes twinkling. He loved it when Finn called him champ. It had started when the little boy had beaten him in a game of Go Fish when he was only four. Finn told him he was a champ, and the name had stuck. 'Okay.'

Finn quickly sluiced his face with cold water, slipped his feet into a pair of sandals and took his and Sandy's hats from the hook by the door. Even though it was late afternoon, the February sun had a bite in it and the UV index was still high.

'No swimming,' Sandy said, his eyes clouding over again, as he took Finn's hand.

'No swimming,' Finn agreed. Sandy had suffered another nightmare the previous night, his loud scream at two a.m. wakening Finn who had taken him into bed with him. It had been difficult to get back to sleep with the small, hot, wriggling body beside him, probably why he'd fallen asleep in the chair. 'How about we take your bucket and spade? I bet we can build a great sandcastle. I'll just let your mum know where we're going,' he said, taking out his phone to send a quick text. 'Maybe she can meet us there.'

At the beach there were a few teenagers messing around in the sea, enjoying the release after a day in the classroom, several surfers who never seemed to have anything else to do but spend their days searching for the best wave, and an elderly woman with long, white hair and wearing an ankle-length skirt which trailed in the water was walking with her dog at the edge of the ocean.

'It's the pelican lady,' Sandy said, clinging to Finn's hand as they made their way across the sand.

Old Agnes was sometimes called the pelican lady because she cared for rescued and injured pelicans and other seabirds. It was said she cared more for her wild creatures than she did for people, living as she did on a piece of land by the river and looking like an aging hippie. Finn had met her soon after he arrived in Pelican Crossing and had been impressed by her knowledge of the birds and her apparent fitness for someone of her years, though no one seemed to know exactly how old she was.

'Would you like to talk to her dog?' Finn asked. It might be a way to help Sandy overcome his fear of the sea. But the little boy recoiled as if he'd been stung.

'Can we get a dog?' he asked, watching the spaniel sniffing around in the shallow water.

'Maybe.' It was something Finn hadn't considered, but perhaps having a dog would help Sandy's nightmares... or perhaps not. 'Shall we build that castle?'

'Yes, please.' Finn noticed how Sandy ensured they were some distance from the edge of the ocean before he set down his bucket and spade.

*

'Wow, that's quite a castle. Did you build it all by yourself?'

Finn stood up at the sound of Adele's voice.

'Grandy helped, but I did the turret,' Sandy said beaming with pride.

'A castle needs a turret,' Finn said seriously.

'It certainly does.' Adele smiled.

'How was it?' Finn asked his daughter.

'Good. I'll tell you later. Hungry, Sandy?'

'Yes. Will my castle still be here tomorrow?' he asked Finn, his forehead creasing with worry.

'It may be, but we can always build another one.'

Sandy didn't look happy but picked up his bucket and spade. 'Can we have fish and chips for dinner?' he asked hopefully.

Finn glanced at Adele who nodded. 'I think we can manage that,' he said, 'but home first to wash off the sand.'

As Sandy ran ahead to the car, Finn drew Adele aside. 'Was the counsellor any help? Will you go to him again?'

'Yes, to both, and she's a woman, Olivia Grace. She's nice, easy to talk to. She thinks Sandy should see her too.'

'Sandy?' Finn frowned. 'Isn't he too young?'

'She suggested he could be suffering from PTSD, and it might help to have counselling. She treats children too.'

'PTSD?' Finn knew what it was but had only heard of it in relation to soldiers returning from a war zone, or more recently police or those who'd experienced some form of terrorism. Sandy was a five-year-old child. Then he remembered the boy's nightmares, how he woke up screaming and in a cold sweat. He was reliving his experience in the surf over and over again. He had suffered a traumatic event. 'If you think it would help.'

'Talk later,' Adele mouthed as they drew near to the car where Sandy was waiting.

'Grandy says we can get a dog,' Sandy announced as Finn started up the car.

Adele turned to look at him, eyebrows raised.

'I said maybe,' Finn said, but he knew he'd be unable to disappoint his grandson.

'I think I'd like one like the one the pelican lady has,' Sandy decided. 'What's it called?'

Adele looked at Finn again.

'A spaniel.' Maybe a spaniel would be okay. From what he knew, they were a friendly breed and good with children.

'A spaniel,' Sandy repeated happily. 'Can we get a boy? I'm going to call him Bluey.'

Finn and Adele exchanged glances. As far as Sandy was concerned it was a done deal; he'd already decided on a name for the dog, calling him after his favourite cartoon character.

'I'll check out if there are any spaniel puppies available,' Finn said, giving in to the inevitable. He'd never been able to deny his grandson anything, and maybe having a puppy to love and care for would help ease his trauma.

Five

Liz stared at the note. Should she, shouldn't she? Why now? She thought back to that time all those years ago, a time which was etched on her memory.

She'd only been fifteen, and like all fifteen-year-olds had never considered the consequences of her actions. When the captain of the school footy team invited her to a party, a real grown-up party with alcohol and other substances, it never occurred to her to refuse. All she could think of was that John Barr had noticed *her*, invited *her*, that the boy she'd spent the past year pining over had finally asked her on a date.

Knowing her parents wouldn't approve, she'd told them she had a sleepover with her friend, Chrissie. And she had gone to Chrissie's, but only to dress in the outfit her parents would never have let her leave the house in, the one she'd bought with the Christmas money from her grandparents, the money she told her parents she'd banked. In this dress and with her makeup, she knew she looked older, old enough for anything.

The party was wilder than she'd anticipated, but she'd joined in the drinking, even agreed when John led her into a bedroom, willing to do anything to please him, even…

After the party he'd dropped her, telling her she was too young, and only a week later was seen with one of the senior girls. She remembered how humiliated she'd felt.

But it was nothing compared to how she'd felt a couple of months later when she discovered she was pregnant.

Her parents had been wonderful. After the initial shock, they'd decided to move from the small country town where everyone knew everyone's business. Liz left school, her dad got a transfer to the city, and Liz agreed to give the baby up for adoption. Until she held her baby girl in her arms, she hadn't realised what a wrench it would be, how she'd never forget the sight of her tiny features or the feel of her soft skin against her cheek.

After the birth they moved again, this time to Pelican Crossing where Liz was enrolled in the local school for her final years. It was as if it had never happened, but it had. And now her daughter had contacted her.

She'd always known it was a possibility when she'd added her name to the contact register. But as the years went by – her daughter's eighteenth birthday, her twenty-first, her thirtieth – she'd given up hope. Now it had happened, she felt numb.

She stared at the note again as if she could conjure up the image of the girl who had written them, no longer a girl, a thirty-four-year-old woman. What would Tara and Mandy think? They had no idea they had an older sister, the result of their mother's youthful indiscretion. Would they be horrified or accepting? Liz had no idea. Then there was her mother… Liz's dad was gone, but her mother lived in comfortable retirement in *The Haven*, a retirement village on the outskirts of town. How would she react to the news that the daughter Liz had given up for adoption had been in touch?

It would be easy to ignore it, but what if Julie decided to turn up in Pelican Crossing? Could Liz wait for that to happen?

It was all too difficult. Placing the card back in the envelope before dropping the envelope back into the drawer and slamming it shut, Liz changed into a pair of three-quarter pants and a tee-shirt and headed to the beach.

The beach was almost deserted. Liz had spent more time lost in the past than she'd realised, and by now most beachgoers would have gone home or to somewhere to have dinner. The tide was out, and she pounded along the hard sand at the edge of the ocean, her thoughts still with the past and the girl who she only remembered as a baby. Julie. It was a nice name. It made Liz think of Julie Andrews and *The Sound of Music* which she'd watched on television recently with Mandy.

By the time she arrived home again, Liz was exhausted but no further forward in her thinking. Pouring herself a large glass of red wine and lighting the scented candle Tara had given her for her birthday, Liz carried both into the bathroom and ran a hot bath into which she sprinkled a few drops of the relaxing oil she'd received from Mandy at Christmas – one of her younger daughter's better gifts. Maybe a relaxing soak would help her decide what to do.

But as she took a gulp of wine and laid her head back against the end of the bath, she knew she didn't have a choice. She needed to meet Julie, to find out what her life had been like, to discover why she had waited till now to contact her, to see what she looked like. Would she resemble Liz, one of her other daughters… or would she look like the boy Liz had tried so hard to forget?

She dried herself off, pulled on a robe, poured another glass of wine, took the envelope out of the drawer, opened her laptop and began to type.

Six

Saturday was usually a quiet day for Finn, the most recent edition of the paper having gone to press the previous day. There was really no need for him to go into the office, but he liked to check on those of his staff who were searching for news for Tuesday's paper.

Today, Adele was taking Sandy for his first appointment with the counsellor, and Finn had decided to search the internet for spaniel pups. Sandy hadn't stopped talking about "his dog", and Finn didn't have the heart to disappoint him. It might be a good idea to have a dog, anyway. He'd had one when he was Sandy's age, a mutt with a touch of cattle dog and terrier called Rebel. He'd taken that dog everywhere, even snuck it into his bed when his mum wasn't looking. He remembered snuggling up to the animal when he was in trouble, which happened a lot. He must have been a worry to his parents.

As soon as Adele and Sandy left, he made a mug of coffee and took it through to the room he used as a study. The house really belonged to Adele, but she'd begged him to live here with her and Sandy, unable to bear what she claimed was the emptiness in the house with Tim gone. So far, it had worked, but sometimes Finn longed for his own place, where he had no need to ensure he left the kitchen tidy, could spread his papers over the dining table without them being in the way, and where he could wander around naked if he wished.

He fired up his laptop, put on his glasses and typed in spaniel pups for sale, to be presented with a range of advertisements.

Half an hour and another mug of coffee later, he had managed to find two breeders who listed pups which would be available in four weeks' time, just before Easter. Sandy's birthday fell around that time too, so all being well, he could have his Bluey as a birthday gift. He picked up his phone.

By the time Adele returned with an excited Sandy, Finn had made arrangements to visit one of the kennels which was situated in the hinterland, an hour's drive away.

'Guess what?' Sandy said. 'Livia gave me chocolate.'

'Chocolate? Mmm, that sounds good.' Finn raised an eyebrow in Adele's direction.

'Later,' she mouthed. 'Why don't you go and wash your hands while Grandy and I get lunch,' she said to Sandy.

Once he had gone, she said, 'She was so good with him, got him to talk about his nightmare, to draw what he saw, made it into a game.'

'Must have been a relief.'

Adele nodded. 'She says he'll need a few sessions but believes she can help him get over the trauma of seeing his dad disappear under the waves.'

'Let's hope so. Lunch?'

'There's some leftover chicken, and I can put together a salad.'

'Let me do it. You've had a stressful morning.'

'Thanks. It was harder than I thought, sitting there watching through a two-way mirror, but it seemed to go well. And he did get chocolate.' She laughed.

It was good to see Adele laugh. There had been times over the past year when he thought she'd never laugh again. But since she'd decided to apply for the job at the school, she seemed to have turned over a new leaf. Finn could still hear her sobbing in her room some evenings, but she was managing to get out more and to put on a brave face when he and Sandy were around. It was going to take her time to get back to normal, if one ever did after the death of a loved one.

'I've been busy too,' he said as he unpacked the makings of lunch from the fridge. 'How do you fancy going to check out spaniel pups this afternoon?'

'Puppies? We're going to get Bluey?' Sandy appeared and caught the end of Finn's conversation.

'Not today, champ,' Finn laughed. 'The puppies are too small to leave their mummy. But we can visit them, and you can choose which one you want.'

Sandy's eyes grew bigger. 'Really? I can choose my Bluey? Can we go now?'

'Lunch first,' Adele said, 'and say thanks to Grandy for spending his morning searching for puppies for sale, when I'm sure he had a lot of other demands on his time.'

'Thanks, Grandy,' a subdued Sandy said, then his excitement rose again, 'but we are going to see them.'

'Yes, mate. After lunch and maybe after your mum has a rest.' He glanced at Adele. 'I said we'd be there at three-thirty, so there's no rush.'

'Thanks,' Adele said.

But Finn could see Sandy wouldn't be satisfied till they were actually on their way.

*

By quarter past two, Finn, Adele and Sandy were in his car, Sandy unable to control his excitement any longer. As they drove up into the hinterland, Finn could sense Sandy bouncing around in the back seat. He hoped he wasn't in for a disappointment. The person he'd spoken to on the phone, Rhana Black, had said they had six pups, four of which were already spoken for. 'Your grandson can choose from the remaining two,' she'd said. 'Both are male, one golden, one a blue roan.' She'd continued, 'Spaniel pups are very energetic and fun-loving. They remain like that all their lives. They are also loving and affectionate. I'm sure you'll be very happy if you do decide on one.'

It was the first time Finn had driven up this way, and he was enjoying the change of scenery as they moved away from the coast into what appeared to be farmland, some of which was planted with sugarcane, the tall green plants bordering the roadway.

'It's lovely up here,' Adele said, 'but I prefer the coast, even though…' Her voice broke.

Finn frowned. She'd been doing so well, but it would take time for her to heal.

'Sorry,' she said. 'Do you know what these tall plants are, Sandy?' she asked.

'Sugar cane,' he said proudly. 'I saw a programme about it on television. There was a boy who lived on a sugar farm, and he drove the harvester when he was only a bit older than me.'

'Where?' Finn asked Adele quietly.

Adele shrugged. 'At school, or when I was asleep. There are a lot of educational programmes on the ABC.'

'He must have enjoyed that,' Finn said in a louder voice.

'I think he did, but it looked hard. I don't think I'd like to live on a farm.'

Just as well, Finn thought. Getting a dog was a big enough challenge.

'Are we there?' Sandy bounced even harder when Finn stopped the car at a gate on which there was a metal sign with a picture of a spaniel and the words *Spaniels Live Here*. 'Oh, look!' he yelled as he caught sight of the sign.

'I guess this is it,' Finn said with a grin. It was so easy to become excited when you were only five.

They drove up the dirt driveway to a house nestling among a mixture of palms and pandanus to where a tall, heavily built woman wearing jeans and a tee-shirt bearing a picture of a spaniel was waiting to greet them.

'You must be Finn Hunter,' she said, 'and this is…'

'My daughter, Adele, and…'

'I'm Sandy and I'm here to get my dog,' Sandy announced before Finn could introduce him.

Rhana laughed. 'Well, you'd best come with me.'

She led them around the house. 'We keep all the puppies in the house with us,' she explained on the way. 'It gets them used to being with people and it's easier to train them. But this is their playtime and they and their mum are in what we call the playpen.'

Now they were about to see the pups, Sandy held back, clutching Finn's hand.

'All six puppies are here,' Rhana said, 'but only two of them are available.'

As they approached a large, fenced, grassed area, Finn could see the pups cavorting around. They were still pretty tiny.

Sandy let go of Finn's hand to press his face against the fence, his eyes wide with delight. 'There's Bluey!' he said, pointing to a whitish dog with black markings. The spaniel looked nothing like the blue heeler the cartoon dog was based on, but it didn't seem to matter to Sandy pointing at the blue roan spaniel.

'Is he…?' Adele asked, clearly worried the dog might already have been purchased.

'He's available,' Rhana said. 'He's a good choice, Sandy,' she said to the little boy, but he wasn't listening, completely engrossed in watching the puppies. Rhana turned to Finn and Adele. 'The blue roan is one of the most common types of spaniel. As he grows, his coat will change in colour. Blue roan is the name given to cocker spaniels which have a blend of black and white hairs throughout their coat, and each blue roan coat is individual with varying combinations of mixed black and white hairs. Most of the time the mix is fifty-fifty, and the coat will often appear greyish in parts.'

'Can we take him home today?' Sandy asked, apparently having forgotten what Finn had told him.

'Not today, Sandy,' Rhana said gently. 'He's still too little to leave his mummy. He won't be ready to leave her until towards the end of March.'

'My birthday's on the twenty-fifth of March,' Sandy said. 'I'm going to be six.'

'Well, I think Bluey might be ready to go home with you by then.'

'Can he?' Sandy looked at Finn, his eyes about to pop out of his head.

'Oh, I think we can arrange that, don't you, Mum?' Finn asked Adele.

'Would you like Bluey to be your birthday present? It might mean you wouldn't get anything else,' Adele said. She'd clearly seen the cost of the pups on the internet.

'Yes, please!'

The three adults laughed. There was something about the child's delight that made them all feel good.

Leaving Sandy watching the dogs, Finn and Adele followed Rhana inside where they paid for the pup and arranged to pick him up in a few weeks' time.

'Home now?' Finn said when they rejoined Sandy, carrying the folder Rhana had given them listing all the items they'd need before taking their pup home.

'Do we have to?' Sandy turned reluctantly from the fence.

'The puppies will want to have a sleep soon,' Rhana said. 'Your puppy will be waiting for you on your next visit.'

'Okay.' With one last look at the pups, Sandy allowed himself to be led away to the car.

'I love my Bluey already,' Sandy said when he had been strapped into his car seat. 'I'm going to take him for walks and feed him. Can he sleep with me, Mum?'

'I don't think that's a good idea,' Adele said with a frown.

'I think Bluey might prefer to have his own bed,' Finn said. 'Rhana gave us a list of all the things we need to buy for him. We can visit the pet shop and you can choose his bed for him.'

Seemingly satisfied, Sandy became silent, so silent that Finn glanced in the rearview mirror to see the little boy had fallen asleep.

'Thanks, Dad,' Adele said, after glancing back too. 'I haven't seen Sandy so excited and happy since… I just hope…'

'Don't worry. I know about dogs. I can teach Sandy how to take care of him. You heard what Rhana said. Spaniels are loving and affectionate animals. It may be exactly what Sandy needs. With a dog and the counsellor…'

'Thanks, you're right. I probably worry about him too much. He's all I have left of Tim…'

'I understand,' Finn took one hand off the steering wheel to pat her knee, 'but he's a good lad. He'll be fine. The dog can't replace Tim in Sandy's life, but it's something else for him to love… and to love him too.'

Seven

Now Liz had sent off the email to Julie, she was impatient for a reply. What if the girl… woman had changed her mind? She couldn't bear to have her hopes dashed. But it had only been three days since she'd laboured over the email before deciding to make it brief. If they did meet, there would be time enough for explanations.

But today, she had something else to think about. Unable to withstand Mandy's continual nagging, she'd given in and booked the hot air balloon ride. This morning, she'd risen before the sun was up to meet her daughter an hour before dawn in a paddock outside town where the balloon was to take off. She was so nervous she hadn't been able to eat anything before she left but had managed to gulp down a cup of coffee.

'You're going to love it, Mum.' Mandy greeted her when she stepped out of her car, sorely tempted to get back in again and drive away. She loved the little, red, soft-topped Fiat she'd bought herself after the divorce. Tommy would have hated it, considered it was a toy car, but it suited her much better than the safe family Volvo he'd always insisted she drive. Maybe her purchase of the car had been one way of thumbing her nose at him and his opinions.

Liz gazed across the paddock to where a small group of people were standing around a basket sitting on its side on the ground, and two figures seemed to be shooting flames into a large piece of material which was gradually inflating to form a balloon. As the basket righted itself, Liz took a deep breath. It was too late to back out. What had Mandy let her in for this time?

'I'll see you when you get back,' Mandy said, giving Liz a hug. 'You can tell me all about it.'

If I survive, Liz thought, but she listened carefully to the instructions of the man who appeared to be in charge and soon she had joined the excited group in the basket, above which floated the balloon. It somehow didn't look big enough to support them in the air. Liz's stomach churned.

'Hold on,' the man said – he'd introduced himself as Steve and spoke with an American accent – and with a few bumps they were off the ground and in the air. Liz closed her eyes. Maybe, if she didn't look down, it would be all right. She had trouble standing in front of a full-length glass window, what would it be like to have only a fragile basket between her and… nothing?

There was the sound of excited chatter from the others in the basket. Liz cautiously opened her eyes. Holding tightly to the edge of the basket, she risked looking out… and down.

It was different from what she'd expected. It wasn't as scary. They were floating with the breeze several metres in the air and gradually getting higher, but… she was no longer afraid. She took in the bird's eye view of the shoreline and the bay below and began to understand how many people found it exhilarating. While she wouldn't go so far as to describe the experience in those terms, and might not choose to repeat it, she was glad Mandy had persuaded her to ditch her inhibitions and come along. Seeing her hometown from this angle brought a whole new perspective. It all looked so beautiful, so calming, and the air up here seemed so very fresh. She breathed it in, enjoying the surreal tranquillity.

Nevertheless, it was a relief to set foot on solid ground again. 'Thanks,' she said to Steve as he helped her out of the basket. 'That was quite an experience.'

'No problem. Glad you enjoyed it. It's Liz, isn't it? You're Mandy's mum?'

'That's right.' How did he know? How well did he know Mandy? He was closer to her age than Mandy's, and wasn't Mandy seeing Gary Whittaker?

'Well?' Mandy greeted her.

'It was… good, better than I expected.'

'I told you you'd like it.'

'But I don't intend to do it ever again,' Liz added, seeing a gleam in her daughter's eyes.

'We'll see. How about breakfast?'

Liz suddenly realised she was hungry. The fresh air and, yes, she had to admit, the exhilaration of the balloon ride had given her an appetite.

'*Blue Dolphin*?' Mandy asked. The café close to the marina was a favourite of theirs, though not one Liz normally frequented for Sunday breakfast.

'Meet you there.'

When she reached the café, the first person Liz saw was her friend, Poppy, who was with Cam Mitchell, the pair looking very loved up. She'd forgotten they made a habit of having breakfast there on Sundays, had done for years. Seeing them together brought home to Liz how much nicer it would be to be having breakfast with a man rather than her daughter.

She smiled at them, then she saw Mandy waving to her from a table in the far corner of the café and chastised herself. She should be grateful for what she had. She walked over to join her.

'What did you think of Steve?' Mandy asked when they had ordered and been served coffee. 'Isn't he hot?'

Liz stared at her. 'Steve? I thought you and Gary…'

'Not for me, Mum. He's more your age.'

'Oh, Mandy, you're not trying to matchmake again?'

'Just saying.' There was a wicked twinkle in Mandy's eyes, one Liz had seen before, when she signed her up for Happy Hearts.

'Well, don't.' Steve had been a fine figure of a man, but what was someone of his age doing arranging hot air balloon rides? It was something for a younger man, one who was still making his way in life. Then she remembered how he'd known her name, known she was Mandy's mother. A sudden thought occurred to her. 'You haven't been talking to him about me, have you? How do you know him?'

Their meals arrived, eggs benedict for Liz, and smashed avocado with roasted tomato and feta on sour dough toast for Mandy, preventing her from replying.

'Well?' Liz asked when the waitress had left, having ascertained they didn't want more coffee.

Mandy shifted uncomfortably in her seat. She took a sip of coffee. 'I do know him,' she said at last. 'He dropped by one of my classes to hand out some brochures. It's where I got the idea for your birthday. Since then, we've bumped into each other a few times. He often eats at the yacht club, seems to be a bit of a loner. I may have mentioned your name, said I had given you a voucher for the balloon ride.' She put up both hands in a defensive gesture. 'I swear that's all. But you have to admit…'

Liz couldn't help smiling. Mandy was incorrigible. 'He's a good-looking man. I'll admit it, but…'

'And he's single.'

'You didn't ask him?' Liz was shocked. Surely even Mandy wouldn't go that far?

'Have a heart. He always comes to the yacht club on his own. It a sure giveaway. He's usually there on Thursdays. You could just happen to be there too…'

'Enough!' If they weren't in a public place, Liz would have hit Mandy with something. As it was, she just glared at her. 'I thought you had enough trouble finding a man of your own without trying to find one for me too.' As soon as the words were out of her mouth, Liz regretted them. 'Sorry, Mandy,' she said seeing her daughter turn red, 'I don't know where that came from. But you have to leave me to live my own life the way I want to. *If…* and only if… I want a man in my life, I'm perfectly capable of finding one for myself.'

'Sorry, Mum. I was only trying to help. I love you and I sense you're lonely sometimes. I want to see you happy. I don't want you to spend the rest of your life alone.'

'I'm sorry too. I shouldn't have spoken to you like that. Shall we forget this conversation ever happened?'

'Let's.'

For the remainder of their meal, they kept to general topics, to how Mandy planned to expand her personal training business, and how Liz would spend Easter with both Tara and Mandy gone.

'I intend to spoil myself rotten,' Liz said, 'binge my favourite shows on Netflix and catch up with my reading. You'll both be back before I know it.'

But after she'd left Mandy with a hug and a kiss, and was driving home, Liz thought back to their conversation. Mandy was right. She did get lonely sometimes. It would be nice to have someone to come home to at the end of the day, to cuddle up to in bed. She had a vague recollection of saying – or of someone saying – something similar at one of the lunches with her friends. They had all been in the same boat, but now Poppy had a man in *her* life.

The image of Steve, the man she'd met that morning, floated into her mind. Would it be too blatant to do what Mandy suggested, to go to the yacht club one Thursday for dinner?

Eight

It was over a week since they'd gone to view the puppies, and Sandy hadn't stopped talking about *his* dog. To keep him happy, Finn had put a picture of a spaniel on the wall calendar in Adele's kitchen on the day Rhana predicted they could pick up the pup. The first thing Sandy did each morning was to place a cross on the day's date and count how many more days he had to wait.

Meantime, life went on as usual for Finn. Today he had a meeting with a world-famous photographer. Martin Cooper, who now lived in Bellbird Bay was coming to Pelican Crossing to take shots of the pelican refuge which was run by old Agnes – if she had a surname, it had been long forgotten – and Finn was hoping to be able to use some of them in a feature about the refuge. He'd known Martin when he lived in Bellbird Bay and was looking forward to reconnecting with the man who had won two prestigious Atlas awards and had now given up travelling the world to settle down in the small coastal town to the south of Pelican Crossing.

'We're off now, Dad,' Adele called to Finn who was enjoying a second cup of coffee as he contemplated the day ahead. Her application for the teacher's aide position had been successful and now, she and Sandy left for school and returned home together. It was good to see her beginning to find her feet again. and so far, it seemed to be going well. Sandy was delighted his mum was working at *his* school, though not in his class.

'Have a good day,' he said, opening his iPad to check the day's news, always on the lookout for an item *The Courier* could expand on. Today, apart from the usual news of fighting overseas, floods in one part of the country and bushfires in another, there was nothing to remark on. He closed the iPad and drained his mug, a favourite with the slogan, *This GRANDAD belongs to Sandy* emblazed across it, the word Grandad in multi-coloured lettering. It had been a Father's Day gift from Sandy the previous September, and Finn treasured it. Then he set off for the office.

Martin Cooper arrived at ten as arranged. He was a tall man, his faded blond hair tied back in a ponytail, a wide grin on his face. 'G'day,' he said, shaking Finn's hand. 'Good to see you again. How are you enjoying it here?'

'Good to see you again too. I'm settling in. It's a good community, not unlike Bellbird Bay. *The Courier* was a bit rundown when I arrived. I've enjoyed bringing it up to scratch.'

'And you've succeeded. Bellbird Bay's loss is Pelican Crossing's gain. I read those articles about the development scare last year… and the explosion. A busy time for you.'

Finn nodded. It was a time he'd rather forget. 'So,' he said, 'you're here on an assignment. Is it Agnes or the pelicans that interest you?'

'Both.' Martin grinned. 'One of the wildlife magazines I've worked with in the past got wind of the pelican refuge and asked me to get some footage. Then, when I looked into it, I discovered it was run by this elderly woman who looks like an aging hippie. Thought there could be a story there. You said you were interested in doing an article too?'

'I am. Agnes is a bit of an institution in the town. She seems to have lived here for ever. No one knows how old she is. She lives with her spaniel and the birds she cares for on a patch of land by the river, and has amazing skills in tending to the injured creatures. Don't know why we haven't featured her before now. It would be a godsend if we could use some of your shots.'

'No worries. I can let you have some of the ones I don't send to the mag. You've been in touch with her?'

'She was a bit difficult about it, but agreed to see us at eleven-thirty, as long as we don't disturb the sick pelicans and promise to behave.' Finn chuckled. 'I felt I was back in school when I was talking with her on the phone. Wonder if she was a teacher back in the day?'

Martin laughed. 'She sounds interesting. Hope I can get some shots of her too.'

'Don't count on it. Thought we could have lunch afterwards, if you're not in a rush to get back.'

'Sounds good. Ailsa is busy today, helping out at the garden centre,' he said referring to his wife. 'You haven't made strides in that direction?' He raised an eyebrow.

Finn flinched. 'Too busy helping out with my daughter and grandson, mate,' he said.

'Sorry, should have asked. I forgot why you moved up the coast. How is your daughter?'

'She's getting there. It's taken a while, but she's seeing a counsellor now and has found a job. No one prepares you for the death of a partner, especially not at her age, and little Sandy…' Finn shook his head, then gave a grin. 'He's hellbent on getting a dog, can't wait for his birthday.'

'Every boy should have a dog.'

Finn nodded. 'Anyway, ready to rock and roll?'

'Sure thing.'

*

Agnes's old spaniel came running to greet Finn and Martin when they parked at the gate to the property.

'Hello, old girl,' Finn said, bending down and holding his hand through the gate to let the dog sniff it.

'You know the dog?'

Finn stood up. 'Not really. Seen her on the beach with Agnes. Here she is now,' he said, as the elderly woman walked towards them, her white hair streaming behind her. Today as usual, she was wearing a long skirt and a loose top.

'You've met Lady,' Agnes said. 'I know you.' She looked at Finn, then turned to Martin. 'You must be the photographer.'

'Martin Cooper.' Martin held out his hand.

Agnes opened the gate to allow them to enter and led them past the house to a large, fenced, grassy area attached to the back of a well-maintained shed.

Martin unpacked his camera and started taking shots of the area. Finn thought he saw him including Agnes in several too.

Once inside the shed, Finn talked to the old woman while Martin continued to photograph the birds which were in various stages of recovery. Agnes was happy to tell Finn about how she'd started the centre when she retired from full-time employment and became aware of the problems the seabirds encountered with fishing lines, fishing hooks and other sea debris. But he wasn't able to learn any more about Agnes herself, sensing she was being deliberately vague about her background.

Despite this, by the time they were done, he had enough for the article he had in mind which would not only publicise her work with the birds but would hopefully assist her in obtaining more funding to continue her endeavours.

They were about to leave, when as they were thanking Agnes and saying goodbye, her old dog suddenly got underfoot, causing the old woman to trip and fall. The dog, clearly sensing she had caused the accident, slunk off in the direction of the house.

'Hell!' Martin said. He was encumbered with his camera, so it was left to Finn to help Agnes up.

'I'm all right,' she said.

But Finn could see she had a cut on her forehead and had gone very pale. 'I think you need that seen to,' he said with a frown. 'We can take you to the hospital.'

'No, not the hospital.' Agnes started to tremble.

Finn and Martin looked at each other. The cut on her forehead needed to be taken care of, and she was clearly suffering from shock. If she was determined not to go to the hospital, they couldn't force her. Finn's forehead creased then, 'What about the medical centre?' he asked. He'd never had any reason to go there himself, but Adele swore by it. It was more than a doctor's surgery, including other sorts of medical practitioners, as well as the counsellor Adele and Sandy were seeing. He thought he'd heard her mention a practice nurse and a clinic too.

Agnes seemed more comfortable with his suggestion, so he and Martin helped her into the back seat of Finn's car.

'The dog?' Finn asked, seeing the spaniel running back and forth behind the gate.

'Lady'll be fine,' Agnes said. 'She has plenty of food and water, and I don't expect I'll be long. This is very kind of you.'

'Not at all.' Finn fastened her seatbelt before getting behind the wheel and heading back into town.

'Here we are,' Finn said, stopping in a parking spot behind the medical centre. He helped Agnes out of the car and, with Martin and him on either side of the old woman, they made their way into the building.

At the sight of a short, slim, dark-haired woman hurrying towards them, Finn felt the breath leave his body. She wasn't beautiful, but with her finely drawn features, mop of black curls with just a hint of grey and eyes so green a man could drown in them, he felt drawn to her as he hadn't been to a woman since he and Karen split up, since long before that if he was being honest with himself.

Nine

Liz was carrying a folder to the reception desk when the trio entered the medical centre. It had been a busy morning, and she was looking forward to her lunch break. At first, she didn't pay any attention to the two men, one on either side of the old woman. 'Agnes,' she said, dropping the folder onto the desk and hurrying over, 'what happened to you?'

'A small altercation with her dog. She didn't want to go to hospital, so I figured this was the best option,' a deep, cultured voice said.

Suddenly aware of the figure on one side of Agnes, Liz looked up to see the tall man with a thatch of white hair. When his face broke into a smile and his grey eyes landed on hers – grey eyes like a stormy ocean – her breath caught and her heart started to pound.

She knew who he was. Finn Hunter was the new editor of *The Crossing Courier*. He'd been in Pelican Crossing for the past year. But he was a bit of an enigma. All she really knew about him was that he'd moved here when his son-in-law died in a dreadful accident.

Liz had seen him around town, and she'd heard him speak at the town meeting last year. But this was the first time she'd met him face-to-face, and he took her breath away.

He wasn't drop dead gorgeous. Far from it. He wasn't even as attractive as the hot air balloon guy. So why was she feeling as if…?

'Sorry?' she said.

'Agnes had an accident. She tripped over her dog. Is there somewhere…?' He gazed around the busy waiting room.

'Of course.' Liz's training came to the fore. 'The clinic. Follow me.' She led them into the small room at one side of the waiting room and helped Agnes to a seat. 'There's no need for you to stay,' she said to Finn when he and the other man who she recognised as Martin Cooper, the photographer, were still standing there. She knew who Martin was because she and a couple of friends had gone down to Bellbird Bay to see an exhibition of his work.

The two men looked at each other, then Finn said, 'We'll be right outside. We can take Agnes back home.'

'Oh, right.' It hadn't occurred to Liz to consider how the old woman would get home. 'It may take some time.'

'No problem.'

The men left, and Liz gave herself a moment to breathe.

'The nurse will be with you shortly, Agnes. Can I get you anything? Maybe a glass of water?'

'That would be lovely, dear. It's Liz, isn't it?'

'Yes.' Liz remembered meeting Agnes with her dog on the beach. She fetched a glass of water, then returned to the waiting room where Finn and Martin were now seated. Liz checked her watch. 'Okay if I take my lunch break now?' she asked the receptionist. She often filled in for the receptionists at lunchtime.

'No problem,' Cheryl replied. 'Take as long as you like. I won't take a break today as I want to leave early.'

'Thanks.' Making an effort to avoid looking in the direction of where Finn and Martin were seated, Liz collected her bag and hurriedly left.

*

Liz was still feeling unsettled when she returned home that evening, the memory of how she had felt at the sight of Finn Hunter still fresh in her mind. She was glad there had been no sign of Agnes or the two men when she came back from lunch. An enquiry in the clinic revealed that Agnes's injury hadn't been serious. The nurse had been able to patch her up and she'd left with the pair of men who'd brought her to the centre, with instructions to rest for the remainder of the day and to return if she experienced any headache or dizziness.

'She's a game one,' the nurse had said. 'We don't see many old dears as healthy as she is. It was good of those guys to bring her in.'

'Yes, it was very good of them,' Liz had replied.

Lacking the motivation to cook, Liz pulled a frozen meal from the freezer, and opened her laptop to check her emails, hoping there would be a reply from Julie. It had been two weeks since she'd replied to her letter.

There was still nothing. Liz sighed.

She poured herself a glass of red wine and took it and her meal out to the deck. It was lovely out here at this time of night, with a fresh breeze from the water a relief after the heat of the day. But tonight, the sight of the boats lined up in the marina, and the sound of the seabirds seeking their evening roost didn't bring her the peace she sought.

She finished the spinach and feta cannelloni, poured a second glass of wine and thought about her encounter with Finn Hunter. She could scarcely call it an encounter. They had barely exchanged two words. So why did she feel as if her life would never be the same again? She could just imagine what Mandy would say. She must never know, or she'd pull out all the stops to bring them together.

Liz was musing over the fact that she'd finally come across someone who could stir her emotions when her phone rang, the familiar tone breaking into her thoughts. She was still so caught up in thinking about Finn Hunter that, for a moment, the voice asking if this was Liz Phillips didn't register. It was a light, educated voice, not unlike Tara's.

'This is she,' Liz said.

'It's Julie.' There was a pause. 'I got your email.'

Liz clutched the phone, her breath coming in gasps, her heart pounding. 'Julie, I'm so glad you called.'

Ten

After dropping Agnes off and making sure all was well, Finn and Martin drove back into town. 'I think we deserve a bite of lunch. *The Grand* serves a good counter lunch, and they have a selection of the local craft beer,' Finn said.

'Sounds good. I've heard about the brewery. Started by a couple of young guys, wasn't it? Doing well?'

'Very well it seems. A lot of the older guys like us prefer the more traditional brews, but the youngsters can't get enough of it. I've developed a taste for some of their lagers. I'd suggest taking you out to the brewery, but I need to get back to the office.'

'No worries. May give it a visit myself one of these days. Would make a good day out.'

Finn nodded his agreement, as they turned into the hotel car park.

He took a seat while Martin, at his insistence, went to the bar to order, the men both having decided on a traditional meal of pie and chips washed down with a lager from the local brewery. While he was waiting for his companion to return, Finn thought back to the woman at the medical centre.

He knew who she was. As editor of the local paper, he made it his business to know residents of the town, and Liz Phillips had earned a name for herself as being able to ferret out local news, sometimes even before his reporters. He'd heard it was really her daughter who collected the gossip and passed it onto her mother, though he guessed Liz's position in the medical centre made her privy to lots of information.

However, this was the first time they'd met.

'Quite a morning,' Martin said when he returned with two overflowing glasses. 'Agnes is a character. I hope she'll be okay. She's pretty isolated out there by the river with only her dog and the pelicans for company.'

'She should be fine. Everyone knows her. She's lived there for years. And it's not as isolated as it looks. There's a development of townhouses not far away… and she has a number of volunteers who help out with the centre. There would be someone with her most days… just not today. Lucky we were there.'

'It might not have happened if we hadn't been there,' Martin said ruefully, rubbing his chin. 'I think the dog became excited in our company. Anyway, I got some good shots. I'll let you have a few once I've had time to go through them.'

'Thanks, I appreciate it. Cheers,' Finn said raising his glass.

'Cheers. Happy to help. Let me know if you come across any other project we can collaborate on. I'm assuming you got enough for the article you have in mind?'

'I did, thanks. It'll make a great human-interest feature for the colour supplement I'm thinking of starting. If you're interested, I might be able to put a bit of work your way, though *The Courier* wouldn't be able to match the sort of fees you're used to.'

'No worries. I find working for a small-town paper like yours has its own rewards.'

'True.' The pair had worked together on a few news stories in Bellbird Bay, and Finn knew Martin often offered his services free to local charities.

'I saw you looking at the woman in the medical centre,' Martin said raising one eyebrow, when they had finished their meals and decided against a second beer. 'Friend of yours?'

'No, not exactly. It's a small town so I know who she is… and I expect she knows about me too, but till today, we hadn't met.'

'Good-looking woman.'

'Yeah.' Finn gazed into his now empty glass, seeing the woman's unruly black curls, remembering her green eyes. But he didn't want to get into a discussion about Liz Phillips. He knew he'd be thinking about her again once he was alone.

*

When Finn arrived home, Adele and Sandy were already there.

As soon as he walked in, Sandy ran up to him. 'Grandy, can you help me?' he asked, pulling on Finn's hand.

'Give your grandad time to get into the house,' Adele said. 'Busy day, Dad? Glass of wine?'

'Yes to both,' Finn said. 'Remember I said I was going out to the pelican rescue centre today?'

Adele nodded as she poured two glasses of white wine and handed him one. 'Did it go well?'

Sandy was waiting impatiently for the adults to finish their conversation.

'It did. Very well until we were leaving. Then Agnes had an accident, tripped over that dog of hers.'

'The pelican lady with the spaniel?' Sandy asked, following the conversation.

'Yes, Sandy.'

'Oh, dear,' Adele said. 'She's not a young woman. How is she?'

'We took her to the medical centre, then home again. She seems fine. But it's a worry. The nurse said falls always are, especially at her age.'

'How old is she?'

Finn shrugged. 'Who knows?'

'She's old,' Sandy said.

Finn and Adele laughed.

'You're right there, Sandy.'

'I bet Liz knows,' Adele said. 'She seems to know everything around here.'

Finn felt himself redden. 'Liz?'

'The practice manager. You must know who I mean. She has the reputation of being a gossip, but I don't think she is really. She just manages to know what's going on. I think it's her daughter who's the gossip. Mandy runs a personal training business and works at the yacht club a couple of nights a week. I bet she hears and sees a lot and passes it on to her mum.'

'She was the one who greeted us. She seemed to know Agnes.'

'Everyone knows Agnes. Hadn't you met Liz before?'

'Haven't needed to go to the medical centre.'

'Of course you haven't.' Adele peered at him, making him wonder if she could sense his interest in the woman.

He shifted uncomfortably. He'd avoided a conversation about Liz Phillips in the hotel, only to come home to one. 'What is it you need me for, Sandy?' he asked, in an attempt to avoid any more discussion about the woman who had sent his senses reeling.

'I have to do a project on my family, and I need you to help me with it,' Sandy said, dragging Finn off.

Finn heard Adele call out, 'Don't be long, you two. Dinner will be ready soon,' as he left the kitchen, relieved at having an excuse to end their conversation.

Eleven

Liz couldn't sleep. She couldn't stop thinking about Julie. She'd actually spoken to her… her daughter, and Julie wanted to meet her. And, even better, Julie had a daughter. Liz had a granddaughter. Her name was Tilly, and she was fourteen years old, almost as old as Liz had been when Julie was born. Liz couldn't contain her excitement. It took a lot of getting used to.

She tossed and turned, trying to picture what Julie might look like… and Tilly. Did either of them have Liz's dark unruly hair, or were they like Julie's father, the person Liz had tried to forget. Perhaps Tilly resembled her dad, who Julie hadn't said much about other than that they were divorced.

It hadn't been a long call. Both Liz and Julie were feeling their way with each other. Liz knew they lived in Brisbane – her daughter had been so close all those years. They may even have passed each other on the street on one of Liz's trips to the city. She'd learned Julie was a librarian and Tilly was causing her some problems. They'd agreed to leave the details of their lives until they met, and they were going to meet. It seemed Julie had already planned a trip north in the Easter holidays. Now, she'd book into a motel in Pelican Crossing. Liz couldn't wait. The timing was perfect. Both Tara and Mandy would be out of town, giving her time to meet her daughter and granddaughter – the very thought of having a granddaughter sent shivers of anticipation down her spine – without their knowledge.

She'd have to tell them, of course, and couldn't imagine what their reaction would be. But it could wait till after Easter, till they returned, till she'd met Julie and Tilly.

It was almost three weeks till Easter. How would Liz survive?

*

Next morning, when Liz arrived at work, the talk was all about how the famous photographer, Martin Cooper, had walked into the centre with old Agnes. There was no mention of the local newspaper editor who'd been there too, and who had made such an impression on Liz. Trying to let the flow of conversation go over her head, she began on her usual tasks. But she couldn't help thinking about the tall man with the thatch of white hair and those smiling grey eyes who had taken her breath away. At least it stopped her thinking about Julie, wondering if her daughter would like her, speculating as to what her granddaughter would be like.

Liz hadn't had much to do with teenagers since Tara and Mandy, apart from those she saw in the medical centre. They were there because they were sick, but from them – and what she'd read – teenagers of today were very different from what they'd been when her daughters were in their teens. These days, they were likely to spend their time glued to their mobile phones, to listen to music which would deafen any sane person and to live in a completely different world to her.

Liz was grabbing a quick coffee break when her phone pinged with an incoming text. It was from Mandy.

RU free for lunch? Something to ask U. Blue Dolphin at 12.30? Mxx

Liz sighed. What was it now? No doubt something Mandy thought was urgent, something that couldn't wait till after work – Mandy probably had other plans for then and took no account of the fact Liz's schedule wasn't as flexible as hers. Luckily, the centre wasn't busy today. It would be easy for Liz to slip away, take a longer lunch break than usual if necessary. After checking with the other staff on duty, she replied.

Yes. See you there. xx

She'd never got into the habit of abbreviating her words the way the younger generation had. She supposed it made her old-fashioned, but she didn't care.

The remainder of the morning passed quickly. Liz didn't waste any time wondering what Mandy might want. She supposed she might need to borrow money for her diving trip. While the personal training business she'd set up seemed to be popular, Liz couldn't fully comprehend how Mandy could make a living from it, even supplementing her income with a couple of nights waitressing at the yacht club.

When lunchtime arrived, Liz grabbed her bag and set off to walk to the café. She needed the exercise, and it was a lovely morning. She ducked down a side street and walked along Main Street, glad the proposed development had been averted. She loved the old buildings on this street, several of which were over a hundred years old. She stopped for a few moments to peer in the window of *The Mousehole*, the narrow shop which always looked as if it had been squeezed between the two neighbouring buildings as an afterthought. It was run by a group of local women, a potter, a couple of artists, and a woman who made the most glorious patchwork quilts. They took turns to man the shop and sell their goods. Liz always loved checking out their window. This morning a collection of painted, wooden cats caught her eye. They were not unlike the white one she'd received from the Secret Santa the previous Christmas. She was tempted to go in and purchase one to add to the one she already owned – or maybe it would be something Julie might like – or Tilly. But Mandy would be waiting, so she walked on.

'Mum!' Mandy was seated at an outside table. She rose to greet Liz. She must have come straight from running a class, as she was wearing a white crop top with lilac leggings and had a sheen of sweat on her forehead.

'Mandy, darling.' Liz hugged her, puzzling not for the first time, how she and Tommy had produced such an athletic daughter. Neither of them had been involved in any sort of sporting activity. 'Had a class this morning?'

'Just finished. Sorry, didn't have time to shower and change. I have another this afternoon. I've been really busy. All these yummy mummies wanting to get back in shape,' she chuckled, as if she could never imagine herself being in their position.

So, maybe this wasn't about money.

'Let's order,' Liz said, picking up a menu. 'I can't take too long, and you probably can't either.'

When they had placed their order – Liz choosing a ham, cheese and tomato toastie with a cappuccino, and Mandy a carrot, chicken and quinoa salad with a carrot, apple and ginger juice – Liz couldn't wait any longer. 'What do you want to ask me that couldn't wait?'

Mandy fidgeted in her seat. 'It's Margot,' she said.

Margot was the old schoolfriend Mandy shared a house with, and who was always getting into trouble of one sort or another. But she and Mandy had been friends since kindergarten and always got along well.

'What's Margot done now? She hasn't involved you in one of her crazy schemes, has she?'

'No. Oh thanks,' she said as the waitress delivered their drinks. 'She's decided to go to Bali.'

'So?' Liz couldn't see how Mandy's housemate's decision to take a Bali holiday led to this lunch.

'She's moving there. She has some idea of setting up a yoga school and…' her voice trailed off.

It suddenly began to make sense to Liz. She stared at her daughter. Surely Mandy didn't mean…? But she did.

'I wondered if I could move in with you for a bit… just till I find somewhere else to live. I can't bear the idea of looking for another housemate, of living with someone I don't know. I thought… maybe… just until I come back from the dive trip. I'll have time to look around then… or maybe Gary and I…' She blushed. 'It won't be for long, Mum. Please?'

It took Liz a few minutes to think of a reply, during which their meals arrived. The thought of sharing her peaceful apartment with her untidy and often noisy daughter filled her with dread, but there was no way she could refuse. She'd never been able to refuse Mandy anything – hence the online dating, the hot air balloon ride. Though at least she'd managed to avoid going to the yacht club on the off chance of seeing Steve. But the timing couldn't be worse, with the prospect of meeting Julie and Tilly.

'Of course, darling.' Liz bit her lip, but what else could she say?

'Oh, thanks, Mum. I knew you'd agree.' Mandy rose and gave Liz a warm hug.

Was she so predictable?

'When…?'

'This weekend?' Mandy said hopefully. 'Gary's promised to help move my stuff. There's not much, really,' she said, clearly seeing the expression on Liz's face as she mentally worked out how she was going to find room for all of Mandy's belongings in her small apartment. 'You have a storage space, don't you?'

'Ye… es.' Liz's storage locker in the basement car park was already filled with items from their family home, things which didn't fit in the apartment, but she couldn't bear to part with. 'Maybe you could hire storage space yourself,' she suggested. 'You'd be more comfortable without cluttering the room up with stuff you don't need.'

Mandy pouted, then smiled. 'I'll check with Gary,' she said. 'He'll have some ideas.'

Gary again. It seemed to Liz this thing with Gary might be serious, more serious than Mandy's previous relationships. At least she'd get to meet him if he helped Mandy move in. Just how much stuff did Mandy have, she wondered, envisaging her tidy apartment disappearing under a deluge of her daughter's belongings.

'Thanks again, Mum,' Mandy said when lunch was over, and they rose to leave. 'I won't be any trouble. I promise. You won't even know I'm there.'

Liz doubted it but hugged her daughter. Mandy would never change, and Liz loved her. But as she made her way back to the medical centre, her mind was working overtime, trying to figure out how she could fit one more person and her belongings into her small apartment.

Twelve

Finn had spent the last few evenings helping Sandy with his school project which proved more difficult than he'd expected.

When he'd allowed himself to be dragged off by his grandson earlier in the week, he'd been relieved to avoid a difficult conversation with Adele, but on discovering the topic of the project was My Family, and Sandy wanted to find photographs of all his relations, he wondered if dealing with Adele talking about Liz might have been preferable.

First, there had been the search for old photographs, resulting in finding ones which featured Tim looking tanned and happy. Adele had appeared as they were choosing which to include, and her shocked silence and the way the colour had drained from her face had put the project on hold.

He had spent the best part of an hour comforting her, only to be asked by Sandy why he didn't have any brothers or sisters.

Then it was Finn's turn, when Sandy insisted they search for a photo of Grandma too, and place it next to Finn's on the large piece of cardboard. After the divorce, Finn had tried to erase everything to do with Karen from his memory, though he knew Adele still kept in touch with her mother. But Karen had never been one for family reunions, so they probably hadn't seen each other since the funeral. If they had, it had been when Finn was at work, and Adele had kept quiet about it.

The rest was easy, with Sandy laughing at the old-fashioned clothes in the old photos of Finn's parents, and Tim's parents and grandparents, all now passed away, and who Sandy had never known. To him they were diving the fictional characters he read about or watched in movies.

But while Finn was consoling Adele, comforting Sandy and becoming sticky with glue as he tried to stick the photographs in the exact spots demanded by Sandy before labelling them, he'd come up with an idea.

'You've had a busy week,' he said to Adele over breakfast on Saturday, 'why don't you take some time to yourself, go to the beach, have a coffee. I can take Sandy to his appointment.'

'Are you sure?' Adele beamed. Finn knew she was aware he hadn't been convinced about Sandy seeing the counsellor.

'Yeah. It does seem to be helping.' Sandy's nightmares had almost ceased, though Finn did wonder if it was the prospect of getting a puppy of his own, rather than his sessions with the counsellor that had effected the change. But he wasn't game to venture his opinion to his daughter.

'If you're sure. One of the teachers at school invited me to a jewellery party she's having. It sounded like fun, but I thought I'd have to take Sandy to the clinic.'

'I'm sure. You go to your party. It's time you had some fun.'

Adele's eyes clouded over. Finn could have kicked himself. The last time she'd had fun would have been with Tim.

'Thanks.'

'No problem.' Finn gave a sigh of relief. Now he'd found a reason to visit the medical centre, he couldn't wait. Until he came up with this one, he'd thought he might have to pretend to be sick.

He couldn't think of any other way to see Liz Phillips again. It was surprising that in a town the size of Pelican Crossing, they hadn't crossed paths before now, but fate was a strange thing. He didn't know her habits, where she went when she wasn't working. What he did know was that he had to see her again, and when he did… well, he'd fly by the seat of his pants.

*

Sandy was delighted his grandfather was to accompany him, chattering away in Finn's ear all the way to the medical centre about how he was so pleased with the way his family project had turned out and sure it would be the best in the class. Finn didn't think it was a competition but let the little boy babble on. He was too intent on working out how he was going to approach Liz to correct him.

It was a long time since he'd felt attracted to a woman, since he'd allowed one to get under his skin. Even longer since he'd invited one on a date, not since he and Karen first met. What sort of wimp did that make him? He was aware lots of people of his age took to online dating to find a partner – *The Courier* had even published an article about it, the advantages and pitfalls – but it wasn't for him. He'd been happy with the single life… until now.

But when they reached the medical centre, there was no sign of Liz.

Finn took a seat in the waiting room while Sandy headed for a small area at the side where there was a selection of toys. It was obviously something he did on each visit. When his name was called, Finn accompanied Sandy, somewhat stunned to realise he had to remain outside the room and observe what was happening through a two-way mirror. Had Adele mentioned this? He couldn't remember.

However, he was impressed by the appearance of the counsellor, who looked like everyone's favourite aunt or grandmother and with how comfortable Sandy seemed with her. Maybe Adele was right, and it was working. He hoped Adele was enjoying herself. He hoped she didn't grieve for ever. She deserved to have some pleasure in her life, to find love again, and Sandy deserved to have someone to call dad, not an old fogey like him. But he knew these things took time. This morning was only the start.

He wondered where Liz was. As practice manager, did she have an office to herself? Last time, she'd been walking through the waiting room. He'd assumed she was one of the receptionists.

He waited till Sandy emerged from the room carrying a chocolate bar from which he was peeling the foil. He was accompanied by the counsellor.

'Hello. Sandy tells me you're his grandad and the editor of our local paper. He's very proud of you. I'm Olivia. It's good to meet you.'

'Finn,' he said. 'He speaks well of you too.'

'Thanks.' She smiled. 'I'm thinking we may not need many more of these sessions,' she said to Finn in a low voice. 'Sandy appears to be overcoming the trauma I could sense in him when we first met.' In a louder voice she said, 'Sandy tells me he's getting a puppy for his birthday.'

'He certainly is. A blue roan spaniel.'

'Bluey,' Sandy said, through a mouthful of chocolate.

Finn and Olivia laughed.

'See you next week, Sandy,' Olivia said. 'Will you…?' she asked Finn.

'His mother will probably be with him again.'

'Right. Good to have met you,' she said.

Once back in the waiting room, Finn glanced around, but there was still no sign of Liz. As he was settling the bill he casually asked, 'Is the practice manager around today?'

The receptionist looked surprised. 'Oh, Liz doesn't work on the weekend. I think she's helping her daughter move in with her today. Rather her than me,' the middle-aged receptionist laughed. 'Once they move out, they're on their own. That's what I told my lot. They haven't dared come back.' She chuckled.

It doesn't always work that way, Finn thought as he pushed open the heavy glass door, Sandy running out ahead of him. Look at what happened to him and Adele. He was glad he'd been there for her, there in a way her mother had never been. But that was another story, another life.

Now he had to find a different way to meet Liz again.

Over lunch, he repeated what Olivia had said to Adele, who was relieved to hear how much Sandy had improved. 'Though he hasn't had a really bad nightmare since we went to see the pups,' she said, confirming Finn's opinion.

'How was your party?' he asked.

'Not really a party as such,' Adele said, 'a lady showing pieces of jewellery which we were then expected to buy.'

'Did you?' Finn was curious. He knew nothing of such events.

'Not me, but several of the others did. The jewellery was nice, but I don't wear any these days other than my rings.' She twisted her wedding and engagement rings on her finger. They were looser than they used to be.

'Maybe you should. You always used to wear earrings. I remember when you pleaded with Mum to have your ears pierced. And there's all Mum's jewellery. I'm sure she'd want you to wear it.'

'Maybe, but it doesn't seem right to get all dolled up when Tim's not here to see it. And I never go anywhere.'

Finn was conscious of having said the wrong thing again. Before he could wonder if he was about to make matters worse, he said, 'Why don't we change that and go out to dinner – all three of us? I've heard the yacht club is good.'

Adele didn't reply immediately, and Finn was beginning to regret his words, when she said, 'Thanks, Dad. What a nice idea. The yacht club is good. Let's do it.'

Thirteen

Liz's day started badly. She overslept, wakening, her eyes blurred with sleep, to see it was eight o'clock. She wandered through to the kitchen and turned on the coffee machine, hoping a cup of coffee would help get her awake.

There was a message on her phone.

Don't forget Gary and I are bringing over all my stuff this morning. Hope to be there around nine. xx

Hell, it was Saturday. Mandy was moving in. Liz had made an effort to clear the spare room the previous evening, carting some of the larger items down to her storage locker, but she'd planned on making an early start to finish it off this morning. She wanted the room to look inviting when Mandy arrived. Too late now. Liz downed her coffee quickly, took a few bites from the toast she'd made while the coffee was brewing and headed for the shower. Maybe a blast of cold water would help her feel more human, more welcoming to the daughter she didn't really want to move in and disturb her peaceful existence.

She was just out of the shower, had pulled on a pair of shorts and a tee-shirt, and dragged a comb through her hair when there was a familiar pounding on the door.

Mandy was standing there, looking as if she'd been awake for hours. Behind her stood a tall young man wearing a pair of board shorts and a tee-shirt with the dive school logo, his blond hair tied back in a ponytail. 'Hi, Mum. This is Gary.'

'Hello, Mrs Phillips. Good to meet you.'

'You too, Gary,' Liz said. She hugged Mandy but didn't know what to do with Gary. He didn't look the sort to shake hands and they weren't on hugging terms.

'We have everything in Gary's ute,' Mandy said. 'I took your advice and rented a storage space for the bigger items. Can we bring it all up now?'

'I suppose so. Do you want to check out the room first, to work out where you want things to go?'

'No, we'll be right. Gary?' They disappeared again.

Liz made another cup of coffee. She had the distinct impression this was going to be a long morning.

She was right.

After so many trips back and forth from Gary's ute Liz lost count, Mandy finally said, 'I think that's it. I'm dying for a coffee, and do you have anything to eat? We skipped breakfast.' She opened the fridge and peered inside.

Liz had forgotten Mandy's annoying habit of doing this. She tended to do it with the pantry too, had done since she was little, and when asked what she was looking for, always answered, "Nothing".

'How about you make the coffee and I do bacon and scrambled eggs,' Liz said. 'You know how it works?'

'*I* do, Mrs Phillips,' Gary said.

'Call me Liz.'

'I think you know my dad?'

'Jamie? Yes. From school… he was in Year Twelve when I was in Year Ten.'

'Mum only came to Pelican Crossing then, didn't you, Mum?' Mandy said, dropping onto one of the stools by the kitchen bench. 'Gary's dad grew up here,' she added for Liz's benefit.

Liz decided not to respond. There was always the danger of revealing more than she wanted to or intended. She took the packet of bacon and six eggs out of the fridge and broke the eggs. 'So, it seems your dive school is going well, Gary,' she said instead.

'Really well, Mrs… Liz. It was lucky Dad had the extra space, and the council have been good with allowing me to use the rock pool. It's been a brilliant summer, though I guess demand might drop off in the cooler months.'

By the time the food was ready, Liz was feeling quite comfortable with Gary. He was a nice boy, well-mannered and communicative which was more than could have been said for some of Mandy's boyfriends in the past. Liz hoped this one might last and judging by the way Mandy looked at him and hung on his every word, her daughter did too.

'Thanks, Mum, that really hit the spot. Have to go now and put the rest of my stuff into storage. I'll be back sometime in the afternoon. I really appreciate you letting me come here. I know I'm putting you out. We…' she glanced at Gary who nodded, '… we'd like to take you to dinner tonight as a thank you. How does the yacht club sound?'

Hiding her surprise and sure it must have been Gary's idea – her daughter would never have been so thoughtful – Liz said, 'Thanks, it sounds lovely.'

'See you later.' With another hug from Mandy, and a smile and a wave from Gary, the young couple were off again, leaving a pool of silence and a table of dirty dishes behind them.

Liz cleared up, then couldn't resist peeking into the spare room. She gasped. Every surface, including the bed, was covered with Mandy's belongings. The floor was home to so many boxes it would be difficult for anyone to move, and what looked like Mandy's personal training equipment was spread around. She closed the door quickly.

This was what it was going to be like with Mandy living here, Liz thought. It would be like having a flatmate, but one who felt no requirement to do her share of the chores. Well, it would be good to have her daughter there, to see her every day, even if it was only for a short time. Mandy had said it would be till she came back from the dive trip. Liz wondered what would happen then.

*

Liz was feeling more cheerful by the time she was getting ready to go to dinner. As promised, Mandy had returned in the afternoon, and they'd enjoyed a lovely walk on the beach together, Mandy reiterating how much she appreciated being able to "come home" even though Liz's apartment had never been her home. Liz had bought the apartment after Tommy left, after the divorce. Mandy had moved out around the same time to a shared house in town.

Now, as she dressed in her favourite calf-length green dress, the one Tara told her brought out the colour of her eyes and which always made her feel good, Liz found herself actually looking forward to having Mandy living with her. Maybe they'd find time to do some of the things she'd always wanted to do with her daughter, but which had been too difficult to arrange.

'Ready, Mum?' Mandy popped her head into Liz's bedroom. 'Wow! Looking good,' she said. 'Gary's just texted he'll meet us there.'

'Ready,' Liz said, taking one last look in the mirror and deciding she didn't look too bad for fifty. *This is what fifty looks like*, she thought, remembering a celebrity saying those self-same words. It was still a shock to realise she'd hit that milestone. She'd read somewhere it was all downhill from here, but it didn't feel that way to her. She had so much to look forward to. There were Julie and Tilly who were coming to visit over Easter, the prospect of Mandy finally settling down with Gary – she crossed her fingers – and… she drew in her breath… the possibility of meeting Finn Hunter again. Pelican Crossing was a small town and just because their paths hadn't crossed till now, didn't mean they wouldn't in the future. She hurried out to join Mandy.

Gary was waiting for them at the entrance to the yacht club, looking very smart in a pair of pressed jeans and a flowered shirt with the sleeves rolled up to the elbows. His ponytail had been tamed into a neat bun. Liz wondered if it was for her benefit or if he felt the yacht club demanded it.

'Hey,' he said when he caught sight of them. 'Liz,' he nodded, then, 'Looking good, babe,' to Mandy who blushed.

Mandy was wearing a pink dress with cut-out shoulders and a handkerchief hem. It wasn't a style Liz admired, but it looked good on her daughter.

Once inside, the three were shown to a table by the window overlooking the marina. Liz always loved the marina at this time of night, as the setting sun's rays turned the sky and the ocean to various shades of pink and gold. It was so romantic. Perhaps one day she'd have someone to share it with, someone other than her daughter and her daughter's boyfriend. But for now, she'd make do with present company.

'This is lovely,' she said. 'You must have booked to get such a good table.'

It was Gary's turn to blush. 'Mandy said I should,' he muttered. 'The club's always busy on Saturday evenings.'

Mandy was gazing around as if looking for someone.

Oh, no! Liz had the awful feeling she was being set up, that Steve, the hot air balloon man, was going to suddenly appear. Mandy had said he normally came here on Thursdays, and this was Saturday, but…

She realised her fears were groundless when a waiter appeared with menus.

'On the other side tonight, Mandy?' he asked with a smile. 'Sorry to keep you waiting.'

'I thought you were on tonight.' Mandy chuckled. 'We expect special service.'

'Always. I'll be back when you've made up your mind.' He glided away.

Liz studied the menu and quickly decided on the crispy skin salmon with salad. Then, feeling more relaxed, she picked up the glass of wine from the bottle Gary had ordered, took a sip and gazed around the restaurant. Her breath caught when her eyes fell on a table on the far side of the room where a small boy was seated with a woman who appeared to be his mother and… it couldn't be, but it was… Finn Hunter.

She quickly dropped her eyes, feeling herself redden. When she dared to glance up again, he was looking straight at her. As their glances met, a blast of heat flowed through her. She began to tremble.

'Is something the matter, Mum?' Mandy asked, her eyes following Liz's. 'Oh, isn't that the editor of the local paper? Do you know him?' Her eyes gleamed.

Liz could read her mind.

'No, not really. We met when he and Martin Cooper brought old Agnes into the medical centre.'

'Martin Cooper, the photographer?' Gary said in an awed tone. 'Wish I could get him to come on one of our dives. His underwater shots are amazing. When he… Sorry,' he said, clearly seeing the glazed looks of his companions. 'I tend to go on a bit sometimes.'

'A lot of times,' Mandy said but there was an affectionate note in her voice. 'Are we ready to order?' she asked as Liz saw the waiter approaching again.

They were waiting for their meals, Gary in full flight describing a dive he'd taken on the Great Barrier Reef the year before, when out of the corner of her eye, Liz saw the three people at the far table rise to leave, the little boy running ahead intent on reaching the doorway first, the woman, presumably his mother, hurrying after him. Where was Finn?

'We meet again.'

Liz looked up at the figure towering over her. She gulped. Her heart began to flutter so hard she thought it might jump out of her chest.

'It's Liz, isn't it, Liz Phillips? We met at the medical centre when…'

'… you brought old Agnes in,' Liz said.

He nodded, seemed to hesitate for a moment, then said with a smile, 'Enjoy your evening.'

Before Liz could reply, he was gone, hurrying after his companions.

'What was that about?' Mandy asked.

'I… I don't know.' Liz stared after the man who'd stirred her emotions, picked up her wine glass and gulped the contents down.

Fourteen

'Who were you talking to?' Adele asked, when Finn joined her and Sandy at the door. 'She looks familiar.'

'Liz Phillips. I told you we met when Coop and I went into the medical centre with old Agnes.'

'Oh!' Adele didn't display any interest. Why should she? Finn had barely exchanged two words with the woman. He'd intended to… he wasn't sure what he'd intended to say. But the sight of the young couple she was with gazing at him, listening avidly, had sent everything he might have said out of his head. He was no further forward.

'I know her, Mum,' Sandy said. 'I've seen her when we go to see Livia. I don't think she's a doctor, but I've seen her go into one of the rooms near Livia's.'

Finn looked at his grandson with something like respect. Sandy had noticed her too. 'Right, champ,' he said.

'Who's Coop, Grandy?' Sandy asked, going back to the earlier part of the conversation as he was wont to do.

'Martin Cooper. People call him Coop. He's a famous photographer. You know the book of photographs I gave your mum at Christmas?'

Sandy nodded. 'The one with pictures of jungles and caves and things?'

'That's the one. He took all those photos. He used to do a lot of travelling, but now he lives in Bellbird Bay where I used to live, before I came here to live with you and your mum.'

But Sandy had lost interest. They had reached the car, and he was wrestling with the car door handle.

By the time they reached home, Sandy was almost asleep.

'Why don't we give his bath a miss tonight? I'll get him ready for bed and you can put your feet up.' It hadn't escaped Finn's notice Adele was looking tired too.

'Thanks, Dad,' she said.

Finn helped the little boy change into his pyjamas, then Sandy chose a book, and Finn settled on the chair beside the bed, opened the copy of *Nate the Great* – an old book, but a favourite with Sandy – and began to read. It wasn't long before the small boy's eyes closed. Finn closed the book, dropped a kiss on Sandy's forehead and tip-toed out of the room.

'Out like a light,' he said when he joined Adele in the living room, to discover she'd poured two glasses of wine.

'We didn't have any with dinner,' she said.

'Thanks.' Finn dropped onto the sofa.

'Sorry if I was a bit grumpy earlier. It was just… seeing all those women at the jewellery thing, listening to them talking about their husbands. It brought it all back. I shouldn't have taken it out on you, Dad.'

'It's okay. I can cope. I know things aren't easy for you. They do say it gets easier with time, but I'm not sure it does.'

'Hmm.' Adele took a sip of wine.

Finn took a deep breath. 'Do you ever talk to Mum about it?'

Adele stared at him. 'What made you think about Mum?'

'Nothing. I just wondered. You are in touch with her?'

'Not recently. She's not the world's best communicator, not the most sensitive either. But you know Mum. She'd probably tell me to get over it.'

'Mmm.' Finn wished he could do more to help his daughter overcome the grief which still shrouded her.

'I worry about you, Dad.'

Finn stared at her in surprise. 'Me? Why?'

'You changed your life to be with Sandy and me. It couldn't have been easy for you. But it's no life for you to spend it caring for us. You're still relatively young. You should be… I don't know… making a new future for yourself, finding a new partner.'

Finn's mouth dropped open, the image of Liz Phillips appearing in his mind's eye. Had Adele read his mind? Did she know he'd been attracted to Liz? Her next words put his mind at rest.

'I know it's probably difficult for you to meet anyone when you spend all your free time with us, but I… there's no sense in both of us spending a lonely old age.'

'I'll never be lonely while I have you and Sandy, and you… given time, Adele, you may find someone to fill the gap in your life.'

Adele shook her head. 'I'll never forget Tim.' Her eyes filled.

'Of course not. No one would expect you to.' It was too soon, he realised. He'd spoken too soon.

'I think I'll go to bed.' Adele drained her glass and took it into the kitchen.

Finn heard the tap run, the sound of the dishwasher door opening and closing, then Adele's footsteps and the closing of her bedroom door. He sighed. He'd done it again. It was so hard to know when to speak and when to stay silent. But the conversation had proven to him yet again that he needed to do something more to connect with Liz Phillips. But what?

*

Finn was no further forward in his thinking by the time Monday came around. The previous day had been spent by the beach, Sandy still refusing to venture near the water, Adele lost in a book – or pretending to be – and Finn trying to work out how to contact Liz Phillips.

A call from the mayor took care of lunch. Finn had met Joe Harris soon after he arrived in Pelican Crossing, and the two men had become friends. Both single, Finn divorced and Jo a widower, they often met for a beer to put the world to rights. Joe was also a good source of information. Today, Joe had intimated he had a juicy piece of news to share.

The morning passed in the usual rush to finalise the first edition of the week, leading Finn to wonder yet again if they should take the option of going digital. It was a decision he'd shelved, knowing many of their readers loved the paper version and several had never mastered anything online. It was a relief to close the office door behind him and make his way to *The Grand* where he was to meet Joe.

Pushing open the door of the old hotel which gave the impression it hadn't changed in decades Finn was greeted by the familiar aroma of stale beer. He saw Joe was already there, sitting at the bar with a half-full glass. He rose when he saw Finn walk in. 'Yours is coming,' he said, nodding to his glass. 'Couldn't wait.'

The pair took their drinks to a nearby booth and ordered lunch – the inevitable pie and chips. Adele, with her insistence on healthy eating, would be shocked. But after a busy morning there was nothing quite like pie and chips washed down by a beer to make the day seem better.

'So, what's the news that couldn't wait?' Finn asked, when they had both downed half of their beers.

'Remember Jordan Butler?'

'Who doesn't?' The man had been big news a few months earlier when his development plans threatened the town.

'Well, from what I've heard, he's finally got his comeuppance. Seems he tried the same thing on the central coast of New South Wales, targeted the wrong people, is up on charges of threats with menaces, maximum penalty five years imprisonment.'

'Wow. Thanks. I have contacts there. Will follow it up. He's not local news, not anymore, but a lot of folk will be interested.'

'What's up with you, these days?' Joe asked, as he squeezed a sachet of tomato sauce over his chips. 'Anything new?'

'No,' Finn said, then thought better of it. 'Actually, I could do with your advice.'

'Always happy to help,' Joe chuckled.

'It's this woman…'

'It always is,' Joe chuckled again. 'Glad I don't have that problem. Who's the lucky lady?'

'Don't know about lucky.' Finn pulled on one ear. 'It's Liz Phillips, she's…'

'Practice manager at Pelican Crossing Medical Centre. I know who she is. She was a great help when Barb…'

Of course Joe would know her. His late wife had been a patient at the medical centre during the illness which had taken her life.

'So, what's the problem? She turn you down?'

'Not yet. I'm trying to figure out how to contact her. We only met briefly, then I saw her at the yacht club, but she was with a young couple, her daughter, I suppose. I was going to talk to her, ask for her phone number but I chickened out. It's been so long, Joe. I think I've forgotten how.'

'I'm not much help to you there, haven't looked at a woman since Barb… My suggestion is to just do it. You know where she works. Pick up the phone and ask for her. It's that simple.'

'Thanks for nothing.' Finn took a gulp of beer. He hadn't needed to ask Joe. He knew what to do, he'd always known. But Joe was right about one thing. He just needed to do it.

When he got back to the office, Finn picked up the phone and dialled the number of the medical centre before he could change his mind, but he almost hung up when he heard her voice.

'Liz Phillips, how can I help you?'

'It's Finn Hunter. We met…' Finn cleared his throat. 'I wondered if… I wanted to invite you to dinner. Are you free on Friday?'

There was a pause, then she spoke again. 'That sounds lovely. I'd love to have dinner with you.'

Fifteen

Liz's heart was fluttering when the call ended. Finn Hunter had called her, invited her to dinner. She'd been surprised when he approached their table at the yacht club on Saturday, wondered if… Then told herself he was only being polite, despite the speculative expression in Mandy's eyes. At least her daughter had kept her thoughts to herself. Mandy had gone back to Gary's afterwards, leaving Liz to her own speculations, none of which made sense. Now this!

She was becoming used to Mandy's presence in the apartment – when she was there. Her daughter seemed to be spending her evenings – and nights – with Gary, making only fleeting visits to the apartment to change her clothes or pick up bits and pieces. Even on the evenings when she was working at the yacht club, there was often no sign of her till the next morning. When Liz dared to ask why she didn't move in with Gary, Mandy's terse reply was that he hadn't asked her and anyway, his place wasn't big enough to swing a cat never mind contain all her stuff. Liz had managed to stop herself from replying her apartment wasn't big enough either. When she'd last looked into the spare room, there was no evidence of Mandy having made any attempt to unpack properly or put anything away in the shelves and drawers Liz had cleared for her.

But tonight was going to be different. Mandy had promised to be home for dinner. It appeared Gary had other plans. Liz wondered what her daughter would say to her going out with Finn. Would she tell her? Probably. If they ate locally, it would be all over town next day.

After leaving work, Liz made a quick trip to the supermarket to replenish supplies, before heading to *The Haven* to make a long overdue visit to her mother. She did try to visit every week, but due to a case of food poisoning at the retirement village which had kept all the residents isolated, it had been a few weeks since she'd been there. So she was looking forward to catching up.

Liz drove through the gates of *The Haven* and along the avenue bordered by palm trees, past the beautiful old sandstone building which held the office and restaurant where residents, unable or unwilling to cook for themselves, could buy lunch or dinner, finally coming to a stop outside her mother's tidy villa.

Joan was waiting at the open door to greet her.

'Hi, Mum. I'm sorry it's been so long.'

'Not your fault, sweetheart. It was the prawns they served for the Friday dinner. I was lucky I didn't have any, but the powers-that-be decided to shut us all down. Anyway, it's over now and good to see you. Come on in.'

Liz followed her mother into the neat front room which overlooked the roadway giving Joan an uninterrupted view of the comings and goings of her neighbours. The coffee table was already set for afternoon tea with a plate of what Liz knew was her mother's homemade carrot cake, and her best china. Liz resigned herself to eating her fair share, even though it wasn't long since she'd had lunch. Besides, her mother's carrot cake was something special, and always reminded Liz of coming in from playing in the yard to a slice of carrot cake and a glass of milk.

'What about Tara? No news there?' Liz's mother asked when they were on their second cup of tea. Liz had just shared the news that Mandy had moved back home, and Joan had nodded her approval.

'No, Mum. She and Mark want to wait, do some travelling first.' Liz was just as anxious as her mother to hear Tara was pregnant, but wishing wouldn't make it happen.

Joan sighed. 'I hope I live long enough to see a great grandchild,' she said. 'Bernadette Riley has three and never stops talking about them.'

Liz almost blurted out the news she already had one, but she wasn't ready to mention Julie and Tilly to her mother yet. *Would she ever be?* She had no idea how the older woman might react.

Finally, it was time to leave with hugs and a promise to return the following week. By then both Tara and Mandy would have left for Easter, and Julie would be here. Liz tingled all over at the thought of being reunited with the baby she'd been forced to give away. But first, there was her dinner with Finn to look forward to.

*

The next few days seemed to drag but finally Friday arrived. Mandy was heading off somewhere with Gary, so Liz was able to take her time getting ready without having to answer to her daughter. She had mentioned briefly that Finn had invited her to dinner, only to see Mandy roll her eyes and hear her say, 'I thought there was something going on when he came over to our table on Saturday. Good for you, Mum.'

Now, as she drew a comb through her hair and fretted whether she'd worn too much makeup, wiping off her lipstick and re-applying a paler shade, she was trying to still the butterflies in her stomach. Not counting the disastrous dates with the men she'd met online – and they really didn't count – this was her first proper date since she and Tommy divorced, and she was a nervous wreck.

It was almost time for Finn to arrive to pick her up when her phone rang. Liz's first thought was that he was ringing to cancel, having changed his mind or had some family emergency. But it was Tara's name on the screen.

'Mandy told me, Mum,' she said. 'Finn Hunter seems like a nice guy. I hope you have a good time. You deserve this.'

Liz muttered something, not sure what *this* was and ended the call as she heard a knock at the door. He was here.

After an awkward few moments at the door, when it seemed neither knew how to greet the other, Liz grabbed her bag and they headed to his car. She was surprised to see he drove a Prius, pleased he showed some concern for the environment.

'I thought we'd drive out of town,' he said as he started up the car. 'I know what these small towns are like and don't relish the prospect of being next week's news. I'm guessing you don't either.'

Liz gave a sigh of relief.

'Have you been to *Addisons*?' he asked. 'I've heard good things about it, and I believe *The Courier* gave it a good review.' He grinned.

Liz grinned too, pleased he had a sense of humour. She began to relax.

The restaurant fulfilled the promise of the review she'd read in *The Courier*, the seafood platter they shared leaving nothing to be desired and the bottle of semillon blanc Finn selected from the extensive wine list was perfect.

'Tell me about yourself,' Finn said when they were waiting for dessert – a delicious-sounding triple flavoured crème brûlée. 'You have a daughter?'

For a moment Liz hesitated, but now wasn't the time to bring up Julie. 'Two,' she said. 'Tara, the oldest works in recruitment. She's married and she and her husband are off to Paris for Easter.'

'Half their luck. The other is the one I saw you with in the yacht club?'

'Mandy. Yes. She has a personal training business. She… and her belongings… have just moved in with me,' she said ruefully.

'You don't sound thrilled.'

'I'm not.' Liz suddenly felt guilty remembering Finn had moved in with his daughter and grandson, but there had been extenuating circumstances. 'My apartment isn't designed for someone like Mandy. She's not the world's tidiest person. But she hasn't been there much. There's a new boyfriend.'

'Ah!' He grinned, his lips turning up and his eyes twinkling with amusement.

Liz felt a flutter in the pit of her stomach at the sight of that grin and those storm-grey eyes. How could he have such an effect on her on such a short acquaintance? She'd heard about such things. Didn't the French call it a *coup de foudre*? It wasn't exactly first sight, but it might as well have been. Liz had never thought it would happen to her, and certainly not at her age. How Mandy would crow if she knew.

'You live with your daughter, too, don't you?' she said, trying to still the butterflies in her stomach at the thought of what it would feel like to kiss him, to have those lips pressing against hers.

'Yes.' He gazed into space. 'I came to Pelican Crossing to support

Adele and Sandy when Tim died. She took it hard… they both did.' He pulled on one ear. 'Some days she seems better, then on others it's as if it only happened yesterday.' He shook his head.

'I'm sorry.' Liz put a hand on his, then pulled it away, lest he think her too forward. She wanted to comfort him, to tell him she understood, but how could she? She didn't. She had no idea what his family were going through. 'You took a lot on,' she said feeling sympathy for him.

'Thanks. But there was no one else to step up.'

'Your daughter's mother?' *Was he widowed or divorced?*

'Karen?' Finn snorted. 'She doesn't care about anyone but herself. There was no way she was going to uproot her life to support our daughter.'

Divorced, then.

'I'm sorry,' Liz said again, wanting to do or say something to make him feel better, but feeling helpless.

'It's not your problem, and I think my being here is helping… both of them. I'm enjoying living in Pelican Crossing too.' He grinned again, sending shivers through Liz. 'I'm guessing you're divorced too? You can probably understand the dilemma of an uncaring ex-spouse.'

'I certainly can. Tommy… well, suffice it to say he wasn't the most faithful of husbands. I've been on my own now for six years. I enjoy the freedom, though it sometimes gets lonely.' As she spoke, Liz realised how lonely she did often feel, mostly on Saturday evenings the time when those who were one part of a couple had someone to spend it with. *Why was she confiding this to Finn who she barely knew?*

It was Finn's turn to say, 'I'm sorry.'

For a moment Liz considered touching his hand again. Then thought maybe he was thinking of reaching out and touching hers… But their desserts arrived, and the conversation moved on from personal revelations to Pelican Crossing and the feature Finn planned on Agnes and her pelican rescue centre.

After the meal, they wandered outside to lean against the wall surrounding the restaurant. It was too dark to be able to admire the view, only a few stars lighting up the night sky, but Liz could visualise what it was like in daylight. Although some way from the coast, she could imagine the ocean in the distance – the water the colour of Finn's smiling eyes.

As if reading her mind, Finn said, 'The view must be spectacular during the day. Next time, we should come for lunch.'

Liz shivered, a shiver that had nothing to do with the slight breeze. Next time. There was going to be a next time.

'If you're willing to risk seeing me again, of course.'

'I think I could… risk it, I mean.' She smiled, to see him smile too.

'That's a relief,' he said. 'I've really enjoyed this evening. It's been a while… I'm out of practice with this dating thing. My daughter thinks…' He coughed. 'Sorry, you don't want to hear what she thinks.'

'I have daughters too,' Liz laughed. 'They always have an opinion as to what I should do.'

'And…?'

'I usually ignore them.' Liz laughed again. She couldn't believe how much she'd enjoyed the evening, how easy Finn had been to talk to, how similar their tastes in books and music were. It was uncanny, as if…

'We should be getting back,' Finn said, interrupting Liz's train of thought and steering her towards the car, the touch of his firm hand on the small of her back sending a sudden shudder of desire down her spine.

When had she last felt like this? It was so long ago, Liz couldn't remember. But she recognised the sensation. Did Finn feel it too… as if they were being drawn together by some unseen thread?

Once in the car, the only indication of Finn's feelings was the way he smiled at her before starting the engine. They didn't speak much on the drive back to Pelican Crossing, Liz busy with her thoughts, and Finn clearly concentrating on the road as a sudden burst of rain began to beat on the windscreen, taking all of his attention.

All too soon for Liz, they pulled up outside her apartment block. 'Thanks for a lovely evening,' she said.

'My pleasure.'

They sat looking at each other.

'I should go in.'

'Yes.'

Neither moved.

'Would it be presumptuous of me to…'

Liz held her breath, her heart pounding as Finn leant across. Their lips met, and parted, and met again.

Her thoughts in a whirl, too stunned to speak, Liz pulled away, jumped out of the car and ran through the rain to her apartment building, only vaguely conscious of Finn promising to call her.

Sixteen

'Wake up, Grandy! It says on the calendar we get Bluey today.'

Finn opened his eyes to see Sandy standing by his bedside, his eyes bright with excitement. He'd been dreaming about Liz Phillips. They'd been sitting on a deserted beach, and he'd been about to kiss her when he felt someone tug on his arm. He blinked.

'Leave your grandad be, Sandy' Adele popped her head through the door. 'I don't think you're going to get any peace till we pick up the pup,' she said to Finn. 'Breakfast will be ready in ten minutes.'

'Okay.' Finn rubbed his face. 'Let me get up and have a shower, champ.'

'Can we go then?'

'After breakfast. You heard your mum.'

'Yeah.' Sandy's mouth turned down, but he went out and left Finn to get up and into the shower without any more fuss.

'Good evening?' Adele asked, when Finn joined her and Sandy in the kitchen. 'You must have got home late. I didn't hear you come in.'

'Yeah.' Finn piled his plate with the scrambled eggs and bacon Adele had cooked. After he'd dropped Liz off, he'd driven round to the beach and sat for a while staring out at the darkened ocean, listening to the waves pound on the shore, wondering what had gone wrong. He didn't know how long he sat there, but he didn't manage to reach any conclusion.

It had been a good evening, the best. They'd talked about books, music, daughters. He'd told her about Sandy's dog. It had all been so easy. No awkward silences, no need to search for something to say. Everything was fine until…

She'd looked so beautiful sitting there in the moonlight, her lips just waiting to be kissed. It would have taken a stronger man than him to have resisted. She had been sitting, waiting, when she could have got out of the car, gone in. But when he had kissed her… and what a kiss it had been, her lips as soft and welcoming as he'd expected… she'd jumped out of the car and run off as if the hounds of hell were at her heels. What was that about? Was his kiss a disappointment? Was he a disappointment? Had he acted too soon? He'd never understand women. It was why he'd steered clear of them after Karen.

'Can we go now, Grandy?' Sandy couldn't stem his impatience. 'I've finished my breakfast.'

'I'll just finish my coffee.' Finn smiled at his grandson, realising that, while he was rehashing the previous evening, he'd managed to finish his breakfast too.

Ten minutes later they were in the car. If Sandy had been bouncing in the back seat on their last trip to Rhana's, this time he almost leapt through the roof in his excitement. It was a relief to Finn and Adele when they finally reached their destination.

'There it is!' Sandy pointed to the sign on the gate. 'I remember it!'

Rhana was waiting to greet them as before. This time she was holding a wriggling black and white bundle.

'It's Bluey!' Sandy yelled. 'My Bluey!'

'Calm down, champ. You don't want to frighten him. Remember he's only little and he might be a bit afraid about leaving his mummy.'

'Oh!' Sandy calmed down sufficiently to climb out of the car and walk slowly towards Rhana. 'Can I touch him?' he asked.

'Of course.' Rhana bent down to allow Sandy to stroke the tiny creature, who tried to lick his fingers.

'He likes me,' Sandy said, giggling. 'It tickles. Can we take him home now?'

'In a little while,' Rhana said. 'I need to talk with your mum and grandad first. But, when we go inside, I'll put Bluey down on the floor with his toys and you can play with him.'

Finn thought Sandy's eyes were going to pop out of his head as they all made their way inside.

After cups of tea for the adults and a glass of juice for Sandy, during which Rhana ensured Finn and Adele were quite clear on how to care for the pup, it was time to leave. Finn fetched the small pet crate from the car and, despite Sandy's insistence he could hold his new pet on his lap, persuaded the small animal inside.

'He'll feel safer there,' Rhana assured Sandy who had shed a few tears.

On the drive home, it was a challenge to keep Sandy in his seat, as the sound of Bluey whining in the rear of the car upset him, and he kept asking Finn if the dog was all right. It was a relief when they arrived home and both boy and dog could be released.

'Can we take him for a walk?' Sandy asked, as soon as they were inside.

Adele looked at Finn who shrugged.

'He hasn't had all his vaccinations yet, but perhaps we can risk a short one. I'll go with them,' he said. 'Do you want to come too?'

Adele shook her head. 'I think I'll stay here. I've had enough excitement for the day. While you're gone, I'll get lunch ready.'

'Right.' Finn showed Sandy how to attach the lead to Bluey's new collar and they set off, the excited pup almost pulling the delighted Sandy off his feet, and making Finn recognise the need to enrol the three of them into puppy school. He knew *The Courier* ran a regular advertisement for one conducted by the local vet surgery. He could enrol them when they took Bluey in to get microchipped. Then he'd have to register Bluey with the council, arrange his vaccinations, check how old he had to be before he could be de-sexed. It was never-ending.

But seeing the expression on Sandy's face made it all worthwhile.

*

'It's the lady from the doctor's,' Sandy said when they turned into Main Street which was deserted apart from one lone figure. 'Look, Grandy!'

Finn looked to where Sandy was pointing with the hand which wasn't trying to stop Bluey from pulling him along. It was Liz.

As they drew closer, he tried to work out what to say, but before he could frame any words, Sandy gave a yell as he lost hold on the lead and Bluey, suddenly free, dashed off up the street towards where Liz was walking towards them.

'Bluey!' Sandy yelled giving chase, but he was no match for the small dog who was enjoying his first taste of freedom.

The dog, unaccustomed to the freedom, ran straight into Liz who scooped him up.

'Does he belong to you?' she asked the now breathless little boy.

'He's Bluey… my new dog. He's my birthday present,' Sandy said, as Liz set the animal down and handed Sandy the lead.

'Thanks, Liz,' Finn said. He turned to Sandy. 'Sandy, maybe I should…' He reached out his hand for the lead.

'No, Grandy. We'll be fine, Bluey and me.'

As if understanding, the little dog sat down at Sandy's feet and gazed up at him with a soulful expression.

Finn and Liz laughed. Then there was an awkward pause.

Liz spoke first. 'Last night. I'm sorry. I…' She blushed.

'No, *I'm* sorry. It was presumptuous of me. I shouldn't have…'

'No, it's not… It was good, maybe too good. It's been a while…'

'For me too.' Finn smiled, pleased to see a matching smile appear on Liz's face. He cast around for something to say, glanced about him, noted they were standing outside the new gelato outlet.

Liz must have noticed too because before he could speak, she said, 'Why don't we all have an ice cream?'

Sandy's eyes lit up. 'Bluey too?'

Liz laughed again. It was an attractive laugh which gave Finn hope all was not lost. 'I don't think ice cream is good for your dog's tummy, but I suspect you'd like one.'

'Yes, please!'

'I'll get them,' Finn said, glad to have something to do before he said the wrong thing. 'What flavour?'

'Surprise me,' Liz said.

'Can I have chocolate, Grandy?' Sandy asked.

When Finn returned carrying three ice creams, he found Liz had taken Sandy and Bluey across the road to sit at one of the tables located in front of the beach. 'Here you are,' he said, handing the chocolate one to Sandy. Then he held the other two to Liz. 'Which do you prefer – strawberry or mango?'

'Mango, thanks.' She smiled again, and Finn felt a warm glow encompass him.

They ate their ice creams in silence apart from a warning to Sandy when he made an attempt to share his with his pet.

When they had finished, Liz said, 'That was delicious, thanks. Lovely to meet Bluey, Sandy,' she said to the little boy. 'I'm sure Bluey will be very happy with you. Just make sure you keep a firm grasp of his lead.'

Sandy nodded, a serious expression on his face.

Liz looked back up at Finn. 'I'm sorry. I have to go now. I'm having a pre-Easter thing with my girls tonight and need to start to cook. It's been…'

'Look, before you go. I did intend to call you after last night. I hope we can do it again. Tomorrow? Lunch? Are you free?'

There was a pause during which Finn experienced a tingling sensation in his chest, then she said, 'Thanks, I'd like that.'

'Great!' Finn heaved a sigh of relief. 'I'll pick you up at half-eleven. How do you feel about picnics?'

'I love a good picnic,' she said, smiling. 'Thanks,' she said again.

'She's a nice lady, Grandy. Is she your girlfriend?' Sandy asked, his mouth rimmed with chocolate.

'Maybe she is, Sandy,' Finn replied with a grin as he watched her walk off. 'Maybe she is.'

Seventeen

Liz had a spring in her step as she left Finn and Sandy and headed to where she'd left her car, glad she'd made the trip to Main Street to buy a few last-minute items for dinner.

As soon as she got back into her apartment the previous evening, she'd berated herself for acting like a fool, like a prim miss who'd never been kissed before. It had been the perfect ending to a perfect evening… and she'd spoiled it.

The kiss had taken her by surprise. Not the kiss itself. She'd wanted… expected it. It was her reaction to it, to his lips on hers; the wave of emotion which swept through her was unlike anything she'd experienced before. It scared her. That was what made her jump out of the car and run through the rain.

She'd made up her mind she'd never hear from Finn again. What man would want to pursue a woman who ran away at the first sign of affection? But it had been more than affection. It had been a kiss which promised the world, a world which she hadn't known since she was eighteen and in the throes of her first love… if even then.

Now, she was going to have a second chance and she promised herself she wouldn't ruin it this time.

But in the meantime, there was dinner to prepare, the Easter dinner for her family. Tara and Mark would be there, along with Mandy who had asked if she could invite Gary. Liz had been delighted to agree, hoping Mandy might finally have found a relationship which would last.

Liz enjoyed cooking. She hummed to herself as she prepared the large piece of salmon she'd purchased at the market and set it to steam slowly in a bath of white wine and herbs, then prepared a variety of salads to accompany it. Maybe next year, they'd be joined by Julie and Tilly, or was that too much to hope for?

The salads done and waiting in the fridge, Liz set the table, positioning the Easter gifts for the girls lovingly at their places – two small owls she'd purchased at *The Mousehole* only moments before she'd bumped into Finn and his grandson. Now they were older, she'd dispensed with chocolate eggs but still liked to give them something to mark the occasion. For a few moments her thoughts took her back in time to the years when they were small, when she and Tommy had hidden the Easter eggs in the garden and watched with delight as Tara and Mandy searched for them, each trying to collect more than the other. She sighed, wishing yet again she had grandchildren with whom she could repeat the process. At fourteen, Tilly would have outgrown that too, but maybe not the chocolate eggs. She made a mental note to buy one for her on her next shopping expedition and perhaps to make another visit to *The Mousehole* too, to find something for Julie.

Everything was ready. Liz poured herself a glass of wine as she waited for her family to arrive. She had hoped Mandy might have been there to help, but the girl was spending more and more time with Gary, making Liz feel her apartment was only a dumping ground for her daughter's belongings.

At last, there was the sound of voices and a loud knock at the door. Everyone arrived at once and there was a flurry of hugs and kisses. Tara presented Liz with a bunch of flowers, while Mandy handed her a box of chocolates with the instruction not to eat them all at once, and the two men stood around looking awkward.

They were halfway through the meal when Tara asked, 'What gives with Finn Hunter, Mum?'

Liz bit her lip and looked down at her plate. She'd forgotten both of her daughters knew about her dinner date.

'At least he must have been an improvement on those you met on the internet,' Mandy said. 'Sorry, Mum, but at least you tried.'

'We had a nice dinner at *Addisons*,' Liz said, blushing to remember how it had ended.

'*Addisons*? Very upmarket,' Mark said.

'You should take me there,' Tara said, glancing at her husband. 'I've heard the food's something special.' She looked back at Liz. 'Is that all you have to say?'

'Are you going to see him again?' Mandy asked.

'I may do.' Liz felt uncomfortable with this interrogation. She wanted to keep her relationship, if it could be called that on the basis of two dates, private, not something to be bandied about over the dinner table, even by her daughters, especially by her daughers.

But Mandy wasn't finished. 'I think he'd be good for you, Mum. He's the right age, single, been married…'

'That's enough, Mandy. You make it sound like an ad for a partner. I'm not in the market for another husband, and even if I was…' Her voice trailed off at the realisation Finn was exactly the man she'd choose.

'Leave it, Mandy. It's your mum's life.'

Liz looked across the table at her son-in-law. It was unlike him to comment like this. But she was grateful for his timely intervention. She nodded her thanks.

'You must be looking forward to Paris, Tara,' Liz said, eager to change the topic, and for the rest of the meal the conversation consisted of Tara listing all the places she and Mark intended to visit.

Liz was glad no one asked about her Easter plans. She remembered when Mandy had asked her earlier, what her reply had been. Now she buzzed with excitement at the prospect of meeting Julie – and perhaps Tilly – and seeing Finn again. A lot could happen in the next two weeks while both Tara and Mandy were gone.

*

Liz had felt a little teary as she hugged everyone goodbye the previous evening. Even Gary had surprised her with a hug. Tara and Mark were due to fly out in a few days' time, though Mandy wouldn't be leaving till Thursday and would be popping in several times before then.

Liz couldn't suppress her excitement at the prospect of seeing Finn again. He'd mentioned a picnic, so she dressed in a pair of jeans and a white top, threw a blue shirt around her shoulders and pulled on a pair of comfortable canvas shoes. Finn had said he'd provide all the food and drink, so there was nothing else for her to do. One final glance in the mirror and she was ready just as she heard him knock on the door, sending the butterflies in her stomach into freefall.

'Hi!' Liz said as she opened the door, suddenly feeling shy.

'Hi! You're looking lovely.'

'Thanks.' Liz blushed. It was a long time since anyone had called her lovely. It made her feel… cherished.

'Shall we go?'

'I'm ready.' Liz picked up her bag and a wide-brimmed hat.

'Where are we going?' she asked when they were in his car.

'Surprise.' He grinned, his face creasing into the wrinkles she remembered. He really was a good-looking man. Not regular good looks with his thatch of prematurely white hair and the nose which looked as if it might have been broken at one time, but a rugged good looks which Liz decided she liked better, and gorgeous grey eyes which made her think of the ocean on a stormy day.

They drove across town to where the River Boodalang entered the ocean, then along the side of the river till they came to a quiet spot where a barbecue area had been set up beside two tables. It was deserted.

'I didn't know this was here,' Liz said looking around and seeing a pair of pelicans alight on the water, seemingly attracted by their presence.

'Not many people do,' Finn replied. 'I discovered it soon after I arrived in Pelican Crossing. It's close to where old Agnes has her pelican rescue centre. It appears the council built this spot, then forgot about it, as did everyone else.'

'It's lovely,' Liz said. 'So close to the ocean yet secluded. It's like a secret retreat.'

'Exactly. I hoped you'd like it.' Finn began to unload an esky from the car, while Liz wandered over to the edge of the river to watch the antics of the pelicans. They were such elegant creatures. She took out her phone and tried to take a photo, but it was impossible to capture them accurately. She was no Martin Cooper. She gave up in frustration.

'Can I help?' she asked, seeing Finn open the esky and start to unpack it.

'You could open the salads – I'm afraid they're pre-packed ones from the supermarket – while I organise the barbecue. I hope you like steak.'

'Yum.' Liz loved barbecued steak. It always reminded her of growing up in the bush, of her dad lighting up the barbecue on Saturday evenings, of happy family dinners, before they had been forced to move.

Finn poured two glasses of wine while Liz unpacked the salads. There was a tub of Greek salad and one of what appeared to be potato, egg and bacon. Both looked delicious, making Liz wonder why she bothered making her own.

When they began to eat, the two pelicans stepped out of the water and waddled closer. Seen this close, the birds, which didn't show any fear, were larger than Liz had anticipated, with their enormous pink bills and the yellow rim around their eyes. They seemed to be hoping for food, and when none was forthcoming, they waddled back to the river.

The steak was done to perfection. The salads complemented it perfectly. And the company couldn't have been better. It was as if Liz had known Finn for much longer as they chatted about their lives and shared family anecdotes. She liked the way he had moved in to help his daughter and was tempted to tell him about Julie. But it was too soon. What if their meeting didn't work out? It was best to wait.

They were beginning to pack up when the sky darkened and suddenly the heavens opened to a torrent of rain, much heavier than the one which had fallen on their previous date. It was one of those sudden storms Queensland was renowned for. It seemed their dates were fated to attract the rain. By the time they'd packed the car and were safely inside, both Liz and Finn were soaked to the skin, and laughing. His hair was plastered to his skull, his shirt sticking to his skin showing off a muscular body. Liz was sure she looked much the same. By the time they reached her apartment block, the steam was rising from their clothes with the heat in the car.

'Why don't you come in and have a hot shower?' she said, without thinking. 'You should get out of these wet clothes. I can pop them in the drier before you go home.'

Now she was blushing at her words, at the images those words conjured up.

Finn didn't immediately reply, and she wondered if this time, it was she who was being too presumptuous. Then he gave the lazy grin with which she was becoming familiar and said, 'Good idea.'

Leaving the esky with the remains of their lunch in the car, they both jumped out and, holding hands, raced for the doorway to the apartment block, each giving a sigh of relief when they were inside.

Liz and Finn stared at each other, the water from their clothes dripping down to form puddles on the tiled floor. She smiled and pointed to the bathroom, then made her way to her bedroom and the ensuite.

Standing under a hot shower, Liz tried to figure out what she was feeling. It was crazy. She barely knew Finn, but her body was telling her a different story. It was telling her this was a man she could care for, desire, maybe even love. As she turned off the shower and wrapped herself in a soft white towel, she remembered her clean clothes sitting in the laundry; she'd been too lazy to put them away before she went out. She stepped over the ones she had taken off which were lying in a wet puddle on the floor of the ensuite. Maybe she could make it to the laundry and fetch her clean clothes while Finn was still in the shower.

Peering out to make sure the coast was clear, Liz was tiptoeing along past the bathroom when the door opened and she was confronted by the half-naked figure of Finn. Instead of hurrying by, she stopped in her tracks, stunned by the perfection of his ripped body.

Tossing his still wet hair out of his eyes, Finn returned her gaze as if unable to believe Liz was standing there and there were only their towels between them.

It was as if time stood still. Finn reached one hand to stroke Liz's face, holding firmly to his towel with the other.

She felt an unexpected stirring at the base of her stomach as his fingers traced down her cheek… to her mouth… and around her lips.

'Liz,' he murmured as he moved closer to place his lips on hers. This was not the brief, tentative encounter of Friday evening. This was a deliberate and sensual kiss which deepened as he discovered it was returned. Liz felt as if she was floating on air. The thrill of Finn's lips on hers made her realise she was aroused as she hadn't been since the early days with Tommy, aroused as she had thought never to be again. She felt herself sink into his embrace, his arms reached around her and both towels fell to the ground unnoticed.

As they sank to the floor, it was Finn who stopped, removed his lips and, keeping hold of Liz's welcoming body spoke. 'Your bedroom,' he said hoarsely. Unable to speak, Liz indicated her room with one hand, and picking her up lightly, Finn carried her to the bed.

It was too soon, much too soon… but it felt so right.

Eighteen

It was still light when Finn opened his eyes, the late afternoon sun shining in through the window as if the storm had never happened. But it had, and afterwards…

Hearing a slight sound, he turned. Liz was awake and gazing at him, her eyes filled with emotion. 'Have you been awake for long?' He was embarrassed to think that she might have been lying there watching him sleeping.

'Not long,' she said, in a tone of voice Finn didn't recognise.

'I don't… I didn't intend… I'm sorry.' He attempted to rise, thinking she was regretting their lovemaking.

'No need to be,' she said with a smile. 'I have no regrets, far from it.'

Finn gently stroked her forehead and dropped a kiss on her lips. 'I intended to take my time with you, to court you properly. Sorry, I know it's an old-fashioned word. I'm an old-fashioned guy. This isn't how I meant to behave. I should have been more restrained. But seeing you there, glistening from the shower.' He smiled tenderly. 'It was more than this man could stand. But I'm sorry, I can't promise you anything. I have…'

'Obligations. I know.' She sat up in bed and pulled the covers up to her chin, as if suddenly aware of her nakedness. 'I understand. I have them too.'

Finn wasn't sure what she meant. He knew she had two daughters, but weren't they independent – one married and one in a relationship? Unlike him, who had a daughter and grandson dependent on him.

Adele might encourage him to make his own life, but he was aware how she still cried herself to sleep some nights, hiding her red eyes next morning with makeup, how she relied on him to be there for Sandy, to provide the male role model denied to him when Tim died.

Finn saw Liz's disappointment, the smile that didn't quite make it all the way up to her eyes. 'It doesn't mean…' he began, '… I still want to… What I'm trying to say is that I do want to see you again, to continue what we… Hell,' he dragged a hand through his already dishevelled hair, 'I'm no good at this. It's been so long.'

'For me too.' Liz spoke so softly he could barely hear her. 'Let's just play it by ear, shall we?'

Finn felt as if a huge weight had been lifted from his shoulders. Play it by ear. He could do that. And perhaps things would change. *They always did, didn't they*, he thought, ignoring the tiny voice in his head which was saying, *And pigs might fly*.

'Hungry?' Liz asked, defusing the emotion which filled the room. 'I have some leftovers from last night.'

There was nothing Finn would have liked more than to stay here with this warm woman eating leftovers, perhaps drinking a glass of wine, then coming back to bed for a repeat of the lovemaking they'd enjoyed earlier. But he knew Adele would worry if he didn't come home, and Sandy would want to tell him about Bluey's latest antics. 'I'd love to,' he said, 'but…'

'I know,' she said, 'obligations.' She gave a gentle laugh. 'It's okay, remember?'

'You're a good woman,' he said, 'good *and* sexy. But I really must go.'

*

Liz sat on the deck watching the sun go down. She couldn't believe what had happened, that she and Finn had ended up in bed together. She hugged herself remembering how he had made her feel, how nothing else had seemed to matter except this man, this moment.

And now he was gone. She understood. Totally. He had family to take care of – his daughter and grandson relied on him. But Liz suddenly felt lonelier than she ever had before.

Her phone rang. Mandy. 'Hi, sweetheart, what's up?' Liz asked, trying to sound normal, as if her world hadn't suddenly been turned upside down.

Mandy's voice was filled with excitement. 'We're leaving sooner than expected,' she said. 'Gary has arranged to meet an old mate up there and check things out before the trip and he wants me to go with him. Can I drop round and pick up some of my stuff?'

'Of course you can. You know you don't need to ask. Why don't you stay for dinner? I've barely seen you since you supposedly moved in.'

'Sorry, Mum.' There was the sound of a conversation in the background, then, 'Sounds good. I may stay over too. Gary's busy tonight.'

'It'll only be leftovers…' But Liz was talking to empty space. She went inside to check what was left from last night's dinner, poured herself a glass of wine and went into the bedroom which looked as if a bomb had hit it. She remade the bed, then stared at her face in the mirror, trying to work out if the passion she had experienced with Finn had left its mark. But her face looked the same as ever, perhaps a touch flushed, but that could be with the effort of making the bed. By the time Mandy arrived, she was feeing calmer.

'You saw Finn Hunter again today.' Mandy wasted no time in mentioning him. She and Liz were seated on the deck with the bottle of wine Mandy had brought.

'I did. We had a picnic by the river. A barbecue.'

'Sounds like fun. You need more fun in your life, Mum. You're seeing him again? Maybe he can be company for you over Easter.' Mandy took a gulp of wine.

Liz flinched. It wouldn't be Finn who was keeping her company over Easter. 'I expect he'll be spending it with his family,' she hedged. 'He lives with his daughter and grandson. Easter is a time for children.'

'Oh, that's right. Wasn't it his son-in-law who drowned trying to save his son? It must have been traumatic for the little boy. He's quite young, isn't he?'

'Six. He got a spaniel pup for his birthday.' Liz knew the little boy had been traumatised. He'd been right there, seen his dad go under the waves. He was seeing the counsellor at the clinic. She thought his daughter was receiving counselling too. It was a lot for Finn to handle. He wouldn't have much time to spend with her. She winced, castigating herself for having such a selfish thought.

'Not a cat?' Mandy laughed. She knew her mother's predilection for cats over dogs. 'Pity you can't have one here.'

'It wouldn't be fair on the poor creature, and I doubt the body corporate would permit it.' Liz's small apartment was on the third floor of the building. 'I have to make do with the one I have.' She glanced regretfully inside to where the small, white, wooden cat sat on one shelf of the bookcase.

'I guess.' But Mandy didn't look convinced.

'I'm glad you're here tonight, Mandy. When you said you wanted to move in, I expected to see more of you.' Liz forgot her initial concerns. 'Gary… you and him… is it serious?'

Mandy reddened. She ran a finger around the edge of her glass. 'I'd like it to be, and I think… Oh, Mum, how can you tell if a man's serious? He says I'm special, enjoys being with me, but…'

'He hasn't said he loves you?'

Mandy shook her head.

'You love him?'

'I've never felt like this before. When I'm with him it's as if everything is better, brighter. It's difficult to explain.'

'Have you told him how you feel?'

'No! I don't want to scare him off.'

'You think it would?'

'I don't know. What if it did? I couldn't bear it.'

'Men are different from us,' Liz said. 'They sometimes find it hard to express their feelings, to put them into words. What's your gut feeling?'

'I don't know.'

'Maybe this trip…?'

'Maybe.' Mandy took a sip of wine, stared out into space then asked, 'What about you and Finn? I get the feeling there's something there. Have you…?' She waggled her eyebrows.

Liz felt herself redden. This wasn't the sort of conversation she wanted to have with her daughter. While it seemed okay to talk about Mandy's sex life, hers was so new and surprising she preferred to keep it to herself. Though she was pleased her daughter didn't consider her too old to have one.

'Oh, Mum, you have! You deserve it. It's time you had a man in your life, one who's single, one who can…'

'Steady on. This is my life you're talking about. And Finn may be single, but he isn't free.'

'Not…? Oh, you mean his daughter and grandson? But surely they…?' Mandy's voice trailed off as Liz's expression changed. 'Oops, did I overstep the mark? Is there something about our local newspaper editor I don't know? Does he have some dark secret hidden in his past?'

Liz felt the colour drain from her face. It wasn't Finn who had a dark secret. What would Mandy think if she knew… *when* she knew, because Liz couldn't keep Julie and Tilly a secret for long. 'That's enough, Mandy. It's becoming cool out here. We should go inside and eat,' she said, desperate to change the subject.

'But…' Mandy began.

But Liz had already risen and was walking inside.

Nineteen

Liz was glad to reach the medical centre next morning after the chaos in her apartment. Mandy and Gary were heading off today, and her daughter had left it to the last moment to pack, seemingly unable to do so without behaving as if she were leaving for several months instead of two weeks.

The centre, with its rapid turnover of patients and the occasional emergency, seemed an oasis of calm after Mandy's rushing around cursing when couldn't find what she was looking for. Liz had been forced to bite her tongue to stop herself from reminding her daughter that she wouldn't be having this problem if she'd put her belongings away in the first place. She dreaded to think what state the apartment would be in when she returned. But Mandy would never change. She was her daughter. And Liz loved her, even if she was sometimes difficult to cope with.

Liz was bringing the accounts up to date when her phone buzzed. She normally kept it on silent when she was at work, but this morning, she'd merely muted the tone in the hope Finn might contact her. He'd left so hurriedly yesterday there had been no mention of seeing each other again, and he had said…

She checked the screen to see a withheld number. When this happened, she usually ignored the call but this morning, something made her answer. Her heart leapt when she heard Finn's voice. She'd never been in the newspaper office, but she could picture him, his glasses perched on his thatch of white hair, his lips turned up in the now familiar grin.

'How are you this morning? Sorry I had to rush away.'

'That's fine, and I'm fine too.' *All the better for hearing your voice.*

'Are you free for lunch? I can manage to sneak out around one.'

'I should be able to.' Liz knew the reception desk had a full complement of staff today so she wouldn't be required to fill in for anyone over lunch.

'How about we meet in *Books and Coffee*? It's along from the newspaper. I can't be away for long.'

'That would work.' Liz loved the combined bookshop and café. It was located on a corner with the bookshop entrance on one street and the café entrance on the other. Lou, the lovely woman who owned it and ran the bookshop part must be in her sixties but was as lively as many half her age. The café section was run by Ron and Denny, a gay couple whose witty repartee was well known, and whose cakes were to die for. It wasn't too far from the medical centre, and the walk would do her good.

Knowing she was going to see Finn for lunch made the rest of Liz's morning pass in a flash. Before she knew it, it was quarter to one, and time to go to meet Finn.

As Liz neared the venue, she could see him sitting at one of the outside tables reading a newspaper. She supposed it was part of his job to keep abreast with what all the other papers were reporting. Seeming to sense her approach, he looked up and rose, folding the paper as he did so.

'Hey,' he said softly, giving her a kiss on the cheek and sending shivers down her spine.

'Hey,' she replied, shocked at his effect on her after such a short time.

Finn held out a chair and Liz sat down, hoping he couldn't see her trembling. She took a deep breath to calm herself. This was crazy.

'What'll you have?' he asked. 'I often eat here and can recommend the… What?' he asked at her expression.

'Sorry,' she said. 'It's just… you sounded so…' She laughed.

Finn laughed too. '*I'm* sorry,' he said. 'You've probably eaten here before too. What would you like to order? Do you need a menu?'

Liz shook her head. 'I love the bruschetta.'

'Two bruschetta,' he said, rising again to go in to order. 'Coffee?'

'Cappuccino.'

'I should have guessed. You look like a cappuccino lady.'

Before Liz could ask what he meant, he had gone inside. She picked up the paper he'd been reading, surprised to see it was a copy of *The Crossing Courier.*

'You're reading your own paper?' she asked when he returned.

'Someone has to,' he laughed, then became more serious. 'I like to reread it once it's gone to press, see how we can improve the layout.' He sighed. 'The owners are a consortium who own a number of regional papers and are urging me to go completely digital, but I know a lot of our readers rely on the paper version. They'd be lost without it.'

'You're right.' Liz thought of her mother who loved her local paper, and all the others like her in Pelican Crossing who had never moved into the digital age and never would. 'So, what can you do?'

'Try my best to increase circulation to prove how much the community value and need it. It's why I spend hours poring over it. But enough about me. I'm sorry I rushed off without making arrangements to see you again.'

'No worries.' Liz felt an arc of desire shoot through her at the expression in his eyes. 'We're here now.'

'We are.' He thrust a hand through his hair. 'This week's going to be hectic for me. It's Sandy's birthday, and Adele has arranged a few activities and treats. I need to be there.'

'I understand.'

'But next weekend. Easter. Perhaps we could do something then?'

Liz felt a flash of disappointment mixed with the rush of excitement she always experienced at the prospect of meeting her long-lost daughter. 'Oh, not next weekend,' she said, only to see his face fall. 'I'm sorry, I…'

'I thought you said your daughters would be away?'

Had she? She couldn't remember. Possibly. Now he'd think she didn't want to see him. But she couldn't tell him. She met his eyes, seeing their tenderness, his willingness to understand. Maybe this was the one person she could tell. 'It's like this…' she began.

*

Finn was still trying to get his head around what Liz had told him as he walked home that evening, choosing to leave his car in the office car park. He needed time to think, to digest the fact that she'd had a child when she was scarcely more than a child herself, that her parents had moved – twice – to help hide her pregnancy, ending up here in Pelican Crossing, and that now, this coming weekend, after thirty-four years, she was to meet her daughter. He couldn't imagine how it must feel, the excitement mixed with dread. What an Easter it was going to be for her. And there was a granddaughter too.

When Finn thought of all the pleasure he had from his own grandchild, the thought of her having missed out on all of that… It had made him want to pick her up and hug her, right there on the sidewalk. Only the fear of embarrassing her had stopped him. Instead, he'd muttered meaningless platitudes and hoped she understood. At least he'd been able to offer her a handkerchief to wipe away the tears which had trickled down her cheeks as she told him her story.

He knew her parents had acted in her best interests. At least they had supported her, helped her move on with her life. He had no idea how he'd have reacted if Adele had been in the same position – at fifteen. But to go for so long with no contact, no idea if her daughter was alive or dead. What must that have been like? He thought he'd detected an underlying sadness in Liz when they first met. This could have been the cause. And to think he'd burdened her with *his* obligations…

He was still lost in thought when he arrived home to be greeted by an excited Sandy. 'Guess what, Grandy? Bluey did a poo on the kitchen floor!'

'Sorry, Adele.' Finn gave Adele a rueful grin, sure it hadn't been the highlight of *her* day. 'We need to teach him to go outside,' Finn said to Sandy, reminded again of the puppy training class he'd intended to book.

'Mummy cleaned it up,' Sandy said cheerfully.

'Sorry,' Finn said again to Adele. He hadn't intended the dog to make more work for her.

'It's okay, Dad. I can see how much Bluey means to Sandy. Having the dog has done him the world of good.'

It was true. Since Bluey had joined them, Sandy's nightmares had stopped. He was sleeping through the entire night, and he was happier.

'You okay?' Adele asked Finn, making him realise he'd been frowning.

'What? Yeah. Just have a few things to think about.' About Liz, about the momentous event she was having to face this coming weekend. Thinking of Easter, he said, 'I know you have a few things arranged this week for this one's birthday,' he tousled Sandy's hair, 'but do you have any plans for Easter?'

'Will the Easter bunny be coming this year?' Sandy asked, his eyes wide.

'Sure thing, champ.' Finn remembered how the previous year, Adele had been so wrapped in grief, both Sandy's birthday and Easter had passed in a daze. Finn had tried his best to compensate, but the little boy was feeling bereft too. It was the year the Easter bunny didn't pay his usual visit.

'You'll be around? I thought…' Adele gave him a strange look. She knew he'd started seeing Liz.

'All weekend. It's complicated.'

'Oh, okay.'

Finn could see the questions in her eyes and knew he'd be in for an interrogation later when Sandy wasn't around. He'd work out how to deal with it then, without giving away Liz's secret.

Sandy was still focussed on Easter. 'We're making hats and chickens in my class,' he said, 'and there's to be a special 'sembly.'

Adele smiled. 'All the infant classes are making hats for a special Easter assembly and hat parade on the last day of term.'

'Which is? Remind me.'

'Classes wind up on Thursday, right before the Easter weekend.'

'Right, and…'

'Since you're going to be free, maybe we could do something special as a family. Almost everything will be closed on Good Friday, but there are three days left.'

'Can we go up in a balloon, Grandy? Can we, can we? You promised.'

Finn had a vague recollection of making a wild promise to Sandy one morning when they had watched the hot air balloons in the sky. He should have known better. He saw the fear in Adele's eyes. 'Maybe not a balloon ride this time,' he said, 'but we will do something special.' He just had to work out what it could be.

It wasn't till Sandy was in bed and had been read a story, that Finn was faced with Adele's questions. He managed to fend her off by saying Liz was busy with visitors on the weekend and that, yes, he intended to see her again. He tried to make light of it, not wanting to worry her. He had no wish for his relationship with Liz to make any difference to his life with Adele and Sandy, but wondered if he was being fair to Liz. She had a lot to handle at the moment. Was he adding one more complication to her already complex life?

Twenty

When Liz awoke on Good Friday, she wondered for a few moments why there was this empty feeling in the pit of her stomach. Then she remembered, and her heart began to race. This was the day she was going to meet her daughter, meet the adult version of the tiny baby she'd held for such a short time.

She slipped out of bed and headed for the ensuite, hoping a hot shower would still the butterflies in her stomach. But it didn't. She was still trembling with excitement when she pulled one outfit after another out of the wardrobe before deciding on a pair of white pants and a pink V-neck top, turning this way and that in front of the mirror wondering what Julie would think of her.

The sun was shining through the kitchen window. It was going to be a lovely day. The noisy myna which visited every morning was sitting on the deck railing hoping to be fed. A car started up and drove off, its tyres squealing as it turned the corner. Liz could hear the children in the yard outside yelling as they searched for Easter eggs. And she was a bundle of nerves.

Liz made herself coffee and toast, but the toast stuck in her throat. She had no appetite. In one part of her mind – the part that wasn't worrying about meeting Julie – Liz wondered what Finn was doing today. It had been a sudden impulse to share the information about Julie with him, and his reaction had been all that she could have hoped for. Liz could almost see him wondering what he'd have done if she had been his daughter, if it had been his daughter who'd become pregnant at fifteen. He had shared her pain, her fear about meeting the daughter she'd given up for adoption, the daughter who'd be here in – Liz checked the time – less than an hour.

She swallowed. They'd arranged for Julie to come to the apartment. Liz couldn't face the idea of the meeting taking place in public, and anyway, most of Pelican Crossing would be closed on Good Friday. At least in the apartment there would be no one to see her tears or to hear if they argued. She had no idea what might happen.

The knock at the door came before Liz was ready. With one last glance in the hall mirror, she smoothed down her unruly hair and opened the door to see…

'H… hello,' stuttered a woman who looked so like a younger version of her that Liz did a double take. The woman stared too, clearly equally shocked.

'Julie.' It couldn't be anyone else. Neither Tara nor Mandy shared the same features as their mother; they were a mixture of her and Tommy. The woman at the door resembled her exactly. It was like looking in a mirror and seeing herself as she'd been sixteen years ago, before the grey hair and wrinkles, before age took its toll.

Liz's eyes filled with tears. 'You'd better come in,' she said.

'Thanks.'

Liz led Julie into the apartment. She wanted to throw her arms around her daughter and hug her and hug her, but she sensed from the younger woman's tense figure and strained expression, that such an overt show of affection might not be welcome. 'I'm so pleased to see you,' she said. 'I never thought…'

Julie sat down, knees together, ankles crossed, hands clasped on her lap, eyes downcast.

'Tea? Coffee?'

'Coffee would be good, thanks.'

Relieved to have something to do, Liz went to the kitchen and turned on the coffee machine. She held on to the edge of the sink and stared unseeing out the window. What if she was a disappointment to Julie? What if…? Hell, this was more awkward than meeting any of the weirdos from the online dating app. This was her daughter, her own flesh and blood, the baby that had grown inside her for nine months. The baby she'd given away, she reminded herself. It was no wonder if Julie didn't immediately connect with her.

'Here we are,' Liz said, carrying in a tray with the two cups of coffee and a plate of Tim Tams. She didn't normally buy chocolate biscuits, but this was a special occasion, and it was Easter. She handed one cup to Julie.

'Thanks.' Julie shook her head at the biscuits.

There was an awkward silence, then Liz decided to break the ice. 'Why now?' she asked. It had been thirty-four years. Julie could have contacted her at any time in the past sixteen, ever since she turned eighteen.

'It's complicated.'

Liz waited.

'I've always known I was adopted, and when I was about twelve, I started to hate the woman who'd given birth to me. My adoptive parents were good to me, I loved them, and they loved me. But I hated the person who had given me away as if I was a bag of old clothes.'

Liz's breath caught, her eyes wet with tears.

'They told me you were too young to take care of me, that it was for my sake, but I didn't care. I wanted nothing to do with you.' She took a deep breath. 'When I turned eighteen, Mum encouraged me to contact you. She and Dad were getting older. Their health wasn't good. Mum thought it would help me to get in touch with you. But I knew better. I met Billy, got pregnant, married. It didn't last. Mum and Dad died, but I still resented having been given away. Nothing would have made me give Tilly away.'

Liz's eyes grew wider. She began to tremble. Julie's daughter, her granddaughter. 'But why now?' she repeated.

'It's Tilly.' Julie took a gulp of tea. 'She's fourteen, going on twenty-five. I was doing all right as a single mother until she hit high school. She got in with a bad crowd…' She gave a bitter laugh. 'Isn't that what all parents say when their kids get into trouble? Anyway, she and her friends were caught with a group of boys behind the bike shed at school. Then I found her sending photos of herself to a boy – not the sort of photo you'd want your daughter to take, never mind send to anyone. She finally confessed and told me he'd threatened to put it on social media if she didn't…' She broke down in tears. 'I was at my wits' end, then I remembered you'd had me when you weren't much older than Tilly is now. It made me think, made me wonder if I'd been too harsh on you, made me want to meet you. So, here I am. I can understand if you don't want anything to do with us.'

'Oh, my dear! You had no one else to turn to?'

Julie shook her head. 'I'm sorry it's taken this happening for me to reach out.'

'It doesn't matter, but I'm so sorry for Tilly, for you.'

'I don't know what to call you.'

'Liz is fine. Can I give you a hug?'

Julie moved forward into Liz's arms.

It was as if all Liz's Christmases had come at once. The baby she'd only held for an instant before she was taken away was in her arms again. She was a grown woman now, but the love Liz felt was the same.

'Where is she now – Tilly?'

'In the motel. I didn't know…'

'Can I meet her? Does she know about me?'

'I told her what I knew. She's… curious. I'm not sure how she'll react to meeting you. She can be unpredictable.'

'She's a teenager. I remember what Tara and Mandy were like at that age.'

'Of course. Your other daughters.' Julie looked down. 'Do they know about me?'

'No, I wanted to wait… till we'd met.'

'Till you decided if I was acceptable enough to be part of your family?' Julie said bitterly.

'No, not at all. You might have decided you didn't want to see me again, still might.' Liz's heart plummeted at the possibility this might be their only meeting.

Julie gave a slight smile. 'You don't seem too bad.'

Liz relaxed. 'More coffee?' she asked, seeing Julie's cup was almost empty. Her own was still full… and cold.

'Thanks.'

'It's nice here,' Julie said, when Liz returned with two fresh cups of coffee.

'The apartment or Pelican Crossing?'

'Both.'

'What's it like where you and Tilly live?'

'Busy. We live in the suburbs. Lots of houses, traffic. A long way from the ocean.' She stood up, walked to the window and gazed out at the view Liz loved but often took for granted. 'Have you lived here long?'

'In Pelican Crossing since I was sixteen, this apartment, six years, since my divorce.'

'You didn't live here when I was born?'

'Brisbane.' Liz shivered at the memory of that time, of the impersonal hospital ward, then the move to Pelican Crossing and the pretence that nothing had happened, that her life hadn't been torn apart.

'How did it happen?'

Liz took a deep breath.

*

'I didn't know,' Julie said when Liz had finished.

'How could you? My parents took every precaution. No one knew. Only us.'

'I'm sorry.'

'For what?'

'Sorry for what you had to go through, sorry I didn't understand, sorry I hated you, sorry I waited so long...'

'You're here now.'

'Yes. It must have been hard... to start again.'

'It wasn't easy, but Pelican Crossing is a friendly town. It was relatively easy to make new friends. It helped that no one knew...'

'They didn't ask?'

'We were newcomers to the town, said we'd moved from the country. That was all they needed to know.' But Liz remembered how it had felt to be the new girl in town when everyone else had known each other since kindergarten. Olga, who had now left town, had taken her under her wing, then there had been Tommy...

'Tell me about your daughters, my... half-sisters. Do they look like me?'

'A little. You look exactly like I did at your age. Tara and Mandy both have a little of their dad in them.' Liz realised Julie hadn't asked about *her* dad. She was glad, hoped she wouldn't. That part of her past was somewhere Liz didn't want to go.

Julie's eyes alighted on a photograph on the wall beside the window. It had been taken the previous summer and showed Tara and Mandy laughing wildly at the camera. 'Is that them?'

'Yes.' Liz joined her. 'We were celebrating my birthday last year.' Liz remembered the day like it was yesterday. Her girls had decided to treat the three of them to a spa session for her birthday. They'd driven down to Bellbird Bay to the new spa in *The Leonard Family Resort*, spent the morning there, then enjoyed lunch in the hotel restaurant.

'Tara's the oldest?'

'She's thirty and married. She and Mark are in Paris right now. Mandy's twenty-four. She's a personal trainer and she and her boyfriend are up north on a dive trip.'

'Wow! So, I won't be able to meet them?'

'Not this time.' Liz would need to prepare them, tell them about Julie and Tilly. She wasn't looking forward to it.

'I can't quite get my head around the fact I have two half-sisters I knew nothing about. I've always wanted a sister.' She stared at the photograph. 'And your parents?' she asked, turning to Liz.

'Dad's passed, and Mum lives in a retirement village.' As soon as she spoke, Liz realised she had opened a can of worms.

'A retirement village? Here in Pelican Crossing?'

'Yes. She doesn't know we've been in touch.'

'Oh!'

Suddenly Liz was swamped with guilt. Why hadn't she told her mother about Julie… and Tilly. While Joan had been glad to sweep her birth under the carpet at the time, to start a new life, surely after all those years she could forgive Liz and accept Julie and Tilly into her life? Her reluctance to let her mother know about Julie contacting her now seemed foolish, selfish… even if she'd done it with the best of intentions.

'Could I meet Tilly?' she asked, to cover her confusion, and to avoid having to answer any questions about her mother, who was Julie's grandmother, after all. It was only natural she'd want to know about her and meet her – and open that can of worms.

A variety of expressions flitted across Julie's face leading Liz to believe all wasn't going to be smooth sailing there either.

'If she doesn't want to come here, maybe we could go to the beach?'

'I'll call her. Can I…?' Julie took out her phone and gestured to the deck.

'Sure.' Liz picked up the cups and the plate of uneaten biscuits and took them into the kitchen while Julie made her call. Peeking out the kitchen window, she could see her pacing up and down and gesticulating as she spoke.

When she returned to the living room, Julie was already there, slipping her phone into her bag. 'Tilly's agreed to meet us at the beach,' she said. 'She says she'll wait by the marina.'

Twenty-one

Tilly was waiting at the gate to the marina, tall for her age with the same unruly dark hair as Liz and Julie, wearing a pair of knee-length dungarees and a grey tee-shirt. She was leaning against the gate, a sulky expression marring her pretty face.

Liz's heart sank. She recognised that expression. It was one she'd often seen on Mandy's face when she was in her teens and had been forced to do something against her will. Tilly didn't want to be here.

'Tilly, this is Liz, your…'

'I know who she is.' Tilly avoided looking at Liz.

'Hello, Tilly,' Liz said. 'I'm so pleased to meet you. Your mum and I have had a nice chat and…'

But Tilly had turned away, deliberately ignoring both Liz and Julie. She stared out across the marina where the lines of yachts and motor cruisers gleamed in the sunlight, and kicked the ground with the toe of her black high-top sneakers.

Undaunted, Liz walked across to stand beside Tilly. 'It's a lovely marina, isn't it?' she said chattily, as if the girl hadn't been rude. 'I never get tired of looking at it and watching the boats come and go. It's even prettier at night when some of them are lit up. I'd never lived by the ocean till we moved to Pelican Crossing when I wasn't much older than you are. Now, I wouldn't live anywhere else.'

Slowly Tilly turned to look at her, and Liz caught her breath. She could have been looking at herself at fifteen. How could fate have made Julie and Tilly in her likeness, with even the same green eyes, while Tara and Mandy bore only a fleeting resemblance?

'We have the same hair,' Tilly said. 'Are you really my grandmother?'

'I am.' Liz wanted to cry and hug her all at the same time. Here was the grandchild she'd hoped for, dreamt about. But instead of meeting her as a tiny baby in her mother's arms, this granddaughter was a teenager with all the angst that entailed. She searched around for something to say, something that wouldn't arouse conflict. 'Are you hungry?' she asked.

'Everywhere's closed,' Tilly said, turning away again as if that ended the conversation.

'Not everywhere,' Liz said, glad her local knowledge could be of some use. She knew the pizzeria close to *Books and Coffee* was open every day, including public holidays. 'Do you like pizza?'

'I suppose.'

Julie threw Liz a grateful glance.

Twenty minutes later, they were sitting on benches at one of the tables by the beach, two pizza boxes open in front of them with takeaway coffees for Liz and Julie and a can of Coke for Tilly. The pizza and Coke seemed to have calmed Tilly who had lost her sulky expression.

'Did you really have Mum when you were only fifteen?' Tilly pushed away the last piece of pizza.

'I did. I thought I was grown up, made some unwise decisions and didn't consider the consequences of my actions. And I didn't learn. I became pregnant with Tara at nineteen, but by then I was old enough to know the score. Tommy loved me and was in it for the long haul… or so I thought. But we were together for over twenty years. It's more than many couples.'

'Tara… she's…?'

'My oldest… sorry,' Liz sent Julie an apologetic glance. 'Tara is one of my other daughters. She's thirty, and Mandy's twenty-four.'

'They're my…?' Tilly sounded as if she was trying to work out the relationships.

'They're your aunts.'

'Wow! Do they know about Mum and me?'

'Not yet.'

'Do they live here too?'

'Yes. They're not here now. They've gone away for Easter. Tara's married and Mandy is with her boyfriend.'

Tilly didn't speak for several minutes, then asked, 'Why didn't you look for us?'

Liz couldn't answer. How could she describe the tears she'd shed, the nights she'd lain awake, the promises she'd made to God if only she could see her baby? Then, as she grew older reality set in. She'd come to realise her parents had allowed her to grow up, to make a life for herself. And she'd learned it was well-nigh impossible for a birth mother to find her adopted child. As soon as she could, she'd added her name to the contact register in the hope her daughter would contact her and now, all those years later, she had.

Julie understood. 'Liz wouldn't have been able to,' she said. 'She had to wait till I contacted her. It's the way the law works.'

'Then the law's not fair!'

'It's designed to protect both parties,' Liz said. 'I agree it may not seem fair, but what if your mum hadn't known she was adopted, and I had contacted her out of the blue? Can you imagine how she might have felt?'

'And remember how long it's taken me to decide to contact Liz,' Julie said.

'It might be nice to have a grandmother… and two aunts,' Tilly said thoughtfully.

'And a great-grandmother,' Julie said. 'Liz's mother is still alive.'

Tilly stared at Liz. 'She must be very old.'

Liz chuckled. 'Don't let her hear you say that. She's a lively seventy-five and enjoys many of the activities in her retirement village.'

'Can we meet her?'

Julie looked at Liz too.

Liz hedged. They couldn't just turn up. 'I'd have to check with Mum first,' she said. 'I was planning to visit her on Sunday, for Easter.' How was she going to tell Joan that her illegitimate daughter was in town… with her daughter.

'I think we've taken up enough of your time for today,' Julie said, rising. 'It's been lovely meeting you, learning more about what happened all those years ago, about your family. Tilly and I need to…'

'Of course. How long will you be in Pelican Crossing?'

'We've booked the motel for two weeks, till Tilly has to go back to school.'

At the mention of school, Tilly's sullen expression re-emerged.

'Why don't you both come to lunch tomorrow, then maybe we can go to the beach?' Liz said, her eyes moving from Julie to Tilly and back again.

'Tilly?' Julie asked.

'Okay.'

'Good. I'll look forward to seeing you then.' Unsure what to do, Liz went with her gut instinct and hugged them both, Julie returning her hug, while Tilly froze. It would take more than pizza and Coke to win over her granddaughter, but Liz enjoyed a challenge.

Twenty-two

'Does the Easter bunny come today?' Sandy asked, his eyes brimming with excitement, as Bluey scampered around the kitchen getting under everyone's feet. He'd asked the same question yesterday, reminding Finn he still had to buy chocolate eggs to hide in the garden.

'Tomorrow,' he said.

'Oh!' Sandy's lips turned down.

'But maybe we can buy you an Easter egg today when we go to the shops,' Finn said, unable to bear his grandson's disappointment. He was rewarded with a big grin.

'One of the ones with Smarties inside? Andy got one like that from his grandma,' Sandy said, referring to his schoolfriend.

'Maybe.' Finn knew there was one exactly like that sitting in the fridge waiting for Easter morning.

'Will *my* grandma send me one?'

Finn met Adele's eyes over the top of Sandy's head. It was doubtful it would ever enter Karen's head to send her grandson an Easter egg. She managed birthday and Christmas gifts and seemed to feel she'd done her duty by him. It was a pity Tim's parents hadn't survived. It left Finn and Adele as Sandy's only real family.

Keeping Sandy entertained over the school holidays was going to be a challenge. Finn was free for the weekend, but would be back in the office on Tuesday, leaving Adele to carry the responsibility of the small boy and his dog, the latter proving to be more of a chore than they had anticipated.

Yesterday, Good Friday, had been fine. They had taken Bluey for a walk in the morning, and in the afternoon Sandy and Adele had gone to a party at Sandy's friend's home, leaving Finn to have some time to himself. He'd spent most of it wondering how Liz was coping with meeting her daughter for the first time and had to stop himself from calling or texting her to find out.

'Why don't you and Grandy take Bluey to the beach while I do some shopping?' Adele asked Sandy, raising one eyebrow at Finn.

'Good idea,' Finn said. Bluey hadn't been to the beach. It would be interesting to see how the little dog reacted to the sand. 'What do you think, Sandy?'

'Yay!' Sandy said. 'Can we take his ball, and can we…'

'Steady on, champ. Yes, we can take Bluey's ball for you to throw for him, and if we go to the dog friendly section, Bluey will be able to run around.'

'Awesome!' Sandy had recently heard one of the older boys use this word, and liked to try it out, more appropriately at some times than others. 'Can we go now?'

'Finish your breakfast first,' Adele said, pointing to the half-eaten bowl of cereal. 'Then, when Grandy's ready, you can go.'

Sandy started to shovel up his rice bubbles, milk splashing over the edge of his bowl. 'I'm finished,' he said, his mouth rimmed with milk. 'Can we go now?'

'In a little while,' Finn said, his own plate of toast and marmalade still half-finished. He was on his second cup of coffee and wanted to enjoy it. 'Why don't you brush your teeth and look out what you want to take to the beach while I finish?'

Sandy was off like a shot, Bluey lolloping after him.

With both Sandy and Bluey gone, the kitchen was suddenly silent. Adele made herself another cup of coffee and joined Finn at the table.

'Thanks, Dad,' she said. 'I need to buy some eggs when Sandy's not around, plus a few other things.'

'Like hot cross buns?' Finn knew the shops had stocked them for the past few months, but Adele had resolutely refused to buy them. They were a favourite of his, especially the apple and cinnamon variety. She wasn't aware he'd managed to sneak a few during his morning tea break at the paper earlier in the week, when one of the reporters had shared some around.

'Like hot cross buns,' she agreed. 'I'll get some extra eggs too. I can hard-boil them and perhaps Sandy would like to paint them. I remember doing that with you and Mum when I was his age.'

'Yeah.' Finn remembered too. Karen hadn't always been difficult. They'd had some good times when Adele was younger. It was only in the later years things had fallen apart.

'I'm ready, Grandy.'

Finn looked up to see Sandy with Bluey by his side. He was wearing his wide-brimmed hat, the one he normally wore to school, carrying his bucket and spade in one hand and holding Bluey's lead in the other. The little dog was prancing up and down in excitement at the prospect of a walk with his special person.

'Okay.' Finn swallowed the last bite of toast and drained his cup, before taking his dirty dishes to the dishwasher. He grabbed his hat from its hook by the door and checked his pocket for his wallet. 'We're off, Adele,' he said. 'See you later.'

'You'll be back for lunch?'

'Of course.' Finn knew Sandy – and the dog – would be tired out by then, and he'd be ready for a break too.

'Wait, Grandy,' Sandy said and went running to retrieve Bluey's ball before dropping it into his bucket.

'Well remembered,' Finn said, ruffling the boy's hair.

Once at the beach, Sandy chose a spot well away from the sea as usual, laughing as Bluey began to dig a hole and, dropping his bucket and spade on the sand, began to help him, digging into the sand with both hands, seemingly forgetting all about Bluey's ball.

Tipping his hat over his eyes, Finn settled down to watch as both boy and dog almost disappeared into the hole they were digging. Despite it being Easter weekend, this part of the beach wasn't busy, and it was peaceful sitting here in the sunlight.

Finn let his mind wander.

Suddenly, there was a scream.

'Bluey!'

When Finn looked up, Sandy was standing by the hole they had been digging. Tears were streaming down his cheeks. There was no Bluey. Then he saw him. The dog was frolicking in the shallow water with another dog. It was Lady, the spaniel belonging to old Agnes who… Finn looked again… There she was. She appeared to be collecting shells at the edge of the water, oblivious to the two dogs.

'Bluey!' Sandy screamed again.

Finn jumped up and crouched down beside the little boy, whose cheeks were wet with tears 'He's okay, Sandy. Look, he's playing with the other dog. It's…'

'It's the pelican lady and her dog, but Bluey's too little,' he stammered through his tears. 'He can't swim. Daddy…'

Finn pulled his grandson into a warm hug, realising the boy was reliving the accident which had taken his dad. 'It's not like what happened to your dad, Sandy. All dogs can swim. Look!' He pointed to where Bluey and Lady were coasting the waves together.

'But… what if…' Sandy asked, still teary.

'Shall we go over to check on him?'

'No!' Sandy pulled away, his eyes on the two dogs who were having so much fun. 'I want…'

Finn took a deep breath, realising what happened next could be crucial for Sandy. He took the little boy's hand. 'I won't let anything bad happen to you,' he said, and with Sandy clutching firmly to Finn's hand, they walked slowly to the edge of the water.

'Hello,' Agnes said as they approached. 'Is this your dog?'

'He's Bluey,' Sandy said, still clutching Finn's hand like a lifeline.

'He and my Lady are having fun in the waves, aren't they?'

'Ye… es.' But Sandy didn't sound convinced. 'I don't want him to go into the water. He might drown.'

Finn saw it dawn on Agnes that Sandy was the little boy who'd almost drowned, whose dad had drowned trying to save him. She smiled gently. 'Look, he and Lady, they're both swimming. All dogs like the water. They can't come to any harm. It's quite safe.' Agnes was standing in the shallow water, the waves lapping over her feet. 'Why don't you join me?' she said.

Sandy shook his head and moved behind Finn, but Finn could feel him peeping round at the two dogs… and Agnes who was holding out her hand.

Gradually, still holding onto Finn's hand firmly, Sandy took one step towards Agnes, then another, until first one, then both feet were being lapped by the waves. Then Bluey, seeing Sandy in the water, leapt towards him splashing all three of them.

'Bluey!' Sandy said again, but this time the fear had disappeared from his voice. He released the hand which Finn was holding to grasp his pet. Then, to Finn's surprise, he took a step forward just as a small wave splashed over the dog and Sandy's feet. Sandy took a step back but giggled as the little dog tried to bite the wave.

'He'll be right now,' Agnes said nodding, before calling to her dog and going on her way.

'Can we go home now?' Sandy looked up at Finn, his feet still in the swirling water. 'I think Bluey wants to go home.'

'Sure thing, champ,' Finn said, stunned by what had just happened. He decided not to comment. 'Let's get your feet dried first.'

As they drove home, Finn revisited what had happened on the beach. With the help of the little dog – and old Agnes – Sandy had managed to overcome his fear of the sea. He might not be ready to go swimming in it yet, but it was a start.

After lunch, during which neither Sandy nor Finn said anything about Sandy getting his feet wet in the ocean – Finn would tell Adele later – Adele said, 'Who'd like to paint some eggs for Easter?'

'I would!' Sandy shouted, causing Bluey to leap up in alarm from where he was lying under Sandy's chair. 'Will you help, Grandy?'

Finn, who had been hoping for some time to relax with a good book – he'd recently bought the latest Chris Hammer from *Books and Coffee* – sighed, then said, 'I'd love to.'

Adele boiled half a dozen eggs, and Finn and his grandson spent a companionable afternoon at the kitchen table painting designs on the shells. It wasn't until after dinner and when Sandy was safely tucked up in bed that Finn had an opportunity to talk to Adele.

'A strange thing happened at the beach today,' he said, and proceeded to describe what had happened, finishing with, 'I think it's a step forward but maybe we shouldn't get too excited about it.'

Adele beamed. 'Oh, I agree, but I wish I'd been there. I must tell Olivia about it when I next see her. She's been suggesting there isn't much more she can do for Sandy, but I wonder...'

'I'll leave it to you both.'

'I got the eggs. Should we wait till morning or...?'

'... do it now? Probably. The little blighter will likely be up at the crack of dawn to check if the Easter bunny's been. We can't disappoint him.'

As they crept around the garden in the dark, hiding the chocolate eggs, Finn realised that by the time they finished it would be too late to call Liz.

Twenty-three

By Saturday evening, Liz was beginning to feel more comfortable with Julie, though it was still somewhat awkward with Tilly whose moods swung from curiosity to being downright rude. They'd spent the day at the beach, the relaxed atmosphere allowing Liz to get to know Julie better, then had dinner at her apartment where Tilly had wandered around looking at the photographs and asking Liz questions about Tara and Mandy.

After dinner, Tilly, who had been rifling through Liz's collection of DVDs asked if she could watch a movie and, relieved she had found something to please her, Liz and Julie had retired to the deck with glasses of wine.

It was pleasant out there, with the breeze coming off the water and the sound of the waves in the distance.

'You must love it here,' Julie said.

'I do.'

Julie glanced inside to where Tilly was engrossed in watching *Love Actually*, one of Liz's favourite movies. 'Tilly seems happy. I worry about her.'

'You said it was why you contacted me. What do you expect me to do to help?'

Julie shrugged. 'I don't know. Now we're here, it seems like a crazy idea. I thought maybe you could talk to her, tell her about your experience, help her understand what can happen. Oh, I don't know. Maybe I wasn't thinking straight.'

'Have you thought of putting her on the pill?'

Julie's eyes widened. 'You don't think…?'

'Probably not, but it never hurts to be prepared for all possibilities. If I'd been…' Her voice trailed off as she realised…

'I'd have never been born.'

'I didn't mean…' But had she? Becoming pregnant with Julie had changed her life. She had no idea what her future might have been like if it hadn't happened, if the family hadn't been forced to move, if they'd remained in their small country town. Would she have gone to university, married a local boy? It was all immaterial now, but in those months when she was pregnant, and in the years which followed, she often wondered how different her life would have been if she hadn't met John Barr, hadn't gone to the party, hadn't…

'I made sure Tara and Mandy took precautions,' she said.

Tara and Mandy hadn't been sexually active at fifteen, but as soon as they started showing an interest in boys and Liz had an inkling they might, despite Tommy's protestations, she had taken them to their family doctor to have him prescribe the pill. She didn't want them to follow her path. She didn't want Tilly to, either.

'I thought maybe you could talk to her,' Julie said again, clearly uncomfortable with the way the conversation was going.

'I doubt that would help. At her age, they think they know it all. I remember I did. I don't think any amount of talking from an older relative would have made any difference.'

'Oh!' Julie took a gulp of wine.

'But I'm glad, if it led to your contacting me, to my meeting you and Tilly. I can't tell you how glad I am.' Liz put her hand on Julie's, marvelling yet again that this was her daughter, her own flesh and blood and that her granddaughter was there in the next room.

'Any sort of discussion has to come from Tilly,' Liz said, watching the teenager through the glass. 'Let's see what happens in the next few days.'

'Mmm.' Julie didn't sound very hopeful. 'She can be very tight-lipped about things. I only discovered about the photo by accident. I found her crying in her room and forced her to tell me what was wrong.' She sighed. 'Maybe I was wrong to think you had the answer.'

'No, not at all. But I can't give her a lecture. It would never work.'

*

Now it was Sunday, and Julie and Tilly were going to do their own thing while Liz visited her mother. She normally enjoyed visiting Joan in her villa in the retirement village. *The Haven* was a relaxing place to visit and lunch with Joan was usually a happy occasion. Being Easter Sunday, Liz knew her mother would have prepared a special meal for the two of them and would no doubt present her with a chocolate Easter egg; Joan believed you never grew too old for chocolate Easter eggs.

The call from Finn when she was barely awake had been a surprise. He knew about Julie and Tilly's arrival, so they hadn't made arrangements for the weekend, but he said he'd wanted to check on her, to find out how the meeting with her daughter had gone. It was somehow comforting to curl up in bed, to hear his voice, and to attempt to describe her delight at meeting Julie and Tilly. 'Julie's lovely,' she said, 'and Tilly's a typical teenager, all angst and moodiness.'

'Are you going to be tied up with them as long as they're here or is there a chance we can meet?' Finn asked at last, when they had been chatting for some time, she'd told him about Julie's worries, and he'd related the story of Sandy at the beach.

'I'm not sure. I expect so.' Liz had taken two weeks leave from work and, although eager to see Finn again and see where things led, she was loath to give up any time with Julie and Tilly, not knowing when she might see them again. 'Can I let you know?'

'Sure,' Finn said, but Liz detected a note of frustration in his voice.

'It's not that I don't want to see you,' she said. 'I do, but with them here, it's difficult. This is all so new to me. I don't know…'

'I understand,' he said.

But did he?

'Thanks,' Liz said. 'I'm sorry. What are you doing today?' She wanted to picture his day.

'We're hunting for Easter eggs. It seems the Easter bunny was busy last night. I'm not sure who's the more excited, Sandy or Bluey.'

Liz chuckled. 'The dog's hunting for Easter eggs?'

'You got it. Where Sandy goes, Bluey follows. There are going to be tears if the dog manages to collect more than the boy.'

Liz chuckled again. 'Sounds like you might need to referee. Maybe I should leave you to it. I don't have anything nearly as exciting planned. I'm having lunch with my mother and I have to break the news she has a new granddaughter and great-granddaughter who want to meet her.'

'Wow! She doesn't know?'

'I didn't want to tell her before I had to, in case they didn't come, or we hated each other on sight.'

'Good luck with it.'

'Thanks, I'll need it.'

'I look forward to hearing all about it.' It was Finn's turn to chuckle.

It was no laughing matter, Liz thought when the call ended. She wasn't looking forward to breaking the news to her mother. But both Julie and Tilly were keen to meet her. Liz hoped Joan would agree. It had all happened a long time ago. But she knew her mother, and knew that when they came to Pelican Crossing Joan had put it all behind her and had never expected Liz's illegitimate daughter to reappear thirty-four years later.

*

When Liz parked outside her mother's villa, Joan was at the door to greet her as usual. Liz sometimes wondered how she managed it – if she'd been waiting there for ages, or had been peering out the window, only to dash to the door when Liz's car came into view.

Today, she didn't waste time wondering. She was too busy trying to figure out what to say, how to break it to her mother that the baby she thought was gone from their life for ever was in Pelican Crossing, and had a daughter of her own.

'Hi, Mum. Happy Easter.' Liz greeted her mother with her usual hug and kiss.

'Happy Easter, darling.' Joan held Liz at arm's length. 'You're looking a bit peaky. Are you getting out enough?'

'I'm fine, Mum. How are you?'

'Oh, I'm well as usual, apart from a few aches and pains, but I can't complain. I saw my doctor last week for my annual checkup and she tells me I'm very healthy. She didn't add "for my age" but I saw it in her expression.' She chuckled. 'Come on in. I've made a lamb roast – your favourite.'

'Lovely, Mum.' She handed her mother the bunch of flowers she'd brought. Lamb roast had been her dad's favourite, not hers, but her mother could be forgiven for forgetting. Liz suspected she missed him more, not less, as time went on.

'I'll just put these in water and check the oven, then we can have a glass of wine.' Joan headed for the kitchen where Liz knew she wouldn't be welcome. She went into the living area and looked around.

'You've changed things around,' she said when her mother reappeared, noting how the two armchairs which normally sat one on either side of the sofa were now sitting together on one side of the room, the sofa on the other.

Joan blushed. She handed Liz a glass of wine and took a seat in one of the armchairs. 'It's… when I have a friend round to watch television. We both like the armchairs.'

'A friend?' Liz stared at her mother.

'Don't look at me as if I've grown horns. I do have friends, you know.'

But not friends who cause you to move your furniture around.

'And what's this *friend*'s name?'

'Stan's new in the village. He bought Val's house. You remember I told you she'd passed away, the woman I used to play Scrabble with. It was so sad, she…'

'Mum!' Liz couldn't believe her ears. Her mother had a man friend, one she watched television with, in her rearranged living room.

'What, dear? Surprised to discover your mother can still attract a man?' She patted her recently styled white hair. 'It's not too late for you, either. I was speaking to Mandy before she went on this dive trip, and she mentioned something about you and our local newspaper editor.'

'That's enough, Mother.' This was not the sort of conversation she expected to have with her mother, to hear that her daughter and her mother had been gossiping about her, about her and Finn.

'I have some news too,' she said when they had progressed from the roast lamb and vegetables, through her mother's standard dessert of apple pie with ice cream, and were seated back in the living room with cups of tea. After her mother's revelation, she had less hesitation about bringing up Julie and Tilly.

'About you and the nice editor? He's done wonders for *The Crossing Courier*. Everyone I speak to is full of praise for him.'

'No, not about Finn.' Liz fizzed with annoyance so spoke more irritably than she intended. 'It's about my daughter, the one I gave up for adoption. She's here, here in Pelican Crossing, she and *her* fourteen-year-old daughter.'

Twenty-four

'What do you mean?' Joan stared at Liz as if she'd taken leave of her senses. 'How can she be?'

'I never forgot her and as soon as I could, I registered to say I was willing to be contacted. I'd given up hope when I received a letter from her. I replied and she – her name is Julie – is here on holiday with her daughter, Tilly. Your great-granddaughter.'

'How dare she… after all these years.'

'She's my daughter, Mum, your granddaughter… just as much as Tara and Mandy are.'

'I think we need another cup of tea.'

Tea, her mother's solution to all of life's woes.

'No, you stay there,' Joan said as Liz started to rise. 'I don't need any help.'

Liz stared at her mother's unyielding back as the older woman made her way to the kitchen. She should have expected this reaction, been prepared for it. She had been, but had hoped… What had she hoped – that Joan would welcome Julie and Tilly with open arms? That was never going to happen. The best she could hope for was she'd at least agree to see them, talk to them. Julie and Tilly wanted it so much, and Liz wanted it for them.

Joan returned, handed Liz her cup, then took a seat, back in the armchair she'd been sitting in before. 'Well,' she said with a sigh, 'I suppose you'd better tell me about them.'

Liz took a sip of tea, then placed her cup carefully on a side table.

She clasped her hands together in an almost prayer-like pose. 'They both look like me…. like you, too,' she added, remembering photos of a younger version of her mother and the way Joan used to love telling her how much she resembled her as a young woman. It had always been a disappointment to Joan that neither Tara nor Mandy took after her.

'Hmph.'

'They live in Brisbane,' Liz continued. 'Julie's divorced and works as a casual in her local library, has done since the divorce. Tilly's fourteen and lovely.' Liz mentally crossed her fingers. 'She's been having a few challenges at school and Julie hoped I might be able to help.'

'Hmph,' Joan said again, but there was a gleam of interest in her eyes. 'And have you?'

'Not so far. I'm hoping she may feel she can open up to me.'

'Well, it all sounds a bit strange.' Joan sipped her tea and grimaced. 'I forgot the sugar.'

Liz hid a smile. It was so unlike Joan to make a mistake like that… and admit it. She must be feeling really uneasy.

'And is that all she wants? How do you know she's not after your money?'

'Money? What money? Neither of us is so flush there would be any money to be had. Have a heart, Mum. This is my daughter we're talking about. The daughter I was forced to give up.'

'You were only fifteen, Liz. Your dad and I did what we thought was best. We gave up a good life in the country, moved twice so you could start again with a clean slate. There was no need to dig up your dirty laundry after all this time.' Her hand trembled as she put down her cup.

Liz took a deep breath and counted to ten before replying. 'I'm sorry you see it that way, Mum. I'm thrilled to have Julie and Tilly in my life. I'm only sorry it took Julie so long to decide to contact me. I'm glad she had good parents, people who were kind to her, who loved her. It could have been very different. I do realise I was too young, too young to have a baby, too young to take care of her, but it didn't mean I didn't think of her every single day, wondering where she was, if she was being taken care of, if she was happy.'

Liz had been staring at her hands all the time she had been talking. Now, she looked up, shocked to see tears in her mother's eyes.

'I didn't know. I thought you'd managed to forget. We made sure no one in Pelican Crossing was aware of your past. You seemed happy in school here, made friends, married, had two beautiful children...'

'I was, Mum. I am. But there was always a part of me that longed for the daughter I gave away.' Liz felt her own eyes moisten. 'Oh, look at us,' she said, trying to laugh, but crying instead. She took a couple of tissues from a box sitting close by, handed one to her mother and used the other to pat her own eyes dry.

'I'm sorry, Liz,' her mother said at last. 'But it was all so long ago. I can't undo what we did back then. What can I do to help now?'

Seeing her opportunity, Liz didn't hesitate. 'You can agree to meet them.'

*

'So, she has agreed to meet you both.' Liz didn't think it necessary to repeat all her mother had said. It was enough she'd finally agreed.

'Do I have to?' Tilly asked. 'It's weird. A week ago, I didn't even know she existed.'

Liz shrugged. Tilly's moods seemed to change from one day to the next. She remembered how Mandy's had, too. Had Liz been like that as a teenager? She didn't remember. She'd been forced to grow up too quickly.

Julie's response was more measured, as if she could read what Liz hadn't said. 'Are you sure?' she asked Liz doubtfully. 'And, yes, Tilly, if your great-grandmother has agreed to meet us, you do have to go.'

Tilly pouted.

'She's invited all three of us to lunch on Wednesday. Doesn't that sound as if I'm sure? And I have to warn you, lunch with my mother is full on.'

'Yuck,' Tilly said. 'Didn't you say she lives in one of those retirement places with other old people?'

'*The Haven* is a retirement village, and the inhabitants tend to be in their later years,' Liz said, 'but I don't think many of them consider themselves to be old. In fact, Mum told me she has a new friend – a male friend.'

Julie laughed. 'I think I'm looking forward to meeting her too.'

'Now, what did you two do today?' Liz asked, and the rest of the evening was spent with Tilly going into raptures over their day spent on the beach where she'd seen a group kitesurfing. 'And Mum says I can try it,' she finished.

'Wow, you're a lot more adventurous than me,' Liz said, prompted to tell them about her hot air balloon ride, which of course sent Tilly to check the rides on her iPad as Liz said it was something she had no wish to repeat.

'I've booked us in for Tuesday morning, Mum,' she said, looking up with a grin. 'My treat, I'm using my birthday money from Dad.'

'What, me too?' Julie asked.

'Of course. It'll be great, Mum. You did enjoy it?' she asked Liz.

'Once I was up there, yes. But once was enough.' She remembered the feeling of exhilaration but also the fear, the sense of having nothing between her and the ground. 'I wasn't sure about it to begin with, but once it got going, it was okay.'

'It's going to be better than okay,' Tilly said. 'And it says breakfast is included.'

Mandy hadn't mentioned anything about breakfast being included. Liz was glad. She'd have hated sharing breakfast with the cheerful group from the ride… and their host. Strange how since meeting Finn, she hadn't given any thought to the hot guy who organised the balloon ride.

Finn! When was she going to manage to see him again? Hearing her mother talk about the new man in her life, had made her want to see him, to feel his arms around her. It had only been a week since she'd wakened up in his arms, but it seemed as if it had been much longer.

Twenty-five

It was almost a relief to get back to work on Tuesday. Finn's Easter weekend had been full on. Seeing how exhausted Adele was, he had taken it on himself to spend time with Sandy and, much as he loved his grandson, the young boy was a ball of energy which Finn had trouble keeping up with.

They'd played with Bluey in the back yard, throwing balls for the dog to fetch, till Finn had called a halt, neither the dog nor the boy seeming to tire of the game. Then there had been more trips to the beach where Sandy proved willing to venture into the shallow water as long as Finn kept a firm grip of his hand.

Adele seemed grateful for the respite, but Finn worried about her, noting how the lines beside her eyes and mouth appeared to be deepening. He wondered if she got much sleep, but had given up asking, as she always said she did and told him to stop worrying about her. How could he? She was his daughter, and he hated to see her still so enmeshed in her grief.

Today, she was taking Sandy to an event at the library, so the pair of them should be kept busy. Then he'd promised to meet them for lunch at *Books and Coffee* and to buy Sandy a new book. He might buy one for himself too, though he didn't know when he'd find time to read it. He still hadn't finished the Chris Hammer one.

The office was humming with the sound of voices when he arrived, his staff sharing their Easter stories, the air filled with the aroma of coffee and the doughnuts they liked to bring in to work after a holiday.

'Good weekend, boss?' one of them asked.

'Yes, thanks. Hectic. I'd forgotten how busy Easter is with a six-year-old – and a small dog.'

There was a burst of laughter, and someone muttered, 'You're not as young as you used to be.'

Finn nodded. 'Too right.'

The morning passed quickly as he met with staff to discuss the week's news and how best to feature the upcoming ANZAC day celebrations. There were still a few weeks to go, but one of his reporters suggested interviewing the few remaining Vietnam war veterans in the town. Stan Ross was a neighbour of his who had recently moved into *The Haven*. Finn agreed. It would provide a fresh slant on the day. He suggested taking along a photographer and doing a then-and-now feature.

Lunchtime arrived before Finn was ready for it. He closed his computer and hurried along the street to the bookshop-cum-café where Adele and Sandy were already waiting.

'I chose a book already, Grandy,' Sandy said, holding up a copy of a book with a photo of a golden cocker spaniel on the cover entitled, *Cocker Spaniel, fun facts on dogs for kids*. 'See Grandy, the dog on the cover looks just like Bluey but he's a different colour… and it says it's for kids.'

'So it does, Sandy.' Finn's amusement at Sandy's choice of reading matter sent the worries of the morning out of his head. He caught Adele's glance.

'He was determined to get a book about looking after Bluey,' she said. 'I managed to steer him to this one. The others were designed for adults.'

'Maybe we should get one for me,' Finn said, half in earnest. 'Let's pay for your book, then we can organise lunch,' he said to Sandy.

By the time they had ordered and sat down, half an hour had passed, and Finn could see himself having to stay later than he intended at the office if he was to get through the day's tasks. But he'd promised Adele and Sandy this time, so put work to the back of his mind again to concentrate on his daughter and grandson.

Finn was juggling his coffee with Sandy's book, the little boy intent on showing his granddad the photos inside the book, when he heard a voice he recognised. Turning quickly, he saw Liz enter the café with two younger women who must be her daughter and granddaughter. As he was deciding what to say, the book fell to the floor and the younger of the two women picked it up.

'Is this yours?' she asked, handing it to him.

'It's mine!' Sandy said, grabbing his book. 'I was showing it to Grandy.'

'Hello, Finn,' Liz said. 'I didn't expect to see you here.'

'You're the lady from the clinic,' Sandy said.

Adele smiled.

'Liz.' Finn stood up, unsure whether to shake her hand or give her a kiss on the cheek. He did neither, seized with a sudden urge to take her in his arms. 'And this must be…'

'My daughter, Julie, and my granddaughter, Tilly. This is Finn Hunter, the editor of our local newspaper.'

So this was how it was going to be? Finn's heart plummeted.

Then she smiled, a smile that lit up her face and sent shivers down his spine.

'And a very good friend of mine,' she added.

'Thanks, Tilly,' he said belatedly, but the words fell on deaf ears. Tilly had already wandered off into the bookshop.

'Sorry,' Liz said. 'We'd better…' She gestured to where Tilly was already rifling through a display of new releases. 'I'll call you later.'

When Liz and her daughter had disappeared to follow her granddaughter, Adele looked at Finn, her eyes wide with surprise. 'Her daughter? I thought she only had two daughters. I've met Tara and Mandy. Where did that one come from?'

'It's a long story and not for little ears,' Finn said, even though Sandy was engrossed in his book and deaf to anything they might discuss. 'Later.' He wasn't sure how much of Liz's story was his to share. Maybe Adele would forget about it. He was heartened by Liz's promise to call him later, hoping she might have figured out a way for them to meet.

That hope carried him all through the afternoon, until he was about to leave the office. It was close to seven o'clock, and Sandy would be disappointed he'd missed his story time. When his phone rang, he assumed it was Adele wondering what had happened to him. She did tend to worry. He put it down to her having lost Tim. Finn was all she had left, him and Sandy. And she worried about losing them too.

'Hi, Finn. Sorry about lunchtime.'

It was Liz.

'No worries. How are you? I thought I was seeing double, no, triple!'

Liz laughed. 'They do look like me, don't they? Apart from the grey hair and wrinkles on my part.'

'I love your grey hair and wrinkles. I love every part of you. In fact…'

Liz laughed again. 'I love you too.'

Her words made Finn's heart sing, even though he knew the use of the word love was done jokingly. 'It's good to hear your voice,' he said. 'Dare I hope…?'

'We're having lunch with my mother tomorrow, all three of us. Don't ask,' she said, as if expecting him to question it. 'But as a result, Julie and Tilly have decided to have an early night. They've gone back to the motel, so I have some free time…' Her voice trailed off as if she felt she was being too forward.

Finn didn't immediately reply, wondering how he could explain to Adele that he might not be home till much later.

'I realise you may be busy,' she said, a note of what might be embarrassment or regret in her voice.

'No, I mean yes, I'd love to drop by. I assume this call is an invitation?' He thought it best to make sure it wasn't his imagination working overtime telling him what he wanted to hear. He ran a hand through his hair. 'I'm still at the office. I need to make a call. Half an hour?'

'I'll look forward to it.' Her voice was low and husky sending a sudden rush of desire through his entire body.

Finn should have predicted Adele's response when he haltingly told her he had plans for the evening.

'About time,' she said down the phone. 'I saw how you and Liz Phillips looked at each other in *Books and Coffee*. It's how I remember Tim and I looking at each other in the early days of our relationship. Go for it, Dad.'

'No, Adele. It's not. We're not…'

'Do you think I didn't notice how you glowed when you arrived home from your picnic with Liz last Sunday?' she asked. 'As I think I may have said, you need a life of your own. Sandy and I are fine now, but I worry about you.'

'There's no need, honey. And you know you and Sandy will always come first with me, no matter…'

'That's enough, Dad. Have a good evening. Sandy has had his story – from his new book – and is tucked up and asleep. I plan to pour myself a glass of wine and watch a soppy movie, one of those you hate. Don't worry about us.'

'Thanks, sweetheart.'

'Just make sure you don't wake the dog when you come home.' She ended the call before Finn could reply.

*

Liz was waiting for Finn, dressed in a loose tentlike dress, her hair curling around her face. Unable to resist, he took her in his arms and kissed her, a kiss that released all the pent-up emotion of the past week. She felt good, her soft lips, her hair brushing his face, her body melting into his. All he wanted to do was to pick her up and carry her to bed, but…

'Have you eaten?' she asked, making Finn realise it was some time since lunch. 'Food first,' Liz said, taking his hand and leading him to the living room where on the low coffee table a feast of bread, cheeses, pâté, and fruit was set out, along with a bottle of wine and two glasses. 'When you said you were still in the office, I suspected you'd be hungry.'

'A woman after my own heart,' Finn said to see Liz blush.

While Finn ate his fill, Liz sipped a glass of wine and told him all about Julie and Tilly, finishing with the lunch with her mother.

'At least she agreed to meet them,' he said, when she had described Joan's reaction.

'Yes, and that's not all. My mother has a man friend, a new resident in the village, someone called Stan.'

Finn chuckled. 'She's a lively old duck,' he said, then something clicked. Stan… *The Haven*… Where had he heard these two linked today already. He snapped his fingers.

'What is it?'

'In our news conference today, one of the reporters put up the idea of interviewing some Vietnam vets for an ANZAC day feature article. He mentioned one called Stan who'd recently moved to *The Haven*.'

'There couldn't be two of them, and he'd be the right vintage. Wow, what a coincidence. I bet Mum would love to see him in the local paper. Wonder if he was a war hero. Wouldn't that be something?'

'You don't mind… about her?'

'Why should I mind? I only hope I haven't given up hope of love and companionship when I reach her age.' She blushed again.

'Well, let's see what we can do about it right now.' Finn drained his glass and moved closer to Liz on the sofa, reaching one arm around her shoulders and pulling her towards him. As their lips met, everything else was forgotten.

Twenty-six

Next morning, Liz moved around in a dream. It had been late when Finn left her bed to return home, very late. She hugged herself remembering how she had felt in his arms, how their bodies had been so in tune as their passion mounted.

Then she reminded herself she must focus on today, on lunch with her mother, on Julie and Tilly.

As she showered and dressed in a pink dress she knew her mother would approve of, she chided herself for worrying about her mother's opinion. She was fifty, not fifteen, but lunch today was important. She hoped Joan would like Julie and Tilly, would behave and wouldn't repeat some of the things she'd said to Liz. She hoped Tilly would behave, too.

Liz had arranged to meet Julie and Tilly for breakfast at *The Blue Dolphin*. The café was opposite the marina and not far from their motel. By the time she got there, she was a bag of nerves.

'Hi, Liz,' Julie greeted her with the now familiar hug. It felt so good to be hugged by her daughter… this daughter.

Tilly only muttered a brief 'Good Morning' before dropping into a seat and picking up a menu.

Liz waved away Julie's apologetic glance. She understood teenagers. Tilly was no different from what Mandy had been at that age, though Tara had seemed to bypass the sullen stage completely.

Liz and Julie ordered coffee, Tilly a banana smoothie, and all three opted for scrambled eggs with bacon and sourdough toast.

'Is he a special friend... the man we met yesterday?' Julie asked, while they were waiting for their meals to arrive.

Liz reddened, and Tilly looked up from her phone, clearly interested in the answer.

'You said he was the editor of the local newspaper,' Julie said, 'and a very good friend.'

'Yes, he... we... We've only got to know each other recently, and...'

'He seems nice. Who were the woman and boy with him?'

'His daughter and grandson.' Liz was on more comfortable ground. 'It's a sad story. Adele's husband drowned trying to save their son, and Finn moved to Pelican Crossing to support them.'

'And we hit town just as you were getting to know him. Sorry.'

'No, it's not...' Liz felt herself redden at the memory of the previous evening.

'Please say if you want to spend time with him. We can always find something to do. You don't need to spend every day and night with us.'

'But I want to. I've waited so long for this, was afraid it would never come, that I'd never meet you. And now there's Tilly, too. I don't want to waste a minute,' she said. But she was flooded with guilt. She meant every word, but wished she could fit in time with Finn too. Last night had only made her want to see him again, to spend more time with him. But she didn't want to lose time with Julie and Tilly. She was caught between two competing desires.

Fortunately, their breakfasts arrived, and Liz was able to change the subject, but she could see Julie hadn't forgotten about it. She recognised an expression of her own on her daughter's face.

*

As she drove through the entrance gates to the complex of villas, Liz thought, as she always did, what a peaceful place it was. Although she knew there were always a number of activities taking place, it was rare to see many people around.

Today, as she parked opposite her mother's villa, the door opened, and, instead of seeing Joan emerge as she expected, it was an elderly man who came out, turning at the door to speak to someone inside.

Was this Stan? Liz felt an unexpected flash of annoyance. She'd been anticipating her mother to be waiting for them at the door not entertaining her… she had no idea what to call him.

The man walked smartly away from the villa, his thinning white hair the only sign of his age. As he passed Liz's car, he gave her a wave, adding to her annoyance. She wasn't sure why she felt this way and took a deep breath. 'Ready?' she asked.

Julie nodded.

The door to the villa was still open, and when they reached it, Joan was standing there to greet them, just as Liz had expected.

'Mum.' Liz hugged her mother, then drew forward Julie… and Tilly who wanted to hang back. 'This is Julie and Tilly.' She bit her lip to prevent her from asking her mother to be nice to them.

'I'm glad to meet you both at last,' Joan said, as if she too had been hoping Julie would get in touch.

Liz silently congratulated her mother on her tact. Perhaps this was going to go well.

'You just missed Stan,' her mother said as they made their way inside. 'He wanted to meet you, Liz, but I thought it better to wait till another time.'

'We saw him leave,' Liz said.

Her mother blushed, something Liz didn't remember ever happening before.

'Well, come in and take a seat. Lunch is almost ready. I hope you like roast lamb,' Joan said to Julie. The aroma of the roasting meat permeated the villa, making their mouths water.

'Yum,' Tilly said, making them all laugh and breaking the ice.

To Liz's surprise and relief, the lunch went well. Joan asked Julie and Tilly about themselves and their life in Brisbane, and Tilly seemed happy to chat about what they had seen in Pelican Crossing. The only sticky part came when Joan asked Julie about her adoptive parents, but Julie managed to respond without becoming upset or annoyed, and Joan really appeared to be pleased she'd had a good life. Liz could almost see her thinking how things had worked out for the best, just as she'd predicted.

But she didn't repeat any of her previous prophecies, only saying she was glad Julie had experienced a happy childhood. Then she began to relate stories about Liz growing up, bringing out an old photograph album which both Julie and Tilly seemed to find fascinating. These anecdotes of her younger days embarrassed Liz, who took the opportunity to retire to the kitchen to wash up the lunch dishes – her mother refused to have a dishwasher.

It was mid-afternoon before Liz, Julie and Tilly rose to leave. Their farewells were less awkward than the greetings had been, with both Julie and Tilly joining Liz in hugging Joan and promising to make another visit before they left Pelican Crossing, although Tilly seemed to be somewhat reluctant at the prospect of seeing Joan again. The trip back to Liz's was spent rehashing the visit which all three deemed to be successful.

'My turn to cook,' Julie announced when they arrived at the apartment. 'Will you be okay here if I duck out to do some shopping?' she asked Tilly.

Tilly muttered something indecipherable, and although Liz insisted there was no need, Julie headed off.

This was the first time Liz had been alone with Tilly, and the sense of awkwardness she'd felt when they arrived at Joan's villa returned. What was she to do with the fourteen-year-old till her mother came back? 'Tea?' she asked. It was always a good start.

'Okay,' Tilly scowled, 'or do you have any hot chocolate?'

'I certainly do.' Hot chocolate sounded good to Liz too. She was in the kitchen, taking two mugs out of the cupboard along with the container of chocolate and the Tim Tams which were still uneaten, when Tilly wandered in.

'Oh, yum, Tim Tams,' she said, taking a seat at the table.

Liz smiled. She was becoming accustomed to Tilly's changing moods.

They were peaceably drinking hot chocolate when Tilly gazed at Liz. She took a long drink, played with a strand of hair then said, 'She's cool, your mum. She said to call her Joan as Great Grandma made her sound old. What was it like… when you were pregnant? How did your parents react?'

'They were good. Very supportive.'

'How about school?'

'We moved away till I had the baby – your mum – then afterwards we moved here. No one at my old school knew.'

'So, you left school?'

'For a few months, then I started at Pelican Crossing High. I had to work hard to catch up.'

Tilly picked at a thread on the edge of her shirt. 'I hate my school. I don't want to go back.'

Liz was silent, remembering what Julie had told her.

'They're so mean to me after… I wish I could change schools too, go somewhere no one knows me. Somewhere like Pelican Crossing. Hey,' her face brightened, 'maybe Mum and I could move here?'

Liz's heart began to beat faster. If only they could. How she'd love to have all three of her girls living right here in Pelican Crossing. She didn't reply immediately. It wasn't up to her to comment. She took a sip of her drink. 'Maybe you should talk with your mum about that,' she said. 'I doubt she'd want to move her life all the way up here. And what about all your friends?'

'You don't want us.' Tilly's eyes filled with tears.

'Of course I want you, sweetheart,' Liz said using the affectionate term for the first time. It rolled off her tongue automatically. 'It's not my decision. As I said, it's a big step.'

The front door opened, Julie arrived with her bags of shopping, and no more was said about moving to Pelican Crossing.

But as she lay in bed that night, Liz couldn't stop thinking about Tilly's words, how wonderful it would be. Then she remembered. Neither Tara nor Mandy knew about Julie and Tilly's existence. How would they react when they found out?

Twenty-seven

Finn stared at the computer screen, unable to believe his eyes. He'd worked his butt off for the past year, bringing this paper up to speed, and to receive this news… by email! He read it again, but it still said the same.

Due to financial exigences, it has been decided to consolidate our regional newspapers into one digital edition. As a result, the final edition of The Crossing Courier *will go to press at the end of this financial year. We are aware this will impact you and your staff and wish you all well in your future endeavours.*

He took off his glasses and rubbed his eyes, then read it again, as if by reading and rereading he could change the words.

'Boss.'

Finn looked up to see one of his junior reporters at his office door. What would happen to him and the others who depended on the paper? What would happen to Finn? He'd left his position in Bellbird Bay to come here, to be here for Adele and Sandy, to breathe life into the dying paper, and this was his thanks. *The Bellbird Bugle* was owned by the same consortium. He suspected it would suffer the same fate. These small coastal communities needed their local newspapers to provide local news. A digital edition from the city couldn't provide the same service.

'Boss?' Brad was still standing there. 'It's time for the news conference. Everyone's in the conference room. They're waiting for you.'

'I'll be right there.' Only a few minutes ago, all he'd been thinking about was the morning's news conference, getting updates on what everyone was working on. Now he couldn't remember what he'd intended to say. Picking up the sheaf of notes he'd prepared earlier, he made his way to meet his staff.

As soon as he saw the eager faces waiting for him, Finn decided to say nothing about the email just yet. Maybe there was some way he could persuade the powers-that-be to change their minds. A list of his successes streamed through his mind. Surely they would count for something? He took a deep breath and opened the meeting as if it was just another day.

But it wasn't, and Finn was aware he wasn't paying as much attention to the reports as usual. He was too distracted. But he did manage to find words to congratulate Ed on his interview of Stan, the Vietnam vet living in *The Haven*, wondering if it was indeed the same man who was Liz's mum's new special friend.

Liz! Their relationship was still in its infancy. What would happen to it… and to Adele and Sandy… if he had to leave Pelican Crossing and find work elsewhere? It was all too hard.

The first thing to do was to ring around the other local newspaper editors he knew, to discover how many were being affected. As soon as his meeting was finished, he returned to his office and picked up the phone. Half an hour later, he knew the worst. They were all in the same boat.

Finn was in the process of composing an email to request a stay of execution – which was how he thought of the closure – when his phone rang. Seeing Joe's number, he picked it up.

'Hey.' He tried unsuccessfully to inject a positive note into his voice.

'Hey, what's up? You don't sound your usual self.'

'Got some bad news.'

'Want to talk about it? I was calling to see if you were free for lunch. *Crossings* has a new menu and I thought we could try it.'

Crossings, the restaurant on Main Street, was located in one of the heritage buildings. It was more upmarket than the yacht club where he'd gone with Adele and Sandy, perfect for more special occasions. He'd taken Adele there for her birthday and been impressed with both the menu and the service. She'd told him a bit about the place.

Evidently it was owned and managed by a woman. Poppy Taylor had grown up in Pelican Crossing, married a local man and been widowed as the renovation of the restaurant was completed. Adele knew the story and empathised with the woman whose husband had drowned like Tim. Local gossip, which Finn as editor of the local paper, was always privy to, reported Poppy was now involved with Cam Mitchell who managed *Pelican Marine*.

Finn made a mental note to take Liz there, when she could spare time from her new family.

'Sounds like a plan.'

'One o'clock?'

'I'll be there.'

*

The restaurant was already busy when Finn arrived. When a smart woman greeted him at the entrance, he pointed to a table in the far corner where he could see Joe waving to him.

'Bit rich for lunch,' Finn said, joining his friend.

'Checking it out. We're planning a retirement do for one of my senior staff – he's been with the council since he left school – and my secretary suggested lunch here at *Crossings*, but no one had eaten here recently.'

'Don't tell me it's on expenses.'

'No, the council won't stretch to that. I thought I might treat you.'

'Good of you, but I'm happy to pay my share.' *Though for how much longer if the paper folded?*

'You sounded down when I rang, said you had bad news?' Joe raised an eyebrow.

'Let's order first.' Finn picked up a menu.

When they had ordered, Finn choosing the rump steak with chips and salad, Joe opting for the rack of lamb with mashed potatoes and beans and selecting a bottle of cabernet sauvignon, Joe asked again, 'What's up?'

'It's the newspaper. They want to close us down.'

Joe's eyes widened. '*The Crossing Courier?* You must be joking.'

'Wish I was, though not something I'd joke about.'

'Can they do that… just close a paper?'

'It's not only us. I called around this morning. It's all the local papers on the coast.'

'We can't let it happen.'

'I agree. I've been racking my brains for a solution. It's happening everywhere, going digital, broadsheet to tabloid. It was only a matter of time. I've emailed the big boss, but I'm not hopeful. I'm not sure what else to do.'

'Pelican Crossing needs its paper. I may sometimes have disagreed with the way the council is portrayed,' Joe chuckled, 'but it's the only way the community get to find out what we're up to.'

'And all the local businesses who advertise with us, local schools, charities and fundraisers…' Finn's voice trailed off as he saw a gleam in Joe's eyes.

'That's what we'll do,' Joe said. 'We'll set up a Save the Courier fund, get the community behind it.'

'But what…?'

'I seem to recall reading about something of the sort happening somewhere in the States. May have been an actual event, might have been in a novel.' He pulled on one ear. 'Anyway, what happened was that this town was about to lose its newspaper and the community got together to raise the money to save it.'

'Are you sure you're not thinking of the movie, *It's a Wonderful Life*, where they got together to save the bank?'

'Am I?' Joe scratched his head. 'Same difference.'

Their meals arrived, and the two men continued to throw around ideas. By the time Finn returned to the office, he was feeling more cheerful. But the end of the financial year was less than three months away. They didn't have much time.

Twenty-eight

It was two days since the lunch with Liz's mum and Tilly's amazing suggestion, and Liz had thought of little else. But neither Julie nor Tilly had raised the subject again, and Liz didn't want to pre-empt them.

Liz was meeting Julie and Tilly this morning to go on a cruise. It was the wrong season for whale watching, but that didn't deter Tilly who discovered an eco-cruise setting out from the marina, which guaranteed sightings of dolphins, turtles and dugongs. It lasted for four hours and included morning tea. Liz wasn't sure about the guaranteed sightings but didn't want to dent Tilly's enthusiasm so was willing to go along.

Before she left, she turned on the television to check the latest weather. While it was fine here in Pelican Crossing, there was the threat of a cyclone farther north. It was still out at sea, and she'd been following its progress over the past few days. The cyclone was predicted to be heading for Townsville and Magnetic Island with landfall expected on the weekend. Magnetic Island was where Mandy had gone on the dive trip. Liz hoped she was safe.

This morning the news reported the cyclone was now category three and might be changing direction; residents in the affected areas – between Cairns and Mackay – were warned to take precautions. A further news item reported shopping centres had been inundated with crowds stocking up on water, bread, batteries and other essential items after agencies urged residents to stock up on supplies to last them three days.

Liz's forehead creased, her stomach lurched. She took out her phone and pressed Mandy's number on speed dial, but it went to voicemail. She bit her lip. She could only hope Mandy was safe. It was time to go.

'You okay?' Julie asked when they met at the marina.

'Fine.'

'You don't look fine.'

'It's the cyclone. It's heading for Magnetic Island where Mandy is. I tried to call her but there was no answer.'

Julie put her hand on Liz's arm. 'I'm sure she'll be fine. From what you've told me, there have been lots of warnings. Surely she'd make sure she was safe?'

'I hope so. Mandy can be very headstrong.'

'What about the guy she's with?'

'Gary?' Liz pictured the calm young man who had been brought up on the ocean, whose father had owned a fishing boat and now a fishing charter, whose brother worked at the marina. 'He's sensible. He wouldn't take any risks.' Liz felt better having said this and decided to put the cyclone to the back of her mind and enjoy the day. There was nothing she could do about the weather, and Mandy would contact her if she was in trouble – wouldn't she?

The cruise lived up to Tilly's expectations. Although they didn't see any dugongs, they did see a number of dolphins and turtles and the commentary on the way was very informative.

After a pleasant lunch at *The Blue Dolphin Café*, they were walking along the beach, Tilly trailing behind, eyes on her phone as usual, when Julie said, 'Tilly said she'd spoken to you.'

'She was asking me about when I was pregnant, about my parents' reaction, how they handled it.'

'She said you'd moved away.'

'I was pregnant, Julie. It was a small town. The gossips would have had a field day. I'd always have been known as the girl who… My family would never have lived it down, even if I'd left as soon as I finished school.'

'Sometimes the city can seem like a small town too. Tilly's afraid to go back to school. I'd hoped… coming here… talking with you… she might have found a way through things, but…' Julie shook her head.

'*Could* you move to Pelican Crossing? It would mean a huge upheaval, your home, your job…'

Julie sighed. 'Not as much as you might think. We're renting, so no house to sell, and my position at the library's casual. I would have to give notice, find a job here, somewhere to live…'

'I'd love to have you with me but…' Liz pictured her spare room, all Mandy's belongings scattered about. She'd said till after the dive trip. They'd be back in a week, but *she'd* need to find somewhere to live too.

'I couldn't expect you to…'

'No, I would offer, but at present Mandy's staying there, or rather her belongings are. She spends most of her time at work or at her boyfriend's place. But it is her home.'

'And it's not mine. I understand.'

'That's not what I mean at all.' This was becoming too complicated. If it was this difficult when Mandy didn't know about Julie, when she wasn't even here, what would it be like once she got back? If Liz had considered it at all, she'd thought Julie would have returned to Brisbane and she could gradually bring the conversation round to the fact she had another daughter, that Mandy and Tara each had another sister. 'I'd be thrilled to have you and Tilly living here. We just have to work out the logistics. Can we talk about it tonight?'

'Sure. Sorry if I came on a bit strong. It hasn't been easy… Tilly's troubles at school, contacting you…'

'I know. I'm so glad you did.' Liz knew she couldn't repeat it often enough.

*

After a dinner of takeaway pizza, which was Tilly's choice, followed by chocolate chip ice cream from the local gelato shop, the three moved into the living room where Tilly immediately turned on the television.

'Not tonight, honey,' Julie said.

'But it's *Home and Away*. I always watch it,' Tilly complained.

'Not tonight,' Julie repeated. 'We have something to discuss.'

'Okay.'

'I'll get us some wine,' Liz said, feeling the need for something stronger than tea or coffee to sustain her for the discussion ahead. 'Coke for you, Tilly?'

'Yes, please.'

In the kitchen, Liz checked the weather again to learn the cyclone was still out at sea moving at seventeen kilometres an hour and was predicted to reach landfall that evening. The blood drained from her face as she tried to call Mandy again with no more success than before.

'You okay?' Julie asked when she returned with the wine and Coke.

'Mmm'

'Is it the cyclone?'

Liz nodded.

'I read about it,' Tilly said. 'It sounds scary, huge winds, high seas, heavy rain. But it's a long way from here, isn't it?'

'Yes, Tilly, but Liz's daughter is up there.'

'My aunt?'

'Mandy,' Liz said. 'She's on a dive trip with some friends.'

'Won't the weather be too fierce for diving? I'd love to learn to dive.'

'Yes, it will, and maybe you can… one day.'

'Okay.' Tilly took a gulp from the can of Coke earning her a glare from her mother. 'What are we going to discuss? What's so important it can't wait?'

'I know you spoke to Liz about moving here.'

'Can we?' Tilly's face brightened. 'It would be awesome. Then I wouldn't need to go back to school. Up here, no one would know… *You* moved,' she accused Liz.

'Liz's situation was different.' Julie said sharply.

'But…' Tilly drooped.

'Let's discuss this rationally,' Liz said. She took a sip of wine. 'Tilly, you told me you hate your school, you're afraid this boy will act on his threats if you don't give in to him.'

Tilly nodded.

Julie took her daughter's hand and squeezed it.

'One option is to stand up to him, let him do his worst.'

'I can't…' A wild expression appeared in Tillys eyes.

Liz continued, 'Another option is for you both to leave the city, move somewhere else, start again where no one knows you. The most obvious place to move to is here, to Pelican Crossing.'

'Yay!' Tilly said with a grin.

'It's not so easy,' Julie said. 'We'd have to find somewhere to live. I'd need to find a job.'

'But we could do that, couldn't we?' Tilly looked to Liz for reassurance.

'Let your mum finish,' Liz said.

'We could, but not immediately. These things take time. Even if we find somewhere to live and I find a job, we have a house to pack up, notice to give on our home and at the library, and…' She shook her head as if it was all too much for her.

'Couldn't we stay here?' Tilly gazed around the room.

'Liz doesn't have space.'

Tilly stared at Liz.

'I'm sorry, Tilly. But my spare room is filled with Mandy's belongings. She moved out of her old accommodation and is keeping her things here till she finds somewhere else to live.'

'Oh!' Tilly sagged like a deflated balloon.

'So, even if we do decide to come here, you'd need to go back to school until we sort things out.'

Tilly started to tremble. 'I can't. You don't know what it will be like, with him taunting me, me never knowing what he and his mates are going to do or say next. I can't do it, Mum. You can't make me.'

Julie looked at Liz, an expression of hopelessness on her face. Liz felt for Tilly. This could have been her. She hadn't appreciated it at the time, but now she was so glad her parents had taken the steps they had to protect her and her reputation, even it had meant giving up her precious daughter.

'Let's have a think, shall we?' Liz said, refilling her and Julie's glasses which had somehow become empty.

They sat in silence for a few moments, each lost in their own thoughts, then Liz said. 'What it seems to me is this. There's no way you, Julie, can move immediately. Even if you found somewhere to live and a job here tomorrow, you would still need time to organise everything back home. But for Tilly, it may be different.'

Tilly looked at Liz, a glimmer of hope in her eyes.

Julie appeared puzzled.

'Theres no reason why Tilly can't be enrolled in Pelican Crossing High for the start of next term. It's a good school. I should know, I went there. And I started in Year Ten. We can work something out regarding accommodation. I doubt Mandy will be here for much longer. She's been spending most of her time at Gary's, anyway, and this sofa pulls out into a bed. It wouldn't do for long, but for a bit, until you get yourselves sorted. What do you think?' Liz held her breath, wondering if she'd just set the cat among the pigeons. How would Mandy react if she came home to find Tilly had moved in, that her mother had a daughter and granddaughter who she'd kept secret? She'd face that problem if and when it arose.

'Really?' Tilly beamed. 'Could I, Mum?'

An expression of relief flitted across Julie's face, mixed with one of concern. 'It would solve Tilly's issues,' she said slowly.

'But? I sense there's a but,' Liz said.

'We've never been apart,' Julie said, 'and there's all your stuff, Tilly. How would you manage without it? We only packed for two weeks. And a new school…'

'It would be ace. I love it here. And there's Liz… and Joan… and two new aunts.'

Liz's stomach churned at the thought of telling those two aunts. But they'd have had to know sooner or later. This was only going to be sooner than she'd anticipated… much sooner.

Before Julie and Tilly left, it had been agreed Julie would take Tilly to be enrolled in Pelican Crossing High School the following week and would buy her school uniform and other things she might need in the short term, until either Julie could join them or send up more of Tilly's belongings. Liz didn't want to think about how she was going to find space for everything in her already overfilled apartment, but she'd figure out something. The important thing was to get Tilly settled in a school and place she felt safe from the bullying she'd experienced. Tilly had already checked out the school online and declared it to be cool.

Liz accompanied the pair down to the street entrance to the apartment block and farewelled them with the hugs to which all three had now become accustomed, but which were still a novelty for Liz, one she couldn't get enough of. She had just waved them off when she became aware of a ute stopping nearby and two people getting out.

'Who was that?'

Liz turned to see Mandy standing there, Gary behind her. She was flooded with an enormous sense of relief. 'Oh, my darling! I'm so glad you're safe. I've been trying to call you.' Liz hugged her daughter.

'My phone died. Who was that?' Mandy asked again, pulling herself out of her mother's arms.

Twenty-nine

'Let's get you inside first,' Liz said, 'Gary?'

'Thanks, but I need to get back, Mrs P. Let Dad know I'm safe. Catch you tomorrow, babe,' he said to Mandy, pulling her rucksack from the cabin of the ute and handing it to her, while kissing her on the cheek.

Once inside, Mandy dumped her rucksack in the hallway.

Liz hugged her again. 'I was so worried about you,' she said. 'I was following the news of the cyclone and thinking about you up there.'

'It got a bit hairy. There was no point in staying on when we couldn't dive. So, we decided to come home. Glad we did. We got out just before they closed the airport.'

'Oh, my darling!'

To stem more questions about Julie and Tilly, and seeing Mandy was beginning to wilt, Liz said, 'You must be exhausted. Why don't you have a hot bath while I fix something to eat?'

Mandy gave her a strange look but nodded and disappeared in the direction of the bathroom.

When she had gone, Liz drew in a deep breath. She was racked with guilt. She should have told Mandy and Tara about Julie before this. Now it might be too late. While Mandy was in the bath, she quickly put together a meal of pasta with a sauce made from a packet of mushrooms she had in the fridge and a tin of tomatoes, and poured two glasses of wine. She'd need hers for the explanation she still had to figure out.

Mandy looked refreshed when she appeared in the kitchen, dressed in a long tee-shirt and with a towel around her wet hair.

'Better?' Liz asked.

'Mmm. Thanks, Mum,' she said as Liz handed her a glass of wine and set the bowl of pasta on the table.

'Now,' Mandy said, after taking a sip of wine, 'who were those two women you were hugging? I didn't recognise them.'

Liz took a sip of wine too. 'It's a long story,' she said. 'I should have told you before now, but… anyway, I want you to listen till I finish.'

'Okay.' Looking puzzled, Mandy took a forkful of pasta and another sip of wine.

'It all happened long before you and Tara were born,' Liz began, 'when I was only fifteen…'

'And that's who you were hugging?' Mandy asked, when Liz had finished.

'Yes.' Liz drank the rest of her wine, trying to gauge Mandy's reaction.

'You had a baby, a daughter we didn't know about. Did Dad know?'

Liz shook her head. 'No one knew… apart from my parents.'

'Gran knew… and didn't tell us?'

'It was a shameful thing back then… for a teenager to have a child. In our family, anyway. It was hushed up. As I said, the baby was adopted, we moved here and started a new life. I never expected to find her again.'

As soon as she'd spoken, Liz knew she'd said the wrong thing.

'Find her? You wanted to find her? Weren't we enough for you?'

'It's not a matter of enough, Mandy. Love isn't like that. It can't be parcelled up. I love all of you… all three of you.'

'And her daughter… is your granddaughter?'

'Of course. Tilly's Julie's daughter.' Liz peered at Mandy, but her expression didn't give anything away.

'I'm going to bed now.' Mandy rose and left the kitchen without saying goodnight properly. Liz heard the bedroom door slam.

That went well… not, she thought, wondering how she could have improved on her explanation. She still hadn't mentioned anything about them moving to Pelican Crossing or about Tilly staying with Liz. Time enough for that tomorrow, she thought, before remembering she was taking Julie, Tilly and her mother to lunch at *Crossings* next day. Maybe Mandy could be persuaded to come too, though Liz wouldn't hold her breath.

*

Next morning, after a restless night of tossing and turning, Liz was making breakfast when Mandy appeared in the kitchen. 'Morning, sweetheart,' she said, to be rewarded by a surly expression. 'Coffee?' she asked, fixing a cup for Mandy before she could reply.

'Thanks.' Mandy slid into a chair and picked up her cup, clasping it in both hands. 'What I don't understand,' she said, carrying on the conversation of the previous evening, 'is why you couldn't tell us about this woman. Lots of women have babies and get them adopted. It's the secrecy… Wait till Tara finds out.'

'I did intend to tell you both. I wanted to pick my time.'

'I bet.'

Liz busied herself cooking the banana pancakes she'd decided on for breakfast. They were Mandy's favourite and she'd hoped to mollify her daughter by making them.

'How long will they be in Pelican Crossing?'

The question Liz had been dreading.

'They've booked into the motel for two weeks.' Liz knew she was evading the question but wasn't ready to tell Mandy everything just yet. 'We're having lunch with your gran at *Crossings*. Why don't you join us? You can meet Julie and Tilly then.' Liz held her breath.

'I don't think so.'

Mandy's phone buzzed with a text. She looked at the screen. 'It's Gary. He's picking me up in an hour. Can't make lunch.'

'The pancakes are ready.' Liz took the plate of pancakes to the table along with the strawberries she'd cut up earlier, a tub of yoghurt and the bottle of maple syrup.

'How is Gran?' Mandy asked, indicating the conversation about Julie and Tilly was closed.

'She's well, as feisty as ever, and you'll never guess.'

'What?' Mandy paused, fork halfway to her mouth.

'She has a male friend, someone who's recently moved into the village. I think he's one of the Vietnam vets *The Courier* is interviewing for ANZAC day.' Liz bit her lip again, wishing she hadn't mentioned *The Courier*.

'About that. Still seeing the editor of our local newspaper?'

'Finn and I are still friends, yes.'

'Hmm. Well, don't let yourself get distracted by these new people. Gotta go,' she said as her phone buzzed again. She gobbled up the last piece of pancake on her plate, took a gulp of coffee and was off without the kiss or hug she normally gave her mother.

Liz stared after her. She knew Mandy could be difficult but had at least expected some discussion about Julie and Tilly's sudden appearance in her life, some interest in the younger Liz. She sighed as she cleared away the dirty breakfast dishes, determined not to allow Mandy's behaviour to affect her. But as she fixed her hair and makeup, Liz wondered how she was going to arrange the meeting between Mandy and Julie that she knew had to happen.

*

Liz's mind was full of thoughts about Mandy as she drove to *The Haven* to pick up her mother. Although she tried to hide her worries, Joan was astute enough to notice.

'What's happened?' she asked as soon as she settled herself in the passenger seat. 'I thought we were going out to lunch to celebrate.'

'We were… we are.' Liz glanced at her mother out of the corner of her eye. 'Mandy's home.'

'Oh! Did she meet Julie and Tilly?'

'No, they were leaving just as she arrived, but…' Liz bit her lip, 'she wanted to know who they were. I had to tell her.'

'And I can imagine how she reacted.'

'You know Mandy. Everything's fine as long as it's going her way. The news she has another sister, one she knew nothing about, didn't go down well. I invited her along today to meet them, but…' Liz shook her head.

'Give her time. It was a shock. She needs to adjust. She'll be fine. Mandy's more resilient than you sometimes give her credit for.'

'You think?' Liz wasn't so sure. She knew how pigheaded her youngest daughter could be. She could only hope her mother was right.

They drew into the motel car park to see Julie and Tilly waiting for them, wide smiles on their faces. It was such a relief for Liz to see them looking so happy. She felt her own mood lift.

'Good morning, Liz, Joan,' Julie and Tilly chorused as they took their seats in the back of the car. 'Isn't it a glorious day?'

'It certainly is,' Joan replied.

'Where are we having lunch?' Tilly asked. 'You said something about a special restaurant, Liz.'

'Yes. *Crossings*. It belongs to a friend of mine. Poppy's parents owned it, then she and her husband took it over and renovated it. Sadly, Jack died before the grand opening, but Poppy has done wonders with the place. She's won several awards and been featured on television, on *Weekender*.'

'You watch that, Mum,' Tilly said to Julie.

'I probably saw it there, but I don't remember.'

'I remember the restaurant when Poppy's parents had it,' Joan said. 'Your dad and I used to go there for special celebrations, Liz.'

'Tommy and I went there a few times too, before Poppy and Jack took over. It has quite a different atmosphere now.'

As soon as they walked in, a curvy, blonde woman around the same age as Liz came forward to greet them. 'I saw your name in the book, Liz,' she said, greeting her friend with a hug, and smiling a welcome to the others. 'Good to see you again, Mrs Ellis,' she said to Joan, then, 'And who is this?' She gazed at Julie and Tilly.

Liz squirmed. None of her friends knew about her teenage pregnancy, and she wasn't ready to share it just yet. 'Julie and Tilly,' she said. 'They're visiting Pelican Crossing.'

'Welcome,' Poppy said with a smile. 'And welcome to *Crossings*. I hope you enjoy your meal.'

'Thanks,' Julie returned her smile.

'This is lovely,' Julie said, when they were seated at a table from where they were able to see the entire room. 'And what a wonderful welcome. Your friend is an excellent hostess.'

'Isn't she? I didn't expect to see her here today. She has wound back her time in the restaurant recently.'

'I heard she and Cam Mitchell from the marina are a couple now,' Joan said. 'Time you got yourself a man too, Liz.'

Liz blushed. 'Time enough for that, Mum,' she said, seeing Tilly's eyes widen. Did the girl think she was too old to attract a man? Then a sudden thought occurred to Liz – did her mother know about her and Finn? She snuck a glance at Joan, but the older woman didn't appear to have any hidden agenda for her remark. Liz was being paranoid. And what did it matter if her mother did know? Finn Hunter was a perfectly respectable choice of partner. *Is that what he was?*

'Can I have the fish and chips?' Tilly's voice interrupted Liz's musings.

'You can have anything you want,' Liz said, picking up a menu as she realised the others were already choosing their meals.

After a discussion about whether to choose something they wouldn't cook at home or opting for a favourite meal, Joan chose to order a rib fillet and salad, while Liz and Julie elected to share the seafood experience for two. They were about to order a bottle of wine and a lemon, lime and soda for Tilly, when a waitress appeared at their table with an opened bottle of Squealing Pig pinot gris, courtesy of Poppy.

'So, you haven't met Liz's other daughters yet?' Joan asked, when the meals had been served.

'They're on holiday,' Julie said, then appeared to catch a glance between Liz and her mother. 'What?'

Liz sighed. 'Mandy got back last night. They left Magnetic Island because of the cyclone. She saw you leave and asked who you were.'

'You told her?' Julie asked, putting down her knife and fork.

'I did, and she wasn't well pleased. It's my fault. I should have told her and Tara before now. I suggested she join us here, but...' She shrugged.

'Don't worry,' Joan said. 'Mandy can be unpredictable. Once she gets used to the idea, I'm sure she'll agree to meet you.'

Julie didn't look confident. 'I don't want to cause trouble,' she said. 'Maybe...'

'It's not you,' Liz said, putting her hand on Julie's shoulder. 'She's annoyed I kept a secret from her. Mum's right. Once she's had time to think, she'll come round.'

'Did you know we're moving to Pelican Crossing, Joan?' Tilly said, effectively changing the subject, 'and I'm going to be going to Pelican Crossing High next term.'

Joan threw Liz a surprised glance. 'Really?' she said. 'When did you decide this?'

'Yesterday,' Tilly said, her voice filled with excitement. 'Isn't it great? We'll be living here, close to Liz and you.'

For a few moments no one spoke, then Joan said, 'It'll be a big change. Won't you miss your friends?'

Tilly's face clouded over. 'Not really. I hate my old school. Liz told me how she moved here and started a new life. It's what I want to do too.'

At the expression on her mother's face, Liz was quick to add, 'Tilly's been bullied, Mum. We've talked about this and it's a good solution. There's nothing to keep Julie and Tilly in Brisbane.'

'Where will you live?' Joan asked Julie.

It was Tilly who answered. 'I'm going to stay with Liz when school starts, then Mum will move up once she finds somewhere for us to live.'

'I need to give notice to our landlord and to my employer,' Julie said, seeing Joan's surprise. 'Liz seems to think it won't be a problem for us to find somewhere to live and for me to find work. I can look around in the coming week, before I go back home.'

'Well! I didn't expect this.' Joan took a gulp of wine. 'But it'll be good to see more of you. What sort of work do you do, Julie?'

'I've been doing casual work at our local library, but I can do any sort of admin work.' She shifted uncomfortably in her seat. 'We won't be a burden to Liz or you.'

'You could never be a burden, Julie.' Liz felt her eyes moisten.

A waitress appeared to take their plates and they ordered coffee, but Liz couldn't stop worrying about Julie and her concerns. There was Mandy too, and her sudden departure. She still had to tell her about Julie's decision to move to Pelican Crossing… and that Tilly would be staying in the apartment temporarily.

After she'd dropped her mother off, with a promise to call in the following week, Liz, Julie and Tilly went for a walk along the beach. As usual, the fresh air, the scent of the ocean and the sound of the waves lapping on the shore helped dispel her worries about both Julie and Mandy.

But when she returned home, it was to find Mandy packing her belongings into boxes and large black garbage bags.

'What are you doing?'

'I'm moving out. There will be plenty of space for your new daughter and her kid.'

'Mandy! Theres no need for you to go. Julie and Tilly...'

'You should have told me. I can't believe you kept something like this from Tara and me. If they hadn't come here, if I hadn't seen them, would you ever have told us?'

'I...' Liz knew that if Julie hadn't made contact, her existence would have remained a secret. There would have been no need for Mandy and Tara to ever know. Her silence spoke volumes.

'I knew it! Well, you won't have to worry about me.'

'Where will you go?'

Mandy stopped stuffing clothes into a bag. 'I'm moving in with Gary. We've found a place to rent. It's bigger than where he was. We decided when we were up north, but I didn't expect to have to move out of here so quickly.'

'You don't need to.'

'I spoke to Gran. She told me they're moving to Pelican Crossing, and that the girl plans to start school next week and stay here.'

'She what?' Liz silently cursed her mother. How could she have been so tactless as to tell Mandy Julie and Tilly's plans? She supposed, in her mind, Joan had thought it might help Mandy come to terms with them. How wrong she had been.

Thirty

Finn had been worrying about the future of the newspaper all weekend but had managed to hide his concerns from Adele and Sandy. But now it was Monday morning, and he was back in the office, all his fears re-emerged.

It was strange to see everyone else going about their daily tasks, ignorant of the fact their livelihoods might be at risk. No, he wouldn't let it happen. He was meeting with Joe again for lunch – in the mayor's office this time – and Joe had promised to have figured out a plan.

The morning news conference had just come to a close when he saw he had two missed calls from Liz. His face broke into a smile and his heart leapt at the thought of the woman who had appeared so unexpectedly in his life and given him a new reason to live. As soon as he was back in his office, he called her back.

'Finn!'

The way she said his name made his heart beat faster.

'Liz, sorry I missed your calls. I was…' He dragged a hand through his hair.

'You were busy. I understand. The reason I called…' she hesitated, and Finn could picture her twisting a lock of hair in her fingers, '… Julie and Tilly are tied up today, and I wondered if you were free for lunch.'

Damn! This had to be the day when he already had an arrangement, and he couldn't postpone his meeting with Joe. 'Oh, I'm sorry…'

'That's okay. I had hoped to be able to talk with you.'

Finn could hear the disappointment in her voice. He wanted to see her, to hear what she had to say. 'How about coffee?' he asked. He looked at the unread emails on his computer and grimaced. They would keep. 'I could slip out in an hour's time. *Books and Coffee?*'

'I'd like that,' Liz said sounding happier.

'See you then.' As he finished the call, Finn wondered if something had happened to make Liz want to talk to him. He hoped there had been no problems with her new-found family. Her other daughters were away, so there couldn't be anything wrong there. That only left Liz herself or her mother. Well, he'd find out soon enough.

There was a spring in Finn's step as he made his way to *Books and Coffee*, the prospect of seeing Liz again having brightened his morning and sent his worries to the back of his mind. Though he couldn't dismiss them completely and knew he'd have to tell his staff sooner rather than later. But he wanted to meet with Joe again first and get the next issue of the paper out before he broke the bad news.

Finn arrived first. He ordered a macchiato for himself and the cappuccino he knew Liz liked, then, seeing a tray of blueberry muffins, ordered two of those too, before taking a seat at a corner table where they could talk privately.

Only a few moments later, Liz appeared, her dark curls tumbling around her face, the silver highlights sparkling in the morning light.

Finn rose to give her a hug, enjoying how familiar her body now felt in his arms.

'It's so good to see you,' she said, smiling up at him.

'Good to see you, too. I ordered.'

As he spoke, their coffees and muffins arrived.

'Thanks. These look yummy.' Liz took a seat and picked up her coffee.

'I've been hoping for the opportunity to see you again,' he said.

'Me too.'

They smiled at each other. It was as if they were alone in the world.

'You wanted to talk?' he said.

'Yes.' Liz carefully placed her cup on the table. 'I need to tell someone, and I thought you might understand. It's Mandy…'

'The cyclone. Is she all right?'

'She's back.'

'Oh!' Finn thought what that could mean.

Liz played with her teaspoon. 'She arrived back on Friday. I'm delighted she's safe, but…'

'Did she meet your other daughter?'

'Not yet, but she saw Julie and Tilly leave. I had to tell her.'

'I'm guessing it didn't go down well.'

Liz shook her head. 'She was furious I'd kept Julie secret from her, refused to meet her. She's moved out.'

'Wow! That's a bit harsh. Where has she gone?'

'It seems she and Gary have found a place together. I don't mind. I'm happy for her, but I wish it hadn't happened the way it did.'

'Oh, my dear.' The affectionate term fell from his lips without any thought. 'I'm so sorry. Do you think she'll come round before they leave?'

Liz gazed up at him, causing him to draw breath. She was so lovely, and so vulnerable when she was upset, the green of her eyes seeming deeper than usual. He wanted to pull her into his arms and tell her he'd make it all right. But he couldn't, not this.

'That's the thing,' she said, her expression changing from one of annoyance and turning into a smile. 'They plan to move here, to Pelican Crossing, as soon as Julie can sort out everything in Brisbane. Tilly is starting school next week – at Pelican Crossing High. It's what they're doing today, enrolling Tilly in school, buying her uniform and looking for a place to rent, one they can move into in a few weeks' time.'

'Wow!' Finn said again. 'You said they were staying in a motel.'

'Tilly will move into the apartment when Julie goes home. I had planned for her to sleep on the sofa, but now Mandy's moved out… Oh, I wish she'd waited, talked to me, met Julie and Tilly. I know it was a shock to her. I didn't intend for her to find out like this. But it is what it is. Mum thinks Mandy will come round.'

'You don't?'

'Oh, eventually she will. It's not in Mandy's makeup to be upset with me for long, but I've never seen her quite this annoyed before.'

'I guess you've never produced a new sister for her before.'

'I guess not.' Liz gave a little laugh. 'But enough about my woes. What's happening with you? You seem a little distracted.'

'Sorry.' Finn had been hoping it didn't show. 'I received a piece of bad news last week. The regional consortium that owns *The Courier* – and a lot of other regional papers – have decided to consolidate, close the offices and produce a digital newspaper.'

Liz's mouth fell open. 'But they can't do that. *The Crossing Courier's* an institution in Pelican Crossing. We'd all be lost without it. You can't let it happen.'

'I don't intend to. I've talked with our mayor about it and between us we've come up with a few ideas, one of which is to set up a fundraiser to buy *The Courier* if we can. It's why I couldn't meet you for lunch. I'm meeting with Joe to figure out our plan.'

'Oh, I'm glad. Joe Harris is a good guy. He's very community minded. He's been a bit lost since Barb died but hasn't stopped working for the good of the town and its residents. You'll be right with him. If there's anything I can do…'

'Thanks.' Finn dragged a hand through his hair. He hadn't intended to share his worry with her. Until now, only he and Joe knew. 'Please keep it to yourself. We don't want anyone to know just yet. I need to tell my staff first, and I don't want to do that until I can give them some hope.'

'I understand. Of course I will. I'm good at keeping secrets,' she said with a grimace, 'though up till now, it hasn't done me much good.'

As they rose to leave, Liz looked up at him with a naughty smile. 'One good thing about Mandy moving out…'

Finn was puzzled.

'… it means I'll be alone in the apartment every night this week – after Julie and Tilly return to their motel.'

It took Finn barely a moment to realise what she was saying. 'Is that an invitation?'

'If you want it to be.'

'Tonight?'

Liz smiled. 'They usually leave around eight.'

When they parted, Finn watched Liz walk down the street before he headed back to the office. In addition to the strong attraction he felt for her, he admired her so much. She'd gone through a lot both when she was young, and in the past couple of weeks. He'd like to give Mandy a good shake and tell her to get over herself. But she was a grown woman and would have to do it in her own time.

Meantime, he had tonight to look forward to.

Thirty-one

Liz smiled to herself as she left *Books and Coffee*. The expression on Finn's face had been priceless when she'd practically invited him over that evening – and every other evening that week. But, while she couldn't wait to feel his arms around her again, to sink into his embrace, she couldn't stop remembering how it had come about, and wonder what Mandy was thinking now she'd had time to digest the news she had another sister – and a niece.

Now she'd left Finn, Liz was at a loose end. She'd elected not to join Julie and Tilly this morning, reasoning it was up to them to do the school thing and that she'd be in the way when they were looking at rentals. She really needed someone to talk to, someone with a clearer understanding of Mandy's hurt feelings. As she mentally trawled through her friends, she came to the conclusion Rachel was the obvious one. With two daughters of her own, and several grandchildren, Liz knew Rachel would provide a sympathetic ear and might even offer advice.

A quick call elicited the information Rachel was minding her grandchildren today but would be happy to see her. Liz gave a sigh of relief. Rachel, widowed like Poppy, had turned her large family home into a B&B and between B&B guests and minding her growing clutch of grandchildren, was kept fully occupied. The house itself was situated a short way out of town on a bluff above the ocean where it caught any breeze going, making it delightful in summer, but often blustery at other times of the year.

This morning there was only a gentle breeze ruffling Liz's curls.

She was greeted at the gate by two identical little girls and a small white dog. 'Hello, girls,' she said as she heard Rachel's voice from the doorway.

'Come right in, Liz. These three will be happy out here for a bit longer. We've just had morning tea, but I'm happy to put the kettle on again, or would you prefer coffee?'

'Thanks, Rachel.' Liz reached the door and gave her friend a hug. 'I've just had coffee, but I wouldn't say no to another.' She followed Rachel into the family-sized kitchen which was filled with the delicious aroma of baking. 'Been busy I see,' she said, indicating the tray of cookies on the benchtop.

'The girls helped me make gingerbread cookies,' Rachel said. 'They were such a hit at Christmas, they begged me for more, though I think they got more of the mixture on themselves than on the tray,' she laughed. 'Let me make coffee then we can talk.'

Liz sat and watched as Rachel made coffee. It was peaceful here, a different sort of peace from her apartment. Here there was the distant sound of children's voices and the snuffling of the little dog. 'No guests at the moment?' she asked.

'I do have a family for the school holidays, but they're out all day. Bed and Breakfast is what it says. I have the day to myself to do housework, cook and look after the two terrors,' she said gesturing to where Liz could see the children and the dog through the window. They were playing some game with a ball and seemed totally engrossed in it.

'Now,' Rachel said, joining Liz at the scrubbed wood table which always reminded Liz of one her grandmother had when she was growing up in the country, 'what's up? You sounded worried when you called.'

Liz took a sip of coffee before replying. 'It's Mandy,' she said.

'What's she been up to now? Not more matchmaking? I thought you and Finn Hunter…'

How did she know? Liz sighed. How did anyone know anything in Pelican Crossing? It was impossible to keep a secret. Though *she* had… until now. 'It's more about me, really,' she said. 'About something I've kept secret for years, and Mandy can't forgive me.'

'It can't be that bad, Liz. I've known you since Tara was born. I can't imagine you've been hiding anything that would cause Mandy to act up.'

'It goes back further than that, Rach.' Liz took another sip of coffee and began her story.

'… and they're here in Pelican Crossing now,' she finished. 'It's why I missed our last lunch.'

'And Mandy found out?'

'She did. It's my fault. I should have told her and Tara as soon as they were old enough to understand. But I thought if I never heard from Julie it wouldn't matter.'

'And now it does. Oh, my dear. Who was it who said, *Oh, what a tangled web we weave when first we practice to deceive*? But it was really your parents who set up the deception, and they did it to protect you.' She thought for a moment. 'How has your mum reacted?'

'She loves them, is delighted to have a great-granddaughter, thrilled they plan to move to Pelican Crossing. And Tara still has to find out. She and Mark will be back from Paris at the weekend… if Mandy doesn't contact her before then.' She sighed as the possibility occurred to her.

'Tara isn't as headstrong as Mandy. She may see things from your point of view.'

'Maybe. What am I going to do, Rach? It seems I've found one daughter only to lose another.'

'You haven't lost Mandy. She's taken this opportunity to move in with Gary. Give her time.'

'That's what Mum says.'

'Your mum's a wise woman. Look at what she and your dad did to protect you when you were fifteen and pregnant. I don't know if I'd have had the courage to do all of that to protect one of mine. Although they were different times,' she mused. 'Anyway, the cat's out of the bag, so to speak, now and can't be put back in. You've been reunited with your daughter, have discovered a granddaughter – and I know what a delight grandchildren can be, even if they sometimes make me want to tear my hair out. Be grateful. Mandy loves you. She may be a little confused and angry at the moment, but I'm sure your mum's right. She'll be back trying to organise your life again before you know it.'

'Thanks, Rach, I hope you're right.' Liz clasped Rachel's hand.

'On a brighter note, you and Finn Hunter?' she asked, reverting to an earlier comment.

'It's complicated.'

'Isn't it always? I seem to remember Poppy saying the same thing about her and Cam only last year, and now look at them.'

Liz thought of their friend who was now living happily with Cam Mitchell who owned *Pelican Marine*. They had got together soon after the marriage of Poppy's daughter and Cam's son and it hadn't all been plain sailing, but… 'It was different for them. We both have obligations, family obligations. We can't just…' Liz blushed.

'But you have?'

Liz blushed again. 'We're not teenagers anymore, Rach. We know the score and we know family has to come first. Finn has his daughter and grandson, and I have Julie and Tilly… as well as my other two.'

'But you're both effectively free… single.'

'I suppose. But it doesn't make things any easier.' Liz wished she could change the subject. She didn't feel comfortable talking about Finn like this. Rachel was a good friend, possibly her best friend, but even so, some things were too private to share.

Liz drained her cup. 'Thanks for listening, Rach. It helped.' And it had helped… to tell her about Julie and Tilly and her concerns with Mandy. She hoped her mum and Rach were both right, and Mandy would see sense. Meantime, she'd have to wait.

'I'm always here, anytime you want to talk,' Rachel said. 'And I hope we'll see you at our next lunch.'

'It must be my turn,' Liz laughed, 'so I'll definitely be there.'

As Rachel hugged her goodbye, she whispered in her ear, 'Hang in there, Liz. It'll all work out.'

'Thanks,' Liz whispered back.

On the drive home, Liz reflected that the meeting with Rachel had helped. It had been good to share her story once more – it seemed to get easier with each telling – and her advice about Mandy had been encouraging. Now she had to figure out what to cook for dinner, and there was Finn to look forward to. At the thought of the evening ahead, a bubble of excitement began to build up inside her.

Thirty-two

Finn felt more upbeat for the rest of the morning, the prospect of seeing Liz that evening putting a smile on his face. But it disappeared when he set out to meet Joe. He had no idea what he would do if *The Courier* closed. Newspapers were all he knew.

As he pushed open the door to the town hall offices, the gravity of his situation hit home. No *Courier* meant no job for him in Pelican Crossing. What would that mean for him, for Adele and Sandy, for his relationship with Liz?

'I hope you've come up with a solution,' he said to Joe, when they had shaken hands and exchanged pleasantries. 'If *The Courier* closes, I'm screwed.'

'I don't know about a solution, but I do have a few ideas,' Joe said. 'I ordered sandwiches,' he gestured to a low coffee table, 'and the coffee from the machine is drinkable. Hope you don't mind Coco,' he added, nodding to the chocolate labrador lying at his feet. 'She hates being left at home on her own, so I've taken to bringing her into the office some days.'

'Not at all.' Finn knew the dog had been Joe's sole companion since his wife died. 'And thanks.' He took a seat on one of the chairs by the coffee table and, once he'd made coffee, Joe joined him.

'I've been giving this some thought – don't have much else to do with my time these days – and I have a few ideas.' Joe took a sip of coffee. 'We discussed a fundraiser. I still think that's our best bet. I'm assuming the owners aren't going to change their minds?'

'No chance.'

'Right. The first thing we need to do is to let people know, get the community behind us – A *Save the Courier* campaign. We could use the paper to do that.'

Finn rubbed his chin. 'First, I'll have to let the staff know. I've been keeping it to myself. I wanted to have something positive to tell them before I broke the news.'

'Best do it soon. They'll find out before long anyway if, as you say, it's happening elsewhere too. Then we can get into action – posters, placards, a town meeting. The last one went well,' he said, referring to one held before Christmas which scared off a developer.

'That's all well and good, but we're going to need money, a lot of money, Joe.'

'That's just the start, to get people's ire up. Then we start with the fundraisers and asking for donations. We can have one of those tracking thermometers on the outside of the town hall, keeping track of what's been raised… and a mammoth party when we reach our target.' Joe rubbed his hands together. He was enjoying this.

'It all sounds good, Joe, but…' It wasn't *his* livelihood at stake.

'Oh, ye of little faith.' Joe laughed. 'I haven't felt so energised in ages. This is what the community needs, a reason to pull together for something really worthwhile.' Then he became more serious. 'You're not likely to lose staff when you tell them the news, are you?'

'I hope not. It's difficult to predict how individuals will react. Most of my guys are young with families and mortgages. They may not feel they can afford to sit around and wait till we have a result. But I'll do what I can to persuade them.' Joe's enthusiasm was beginning to rub off on Finn. He could visualise the big thermometer on the wall of the town hall, the amount rising steadily towards their target. 'You know, Joe, this might work.'

'Of course it will work. I have every faith in the people of Pelican Crossing. They always rise to the occasion when help's needed, and this is an issue affecting every one of us. Now, in terms of fundraisers…' he took a bite from a sandwich and a gulp of coffee, 'I vote we contact all the charity groups in town. I believe you belong to quite a few of them.'

'Yes, Lions, Rotary, a few others, when I have time.'

'Good. They're used to raising money. There are also the schools, churches and sporting clubs, then we can ask for individual donations. We have a few well-heeled families who I'm sure would be happy to contribute to keep our newspaper alive.'

'You seem to have thought this through,' Finn said admiringly.

'As I said, I don't have a lot to do these days when I'm not here in the office.'

Finn didn't comment. He knew Joe had developed the reputation of being a workaholic since his wife died, staying late at the office, and even going in on weekends. No wonder his dog was fretting.

By the time he left the mayor's office, Finn's mind was in a whirl. He'd agreed to speak to his staff and the various groups he belonged to, and to put a full-page notice in the paper later in the week. He dreaded to think what his employers would say when they heard about it, but he suddenly didn't care. They'd already decided to cancel the paper. There wasn't much more they could do – except sack him, a tiny voice in the back of his head said. He decided to ignore it.

*

Finn was exhausted by the time he arrived home. The meeting with staff had gone much as he had expected, their shattered expressions mirroring his own initial feelings. He explained what he and Joe intended and managed to raise a cheer, but he was sure there would be a lot of soul-searching when they had time to fully consider the implications.

'Grandy!' Sandy greeted him, Bluey at his heels – the two were inseparable. 'Can you play ball with us?'

Finn stifled a groan.

'Give your granddad time to draw breath,' Adele said. 'Difficult day, Dad?'

'Mmm. Tell you later. I need to freshen up.' He headed to his bedroom and ensuite.

After a shower, Finn felt better. When he walked into the kitchen, Adele handed him a beer.

'You look as if you need that.'

'Thanks.'

'Want to talk about it?'

He didn't, but she deserved to know. 'Sit down. I have something to tell you.'

'Sounds serious.'

'They want to close down *The Courier*.' He took a swig of beer, the icy liquid going some way to improve his mood.

Adele's eyes widened. 'They can't. What will you do?'

'It may not come to that. The owners want to consolidate all the regional papers, go digital. It was coming. I should have seen it.'

'How long have you known?'

'Since last week. Wait…' He held up one hand as she opened her mouth to complain. 'I've been talking to Joe Harris about it. He has a few ideas, ways we can raise enough money to buy the paper. The community needs it. We can't let it disappear. It's not only my job at stake here, there are the staff, and all the residents, shopkeepers and businesses in Pelican Crossing who rely on *The Courier* for local news and community announcements – and for somewhere to advertise.'

'What a brilliant idea. I'll help in any way I can, and I know a lot of others will too.'

'That's what we're hoping. We'll have a full-page feature in the next edition telling everyone what's happening and encouraging them to get behind us, to *Save The Courier*.'

'It's a great slogan. I like it.'

Finn heard a note of enthusiasm in Adele's voice, the first he'd heard in a long time, since… since Tim died. Maybe the potential demise of the newspaper wasn't all bad if it could bring Adele back to the person she used to be.

'I can talk to the teachers and the Mother's Club at school about it,' she said, 'and I can help put up posters and give out fliers and stuff. Maybe we could have tee-shirts made. I know a woman who prints them.'

'That would be great, honey.' If everyone was this keen, they might even succeed.

'Can you play with us now?' Sandy and Bluey appeared in the doorway.

Finn glanced at Adele.

'On you go,' she said. 'Dinner in half an hour.'
'Okay, champ. You heard your mum. For half an hour.'

Thirty-three

It was a few minutes after eight when Liz heard Finn at the door. She'd been on tenterhooks ever since Julie and Tilly left to go back to the motel. What if he didn't come? What if she'd been too forward? She was so out of practice with this dating business. It had been so long. The disastrous dates she'd met through the internet dating website last year hadn't prepared her for anyone like Finn, or for the rush of desire she felt when she was with him.

Liz knew he'd have eaten, as she had, but had prepared a platter of cheese and biscuits and cut up a few pieces of fruit. She checked herself in the hall mirror and opened the door to be pulled into his arms, his lips meeting hers in a passionate kiss. Liz was trembling when they drew apart.

'I've been waiting to do that ever since this morning,' Finn said, producing a bottle of sparkling wine which he had somehow managed to hold in one hand while kissing her. 'I thought we should celebrate the fact we can have some time together.'

'Sounds good to me.' Liz took his hand and led him into the living room. It looked very romantic in the dim light of a table lamp, and with the moon shining through the windows.

Anticipating the wine, Liz had placed two glasses on the coffee table. Finn opened the bottle and filled them, then lifted one towards Liz. 'To us,' he said.

'To us,' she repeated, unsure exactly what he meant. His obligations hadn't changed since they were last together, nor had hers. They had only become more complicated. But she was willing to live for the moment, and this moment was theirs, and theirs alone.

*

They chatted while they drank the wine and spread the cheese on the fig and black olive crackers. Finn told Liz about his meeting Joe and the *Save the Courier* campaign they proposed, and Liz offered to help where she could, suggesting brochures in the medical centre and a petition to the owners of *The Courier*.

While Finn didn't think there was much point in a petition – their minds were made up – he didn't rubbish the idea, pleased she wanted to be involved. If everyone in Pelican Crossing reacted like Adele and Liz had, the project would be a success.

'What will you do if it doesn't work?' Liz asked, when they were almost at the end of the wine, and most of the cheese had been eaten.

'I don't want to think about it,' he said. But he had. He was well aware he might need to leave Pelican Crossing, leave Liz, just as they were beginning to form a relationship.

'Don't let's worry about that now,' he said, pulling her into his arms again and inhaling her sweet scent. Being close to her like this sent his senses reeling. It made him forget all his worries and filled him with such a sense of wellbeing, he couldn't think straight.

It was late when Finn rolled away from Liz, the moonlight shining in through the open bedroom window sending a silvery glow across the room. 'I should go,' he murmured, making no attempt to move.

'Must you?' Liz kissed his cheek, sending shivers of delight through him, and compelling him to draw her into another embrace.

'I must,' he groaned. 'Adele… Sandy… I don't want to, but…' He dropped a gentle kiss on her forehead.

'I understand,' she said, but she wound her legs around his, effectively imprisoning him.

Finn kissed her again, as she slowly untangled her legs from his.

'I know,' she said, 'you have to go.'

'Tomorrow?' Finn asked. 'You did say you were free all week?'

'Tomorrow,' Liz said. 'It can't come soon enough.'

But next week, her granddaughter would be here, and it would be impossible for them to make love like this. It was something neither of them had mentioned. He didn't want some hole-in-the-corner affair with Liz. He wanted more. He wanted... a future.

Thirty-four

'I really like this car. It's so cute.'

'Thanks, Tilly, I like it too.' Liz and Tilly were driving back from the airport, having waved Julie off.

Liz glanced at her granddaughter when she paused at an intersection, but the girl was focussed on her phone again. She was beginning to regret her impulsive offer to have Tilly stay until Julie moved to Pelican Crossing. What did she know about looking after a fourteen-year-old? Teenagers today were a different breed to what they'd been when Tara and Mandy were Tilly's age. It seemed her granddaughter spent most of her waking hours glued to the screen of one device or another.

Liz's mind began to wander. She'd hoped Mandy would have come round by now and she'd have been able to introduce her to Julie and Tilly, but there had been no sign of her youngest daughter, and Liz's calls and messages had remained unanswered. Tara was due back today too, and Liz wanted to make sure she spoke to her before Mandy did. Her plan was to drop Tilly off at *The Haven*, then drive round to Tara's to welcome her and Mark back. She'd baked Tara's favourite lemon slice in the hope of finding her in a good mood and was returning the *life on a rock* plant she'd been minding for her daughter which required daily watering.

'What are your other daughters like?'

Tilly's question pulled Liz back to the present. 'Tara and Mandy? They're very different from each other. I always think Tara is the sensible one. She's married to Mark… well, you know that; you've seen her wedding photo. She works in recruitment and is very focussed on her career. Mandy…' How could she describe Mandy? '… Mandy's always been the baby of the family, spoiled and accustomed to getting her own way. She has her own personal training business and works part time at the yacht club. She tends to be quick-tempered and is currently annoyed with me for keeping your mum secret from her.'

'She doesn't like Mum and me.'

'She doesn't know you. It was a shock for her to learn about you both. I'm sure she will love you when she does meet you.'

'Were you ashamed of Mum?'

'Goodness, no! But it was difficult. As you know, I wasn't much older than you are now. We lived in a small country town. Gossip was rife. It would have been impossible for me if everyone knew I'd been pregnant – and they would have. You can't keep something like that secret. I made a bad mistake, and I was lucky my parents supported me. But I was never ashamed of your mum. You mustn't think that. I always hoped to find her, and you are an unexpected bonus.' Liz threw a grin in Tilly's direction.

'I like that, to be an unexpected bonus.' Tilly grinned back.

'Here we are.' Liz turned the car into the grounds of *The Haven* and stopped outside her mother's villa. 'You'll be all right with Mum while I visit Tara?'

'Of course. I love Joan. She's promised to show me more photos of you when you were growing up, and to teach me Mahjong.'

Liz chuckled. 'That'll keep both of you busy. Mum's fanatical about Mahjong. She plays with a group in *The Haven* a couple of times a week.'

Joan was waiting for them at her open door. 'You'll have time for a cuppa, Liz, before you dash off, won't you? I have the kettle on and there are date scones just out of the oven.'

'Just a quick one,' Liz said, her mouthwatering at the thought of her mother's date scones. She hugged her mother and stepped inside.

The scones were as delicious as Liz expected, but as soon as she had eaten one, she rose to go. 'I need to catch Tara before Mandy does,' she said, her mouth suddenly dry at the prospect of what lay ahead.

'Tara will be fine,' her mother said.

'I hope so.'

Liz's nervousness increased as she drove to where Tara and Mark lived in a townhouse facing the river. It was a little way out of town in a new development. When she reached the complex, she parked and, taking a deep breath and carrying the lemon slice and the plant, walked up to their door.

After the initial hugs and kisses, and Tara's exclamations on the health of her plant, they finally settled in the small courtyard with coffee and Liz's lemon slice. The first half hour was filled with Tara and Mark vying to describe their trip to Paris. They'd loved every minute of it and planned to go back the following year. *So, still no children on the horizon*, Liz thought with regret.

They were on their second cups of coffee, and Tara was talking about lunch, when Liz said, 'I have something to tell you.'

'Mandy left me a weird message about some secret you'd kept for years. Is that what it's about?' Tara asked, seemingly unconcerned.

Liz gave a sigh of relief. At least Mandy hadn't divulged the news about Julie and Tilly yet. 'Yes,' she said. 'I'm sorry I didn't tell you both before now, but… it never seemed to be the right time.'

'So why now?' Tara asked.

'Let me start at the beginning, when I was only fifteen and living with my parents in a small country town…'

When she finished there was a deathly hush. Then Tara said, 'So where are they now?'

'Julie has gone back to Brisbane to settle things there. Tilly is staying with me till her mother gets back. She starts school tomorrow. They've rented an older house near the centre of town and will move in when Julie returns.' She held her breath.

'It's a lot to take in. I can't imagine you pregnant at fifteen. Was that why you insisted Mandy and I go on the pill? What are they like? Has Mandy met them?'

'Your sister…' Liz lifted her cup, realised it was empty and put it down again, 'The short answer is she hasn't met them and doesn't want to. She's not talking to me either, since she learned about them. She moved her things out the next day. As to what they're like. They're lovely. Julie is a single mother, divorced, and works in a library. She's optimistic about finding work here too. Tilly's a typical teenager. She was a bit standoffish at first, but we get on well now. Your grandmother has taken to them both, though she was a bit stunned at first – she thought all of that was in the past and had been forgotten. Tilly is with her now, learning to play Mahjong.'

Tara chuckled. 'Good luck to her with that. She never managed to teach me or Mandy. I'm sorry about Mandy, Mum. But you know what she's like. It must have been a shock. It's a shock to me too, but I can understand how it might have been for you. I… I had a scare when I was fifteen. I never told you. Mandy didn't know either. Amber was the only person I confided in,' she said, referring to her best friend and the daughter of Liz's friend, Poppy. 'It was my first time, and it was such a relief when I got my period. You put me on the pill soon after and I thought you'd guessed. You didn't?'

Liz shook her head, shocked she'd never known of her daughter's fears.

'Don't worry about Mandy,' Tara continued. 'I'll talk her round. It was probably an excuse for her to move in with Gary too.'

'Hmm.'

'What are you doing tonight? Why don't we all go to the yacht club for dinner? We can meet Tilly then. Mark?'

'Sounds good to me,' Mark, who had been quiet during all their conversation, said.

'You're not too tired from your trip?'

'No, it'll probably hit us later. Mandy won't be working tonight. She doesn't do Sundays. So you don't need to worry about bumping into her.'

'Right.' It might not be a bad idea for her to meet Tilly unexpectedly but wouldn't be fair to Tilly.

When Liz left Tara's after an early lunch, it was still too early to pick Tilly up, so she decided to take a walk along the beach, her usual method of settling her mind and working things out. She was surprised and relieved at Tara's reaction, though the revelation her daughter had thought herself pregnant brought back memories of her own teenage terror, of the day she told her parents. Hopefully, Tara was right about Mandy, and she could talk sense into her sister.

Liz was paddling in the shallow water at the edge of the sea, lost in thought, sandals in one hand, when she heard a familiar voice.

'Liz!'

Looking up she saw Finn, his grandson and the small spaniel called Bluey coming towards her. Like her, Finn was walking in the shallows, while his grandson and the dog were running in and out of the water.

'Finn!' Liz's lips curled into a smile as she was suffused with a warm glow. Last week had been magical. Every evening, after Julie and Tilly had gone back to their motel, Finn had arrived with wine or chocolates or both. They'd snuggled up together on the sofa, sometimes talking quietly, sometimes not. Then they'd go to bed to make wonderful love, till it was time for him to go home, leaving her wrapped in the warmth of their lovemaking.

'I thought you were going to see your daughter today.'

'I was. I did.' She smiled as the little boy and the dog rushed past her, splashing salt water onto her legs.

'And?'

'It was okay. I won't go into it now, but she understood. She's going to try to talk to Mandy, so…' Liz held up her crossed fingers.

'I'm happy for you.'

'And she wants to meet Tilly. We're all going to the yacht club for dinner. I hope…' She bit her lip. Tilly could be unpredictable.

'I'm sure it'll go well. I wish…'

'I do too.' Liz knew what he meant. It was going to be difficult for them to see each other while she had Tilly to stay. 'But it won't be for long. I expect Julie to be able to move up in a couple of weeks' time.'

'I can't wait.' Finn gave the lopsided grin Liz had come to love.

There might not be any future in this relationship, given the demands of both families, but she intended to enjoy it while she could.

'Maybe I'll see you at the yacht club,' Finn said, as Sandy became tired of the game with Bluey and insisted it was time for an ice cream.

Liz's heart leapt as she wondered if he meant to join them for dinner.

'Maybe,' she said.

*

Tilly was excited at the prospect of meeting Tara, saying, 'I never thought I'd have an aunt and now I have two.' She spent the drive to the marina peppering Liz with questions about Tara and asking if Liz was sure Tara wanted to meet her.

By the time they parked the car, Liz was ready to scream.

Tara and Mark were already in the restaurant when Liz and Tilly walked in.

'Is that her?' Tilly whispered, when the elegant woman with a cap of short dark hair seated at a window table waved to them.

Liz nodded and steered Tilly towards her. 'This is Tara and Mark,' she said.

'And you must be Tilly. Welcome to the family,' Tara said, rising and giving a diffident Tilly a hug. 'Wow, you look so like Mum.'

Tilly gave a tight smile, as if unsure how to react.

'It's okay,' Tara said. 'Both Mandy and I look a bit like our dad too, but you could be Mum when she was your age.'

'Tilly's mum looks like me too,' Liz said. 'Wait till you meet her.'

'I'm looking forward to it.' Tara smiled.

'Good to meet you, Tilly,' Mark said, holding out a hand which Tilly shook after only a moment's hesitation.

Once they were all seated, Liz began to relax. It was going to be all right.

They had ordered and been served drinks, wine for the adults and a lemon, lime and soda for Tilly, when Liz heard Finn's voice.

'Room for a few more?' he asked. 'You all know Adele and Sandy, don't you?'

Tara's eyes widened. She gazed from Finn to Liz and back again but didn't speak.

Sandy didn't wait to be invited but climbed onto a spare chair next to Tilly who grinned at him.

'I remember you,' she said. 'You had a book about spaniels.'

'I have a spaniel. He's called Bluey,' Sandy said.

'Do join us,' Liz said somewhat belatedly as a waiter hurried to add another table and two chairs to theirs. She wasn't sure if this was a good idea; she knew she'd have some explaining to do to Tara later.

As the evening progressed, however, Liz realised the presence of Finn and his family helped dispel any awkwardness Tilly might have felt at this first meeting with Tara. Young Sandy was delightful, managing to keep everyone entertained by his stories about his puppy, and Tara was able to gently sound Tilly out about her plans and her move to Pelican Crossing.

'She's lovely,' Tara whispered to Liz when they were preparing to leave, 'but you've been keeping very quiet about our local newspaper editor.'

'Isn't she?' Liz said blushing. 'Your sister knew. She didn't tell you?'

'Not a word.'

While Finn and Mark were arguing about who should pay the bill, Tilly pulled Liz aside. 'Sandy wants me to visit him to see his puppy. Will that be okay?'

Liz glanced at Adele who was smiling. 'I guess so,' she said.

'Why don't you both come to dinner next Saturday?' Adele said. 'I think it's time we got to know each other better.'

'Thanks, we'd like that,' Liz replied, looking round to see if Finn was listening. But he was too busy negotiating payment with Mark. She hoped he'd be happy with the arrangement.

Outside the club, the three groups went their separate ways, but not before Tara gave Liz a meaningful look indicating she intended to talk with her about Finn.

'Tara's nice,' Tilly said as they made their way back to Liz's apartment. 'Why doesn't Mandy want to meet me?'

'I'm sure she will soon,' Liz said, hoping with all her heart she was right. Meanwhile, she knew she was in for an interrogation from Tara about her relationship with Finn.

Thirty-five

Liz was barely awake next morning when her phone rang. Stifling a sigh at the sight of Tara's number on the screen, she pressed to accept the call.

'How did I not know you were still seeing him?' Tara asked as soon as Liz answered. 'My mother and the editor of the local newspaper. Am I last to find out?'

'There's nothing to find out,' Liz lied. 'We've become friends, that's all. You and your sister have been encouraging me to live a little. I've only taken your advice.'

'How long has it been going on? We've only been gone two weeks, and we come back to find…'

'Not long, and it's nothing to make a fuss about. He's a nice man. We're both single but we both have family obligations so it's unlikely to amount to anything. But he's good company…' Liz's voice trailed off and she felt herself grow warm as she remembered exactly the sort of good company Finn was.

'I suppose Gran knows, too.'

'Yes.'

'Well!'

Liz almost burst out laughing. It was as if Tara was the parent and she the child. 'I take it you approve?'

'Of course. Mark knows him better than I do. He says he's been such an asset to the town since he arrived. It's so sad about Adele. Mark knew her husband too. They were at school together. He says it was amazing of Finn to move to Pelican Crossing to support her and Sandy when Tim drowned. I'm just surprised…'

'If that's the only reason you called, I need to go. Tilly starts at Pelican Crossing High this morning, and I want to make sure she has a good breakfast and gets a good start.'

'Of course… and I wanted to let you know I plan to catch up with Mandy today. I don't start work till tomorrow, so will try to see her for lunch. I don't suppose…'

'No, I can't get away, and it's best you talk to her yourself. I'm still *persona non grata* with your sister.'

'Hmm. I'll let you know how it goes. Bye, Mum. Love you.'

'Love you too, sweetheart.'

By this time, Liz was wide awake so, although it was still early, she headed to the shower, then dressed in her usual work attire of white shirt and navy pants, before going to the kitchen and turning on the coffee maker.

'Morning, Liz.' Tilly appeared in the kitchen looking too wide-awake for this time in the morning. 'I'm so excited I couldn't sleep,' she said, her eyes bright with excitement.

'You look very smart,' Liz said, as Tilly twirled around to show off her new uniform. The blue and green striped dress with white collar and cuffs suited her perfectly.

'It's a lot nicer than the uniform from my old school,' Tilly said. 'And the blazer's not too bad, either,' she added, pointing to the green blazer on the back of one of the chairs.

'It's changed a bit since my time there.' Liz remembered the old uniform skirt and blouse which all the girls tried to alter into something more fashionable. 'You looking forward to today?' She was aware how daunting starting a new school could be.

'Yes and no. But I know it can't be worse than my old school. I just hope the other girls are friendly and the boys aren't…' Her eyes clouded over, clearly remembering…

'Come here.' Liz pulled her into a warm hug, still thrilled by the knowledge this teenager was her granddaughter. 'You'll be fine.'

'Thanks, Liz.' Tilly was silent for a few minutes then asked, 'Would it be all right to call you Gran? It feels strange to call you Liz when you're my grandmother. It's different with Joan, but… I liked it when I had a grandmother… before my Gran Miller died.'

'Oh, sweetheart, I'd love it.' Liz felt her eyes moisten. She hadn't dared hope Tilly would call her Gran. Now she felt like a real grandmother.

'How about we have banana pancakes for breakfast since it's a special day?' Liz asked, remembering the last time she'd cooked them had been for Mandy. That breakfast hadn't gone well.

'Yum! I've never had banana pancakes. Can I help?'

'Sure. You can mash the banana and cut up strawberries to put on top.'

The pair worked happily together, and the pancakes were a big hit with Tilly saying, 'I must tell Mum about these when she gets back. She called me this morning to wish me luck, and I told her about meeting Tara. She's looking forward to meeting her too.'

'That's good. We'll organise a get-together when your Mum's here.' *Maybe by then Mandy will have come round too.*

An hour later, Liz dropped Tilly off at school, watching nervously as the girl walked confidently through the gate. It reminded her of Tara and Mandy's first days at school, though then she'd taken them into the classroom. But Tilly was too old to be accompanied. Liz could only hope she'd settle in well and make friends as she had done.

*

Although the medical centre was busy, for Liz the day seemed to drag. Her mind wasn't on the job; it flitted between wondering how Tilly was getting on at school and if Tara had spoken to Mandy. It was a relief when the day was over, and she could head for home, though she was disappointed she hadn't heard from Tara.

Tilly had insisted on making her own way back, making it easier for Liz who would have found it difficult to get away; the hours between end of school and the medical centre closing tended to be particularly busy.

As a result, Tilly was already in the apartment when Liz arrived home. It seemed strange to open the door to the sound of music instead of the silence which usually greeted her.

Tilly was in the living room, her legs lying over the arm of the sofa, lost in her own little world, oblivious to Liz's arrival.

For a moment, Liz stood in the doorway enjoying the sight of this young girl who was part of her, part of the daughter she'd thought never to see again. Then she cleared her throat, and Tilly pulled out her earbuds, dropped her legs and leapt up.

'Sorry, Gran. I didn't hear you come in.'

The word, *Gran*, was music to Liz's ears. 'How was your day?' she asked, dropping into a chair.

'It was good. The kids are different here, more laid back. A couple of girls asked me to join them for lunch. They go surfing and play netball and there's a drama group and a school magazine. They've invited me to go cycling with them on the weekend. Is there somewhere I can borrow a bike?'

'Wow! Sounds like you settled in quickly. We should get you a bike. It would help you find your way around. There's a bike shop in Bellbird Bay. Let me think on it. Maybe we can borrow one for next weekend. I'll ask at work.'

'Thanks. It was real cool, and the teachers are awesome. The boys don't seem too bad either.'

'I'm glad.' It was good to see Tilly so enthusiastic. Liz knew Mandy had a bike but wasn't game to ask her to lend it to Tilly. She checked her phone. Still nothing from Tara. She bit her lip. 'I don't expect you have any homework tonight. Why don't we go for a walk along the beach and buy fish and chips for dinner? We can eat them on one of the benches there.'

'Awesome!' Tilly closed the phone she'd been clutching and on which she'd been listening to music. 'I'll change out of my school uniform first.' She disappeared in the direction of her bedroom.

Liz gave a sigh of relief that one of her problems was solved. Now there was only Mandy to worry about. It was a good idea to change, she decided and made her way to her own bedroom where she pulled off her work outfit to replace it with a pair of jeans and a tee-shirt. Slipping her feet into a pair of canvas shoes, she called out, 'Ready, Tilly?'

A smiling Tilly. wearing jeans, tee-shirt and trainers all of which Julie had purchased before she left, appeared. 'All ready, Gran,' she said.

They were sitting by the beach, gazing out at the ocean, eating fish and chips, when Liz's phone rang. Tilly had been describing the peculiar mannerisms of one of her teachers and Liz had been laughing at the way she mimicked him, but the sight of Tara's number on the screen wiped the laughter from her face.

'Sorry, Tilly, I need to take this.' Getting up and moving a little way away from the table to avoid being heard, she answered the call.

'Tara,' she said, her heart in her mouth, 'did you see Mandy?'

'Yes, Mum, but…'

Liz's heart sank.

'It was no good. She wouldn't listen. She accused me of selling out, of being too willing to accept what she called your *other family*. I couldn't get through to her. It was typical Mandy. Once she started, it was as if she couldn't stop. I don't know what to do next. I'm sorry, Mum. I'd hoped I could make her see sense.'

'It's okay, Tara. Thanks for trying. She hasn't turned against you too, has she? I'd hate to think I was to blame for causing a rift between you.' Liz knew how close the two sisters had always been, often teaming up to oppose her.

'No way. It would take more than that. But I've never seen Mandy so determined, Mum. I'm sorry,' she repeated.

Liz sighed loudly. 'It is what it is. I'll give her a few days and try again. I'm not going to let this spoil our relationship for long. She's still with Gary?'

'Oh yes, full of praise for him.'

'That's good. He's a nice boy. I'm pleased she's with him. Maybe he can help change her mind.'

'Was that the newspaper editor?' Tilly asked, when Liz returned to find the remains of her fish and chips had gone cold.

'No, your Aunt Tara.'

'Oh, I love having two aunts. Did she have news of my Aunt Mandy?'

'Still no change there,' Liz said, 'but not to worry. I remembered Tara might still have her old bike and I was right. She's going to look it out and we can pick it up for you tomorrow after I finish work. She's suggested we stay for dinner too.'

'Awesome!'

Liz gazed at the young girl who had quickly become so precious to her, amazed how her life had changed in the past few weeks. Although she was upset about Mandy's reaction, Tara had welcomed the new members of the family, and there was Julie's return to look forward to. Things could be worse.

Thirty-six

'Wow, Dad. It looks great.' Adele held the paper up, open at the full-page spread headed, *Save the Courier*.

Finn put down his coffee and swallowed his last bite of toast before taking the paper from her. He knew what it looked like, he'd been the one responsible for putting it together, he'd seen the rushes, but somehow it looked different over breakfast at his own kitchen table.

The headline shouted out the message. There could be no mistake. Finn was afraid of the reprisals which might come when the owners saw it. But before that, it would be seen and read by everyone in Pelican Crossing.

'What is it, Grandy?' Sandy pushed in between Finn and the paper to see what was taking his attention. Bluey tried to get in too, but Finn pushed the dog away.

'A special page your granddad wrote for today's paper,' Adele said. 'It's a big deal, Dad,' she said to Finn, pouring him another cup of coffee. 'I suspect you're going to need this. You'll have a big day ahead of you once this gets out.'

'I guess you're right.' Finn hadn't really considered how the Pelican Crossing community might react to the news being revealed so starkly in their local paper.

As soon as he walked into the office he found out.

'The phone hasn't stopped ringing,' Chloe said. His PA, usually a calming influence in the office, seemed frazzled, despite it being early in the day. 'I've left messages on your desk, but I don't know how you're going to answer all of them.'

'Thanks.' Finn walked into his office to see a pile of yellow post-it notes on the desk. He groaned.

'Most of the comments were positive,' Chloe said, popping her head round the door. 'The mayor wants you to call him as soon as you can. Coffee?'

'Yes, please.' Finn looked at the pile of messages. It would take him all day to reply, and this was just the start. There had to be a better way. He picked up the phone to call Joe.

'Well done!' Joe said as soon as he answered Finn's call. 'I've been receiving calls about it since I got in here at seven o'clock.'

'You, too.' Finn grimaced.

'All good, Finn. People want to help. I've already had several promises of donations. The thermometer should be up on the wall later today and…'

There was the signal of an incoming call on Finn's phone from a number he recognised. It hadn't taken the owners long to react.

'Sorry, Joe. Can I call you back? The big boss is on the other line.'

'Sure thing. How about we meet for lunch? *The Grand*? You'll likely feel like a beer by then.'

'Thanks, sounds good.' Finn ended the call and picked up the other one. 'Finn Hunter here,' he said, his heart beginning to race.

'Hunter, what the hell were you thinking? That full-page notice in today's issue was way out of line. Why on earth did you agree to print it, and how did some loony local get word of our proposed changes?'

Finn took a deep breath. 'I didn't know it was a secret,' he said. 'These things get out in small towns like Pelican Crossing. The local newspaper is the town's lifeblood. People don't want to lose it. What did you expect me to do?'

'What you were told. There'd be a hefty bonus for you if you toed the line and let things progress as planned. But this…' Finn heard the caller expel his breath, '… you can't expect us to take it lying down. There will be consequences, mark my words. You'll be hearing from us.'

The call ended leaving Finn staring at the phone. At least he'd managed to avoid owning up to creating the page, but regardless of who'd initiated it, he'd approved it. This was the first he'd heard any mention of a hefty bonus, and he suspected it was empty words prompted by the notice of the campaign. He exhaled with something like relief; the battle was on.

*

Liz called as Finn was about to go to lunch.

'Congratulations,' she said, 'that's quite an announcement. Everyone's talking about it here this morning and wanting to help. You'll have no shortage of supporters. What's it like in the office?'

'Don't ask! We're inundated with calls, and I had a threatening one from the big boss. I may not have a job this time next week,' Finn said ruefully, his boss's message finally sinking in. 'But who needs them?'

'Oh, Finn, I'm sorry, I didn't think…'

'I guess it was to be expected. They thought they could close us down quietly and no one would know till it happened. They didn't take into account the Pelican Crossing community.'

'Or the editor of *The Crossing Courier*.'

'I guess not.'

'What happens now?'

'I'm meeting Joe for lunch. I should actually be there now.'

'Well, I won't keep you. Just remember, this is a good thing you're doing. The town needs you.'

'Thanks.'

It was only after he ended the call that Finn realised he had been so full of his own concerns he hadn't asked Liz about Tilly's first day at school or if there was any change with Mandy. He'd call her back later, he decided, when he had more time.

As before, Joe had two beers already poured and sitting on the bar. When Finn walked in, he picked them up and headed to a quiet spot. 'I ordered ham and cheese rolls. Hope that's okay. I thought they'd be easy to eat while we talked.'

'Fine.' Finn didn't care what he ate. He wasn't hungry. The call from the consortium had taken away his appetite. He took a welcome gulp of beer, which went some way to improving his mood.

'What did your boss have to say?'

'About what I expected. He ranted on about the loony local who'd submitted the information and my stupidity and disloyalty for publishing it, threatened all sorts.' Finn took another slug of beer.

Their rolls arrived and Joe bit into one and pushed the other towards Finn. 'Eat. You need to keep up your strength.'

'Hmph.'

'I think we're on the verge of something big, Finn, given the calls I've had already. A couple of thousand pledged and…'

'We're going to need a lot more than that,' Finn said, taking a bite of his roll and grimacing. 'I might not have a job next week.' He repeated what he'd said to Liz. 'They're going to come down hard on me.'

'So what? All the more time to work on the campaign.' Joe wasn't to be discouraged. 'We knew it wouldn't go down well with the consortium, but the town is behind us.'

'I don't know, Joe. What if they won't let us buy the paper?'

'Then we'll start our own.'

Finn stared at his friend. Start their own? It hadn't occurred to him. But they could. The building that housed *The Courier* belonged to the council. With enough money they could replace the fixtures and fittings if the consortium decided to play hardball and remove them.

'It's not like you to give up so easily,' Joe said.

Suddenly, Finn was filled with a new resolve. 'You're right, Joe. You always are. Sorry, it's been quite a morning, but you're right. I can't let the bastards win.'

The rest of their lunch was taken up with plans for the campaign, and by the time he returned to the office and picked up the phone to call Liz, Finn was back on top of things.

'I'm sorry I was so wrapped up in my own problems when we last spoke,' he said. 'How was Tilly's first day at school, and what about Mandy?'

Finn felt himself begin to relax and even managed a laugh as Liz told him about Tilly's impressions of school, but he became more concerned when she told him of Tara's lack of success with Mandy. 'I'm so sorry,' he said. 'I wish there was something I could do.'

'There isn't,' Liz said, 'but thanks for wanting to help. I just have to be patient… not one of my better traits. Can you get away tonight… join Tilly and me for dinner? It won't be anything special, but…'

'I'd love to, thanks. I'm sure Adele won't mind, and I can read Sandy his story before I leave. Around seven?'

'Perfect.'

Finn ended the call with a sense of wellbeing. He was going to see Liz tonight and although Tilly's presence might prevent them from making love, the very thought of her sweet face made him want to whoop with joy.

Thirty-seven

Although Liz had just had a two-week break, the vagaries of the roster meant that Wednesday was her rostered day off and the day when she and her friends always met for lunch. So much had happened since they last met as a group, and she'd missed the previous month. Today, she knew she'd be the focus of the conversation.

It was her turn to host the event, so she spent the morning preparing several salads and setting the table on the balcony. She loved to eat out here when the weather permitted and where all her plants made it seem like an outdoor garden, and today was perfect. As she moved around the kitchen, Liz thought about the previous evening.

Finn had arrived at seven as promised bearing wine for her and a box of chocolates which he handed to Tilly, whose eyes widened at the unexpected gift. It had been a fun evening with Tilly keeping them both amused with anecdotes about school. She was a different girl from the shy, sullen teenager who had arrived in Pelican Crossing with her mother only a few weeks earlier. Then, when dinner was over, Tilly had disappeared to her bedroom claiming the need to do homework. Liz suspected it was more a case of Tilly wanting to give her and Finn some privacy or being eager to spend time with her iPad. Whatever the reason, she was pleased to have Finn to herself.

They spent the rest of the evening snuggled up together on the sofa, till he checked his watch and said it was time for him to go. The warm hug and kiss were lovely, but Liz was left feeling somewhat empty. She wanted so much more.

The sound of someone at the door put an end to Liz's musings as she rushed to answer it, banishing all thought of Finn to the back of her mind.

Poppy and Rachel arrived together, chattering loudly as they walked inside, before taking time to greet Liz with hugs. They were already settled on the balcony with glasses of wine, discussing the full-page article in *The Courier* and the possible fate of the paper when Gill arrived.

'What do you think, Gill?' Poppy asked, when Liz had poured Gill a glass of wine. 'We were talking about the possible closing of *The Courier*.'

'It would be a disaster for the town, but we have to move with the times,' Gill said, taking a sip of wine. 'Oh, I needed that, Liz. Thanks. It's not only happening in Pelican Crossing,' she continued. 'It's happening all over Australia. Everything's moving to the internet. Look at how people are favouring streaming services over cinemas, eBooks over paperbacks. Newspapers are only one more casualty of the digital age.'

'But…' Liz said, '… don't you agree we ought to try to do something about it? The campaign to save *The Courier* appears to have a lot of support.'

'We should do what we can to support it,' Poppy said. 'I plan to give a donation and I'll be happy to have fliers in *Crossings*.'

'I agree,' Rachel put in. 'We all need to do what we can. The paper has been good to me over the years, publishing articles about the B&B, about *Crossings* too, Poppy.'

'I don't dispute that. I'm only saying…' Gill's voice broke.

'Are you all right, Gill?' Rachel asked.

'No, not really.' Gill's eyes moistened. 'Sorry, I've had a bad couple of days. Max… Oh, I'd rather not talk about it.'

The others were silent for a few moments as they tried to imagine what Gill's husband might have done now. Her divorce seemed to have been going on for ever with no resolution in sight. It never ceased to surprise Gill's friends that the woman who successfully handled others' divorces, was herself caught up in an acrimonious one.

They were halfway through the meal, and Liz thought she had avoided questions about Julie, when Rachel said, 'I think Liz has something to tell us.'

They all turned to look at Liz who blushed.

'Rach already knows,' she said, 'but some of you might have seen me around with a young woman and a teenager.' She saw Poppy nod her head vigorously, while Gill seemed surprised.

'Julie's my daughter, and Tilly is my granddaughter.' Liz looked around the group, seeing nothing but support on her friends' faces. 'It's a long story but basically, I became pregnant at fifteen, the baby was adopted, and we've been reunited.'

'How did we not know?' Poppy asked.

'No one did. It was all over before we moved to Pelican Crossing. I never expected to see her again.'

'Wow! What an amazing story. You must be thrilled,' Poppy said.

'I am.'

'What about Tara and Mandy?' Gill asked. 'Her appearance must have put their noses out of joint.'

'Tara is fine with it. She's even given Tilly her old bicycle. But Mandy's a different matter. I just hope…' She bit her lip.

'She'll come round,' Rachel said.

'Don't be too sure,' Gill said. 'Freya hasn't spoken to me since Max left. She's taken his side in our dispute and won't even answer my calls.'

'I'm so sorry, Gill.' It was Poppy who spoke, but all three women knew how devastated Gill was at losing contact with her daughter who now lived overseas.

'And what about you and Finn Hunter?' Poppy asked. 'I've heard a few things about you and our local newspaper editor. What will happen to him if the paper closes and can't be saved?'

Liz felt a chill run down her spine. It was her worst fear, that Finn might have to leave Pelican Crossing. It wasn't something they'd discussed, but she knew it was a possibility, the elephant in the room. 'I don't know. We haven't talked about it. I think he's focussed on ensuring it doesn't happen… he and our mayor.' Seeing everyone had finished eating, Liz rose to clear away the plates and bring in the strawberry flan she'd bought for dessert from the bakery near the medical centre. She knew it would be nicer than anything she could bake.

When she returned, the conversation had changed to a discussion of Poppy's grandchildren. Two of her daughters had produced babies earlier in the year, and her oldest, Amber, would soon give birth to twins after years of trying unsuccessfully to fall pregnant.

'No sign of Tara doing the same?' Poppy asked. Amber and Tara were good friends. They had grown up with Gill's daughter, Freya, and Rachel's Jess. While Freya was still single, Jess now had three little ones who kept Rachel busy.

Liz shook her head. 'No, she seems more focussed on her career and travel than on starting a family. She and Mark are talking about another European trip next year, so it doesn't look like children are on the cards. I'd almost given up hope of becoming a grandmother before Julie arrived with Tilly. I have to say it was a bit of a shock to suddenly find I had a teenage granddaughter, but she's a delightful girl, despite being a typical teenager. You have that in store, Rach and Poppy.'

'They're so lovely when they're little.' Rachel smiled at Poppy, making Liz wish yet again that Tara didn't seem so against having a family.

The group finally broke up, Rachel saying she needed to get back to welcome a new group of guests, and Poppy heading off to meet Cam at the marina. Gill left at the same time as the others but gave no indication of where she was going. She tended to keep things to herself more than the others, perhaps because of the confidential nature of her law practice.

After they'd gone, Liz poured herself another glass of wine and took it out to the balcony where she sat gazing out at the boats on the marina and thinking about the conversations over lunch.

The one about Finn and the closing of the newspaper had really shaken her. What did the future have in store for her and Finn? Did they have a future together, or was what they had between them of a temporary nature, something which could be thrust aside if he decided or was forced to leave the town? At least she had dinner with him and his family to look forward to, she reassured herself. Surely Adele wouldn't have invited her if she didn't think her dad was serious about their relationship?

Thirty-eight

Two weeks had passed since the establishment of the *Save the Courier* campaign and Finn's call from the owners of the newspaper, and he still held the position of editor, though there had been no more mention of the hefty bonus. He supposed he'd forfeited that along with any sort of reference, should he want to apply for another position.

The good news was that donations were flooding in for the campaign, the town meeting had gone well and Joe had kept his word and had arranged for posters and fliers to be printed. These were now displayed in prominent places around town, in almost all the retail outlets, as well as public buildings such as the library and hospital. It would have been difficult for anyone living in or visiting Pelican Crossing to be unaware of what was happening.

The only challenge, according to Joe, was the refusal of the consortium to countenance any purchase of the paper and their absolute rejection of permission to use the name in any future publication. 'We'll figure out something,' Joe said to Finn when he expressed his concern, but Finn couldn't help worrying.

But today, Finn had a smile on his face. Liz's daughter, Julie, had returned to Pelican Crossing on the weekend, and while for the past few days Liz had been busy helping her settle in, she'd called him last night to say she was free and to suggest they get together. He'd booked a table at *Crossings* and couldn't wait to see her. They had met several times over the past two weeks, but he'd been very conscious of Tilly's presence, even if the teenager had tactfully left him and Liz alone. It would be wonderful to have her all to himself again, to be able to make love to her, to relieve all the pent-up emotion of the past weeks.

Things had improved at home too. The confidence in the ocean which Sandy had found with his little dog had grown, and Finn was sure it wouldn't be long before the boy would agree to go swimming again. While Adele still worried about losing him too, she knew she couldn't protect him for ever and, if not entirely happy, was resigned to seeing him in the water again.

Dinner with Liz and Tilly had proved to be a success, with Sandy showing Tilly all Bluey's tricks and insisting she read him his bedtime story, while Adele and Liz had got on well. Finn was starting to believe his daughter was finally beginning to recover from the pall of grief that had shrouded her since Tim's death. It meant that if he did need to take a job somewhere else, he could feel confident she and Sandy would be all right. He didn't dare think about what might happen to his relationship with Liz in that eventuality, only hoping it wouldn't come to that, and Joe was right in his firm belief the campaign would be successful.

At the morning's news conference, they'd had the wash up on the ANZAC edition of the paper which had been a huge success. Ed's interviews with local Vietnam vets had turned out even better than expected and he had proposed a follow-up with Stan Ross who, it emerged, had been quite a hero. But, more importantly, it had given Ed the idea of devoting another edition to the elderly residents of Pelican Crossing and their contributions to the community. Through Stan, Ed had met Liz's mother and reported to Finn that Joan was a wealth of knowledge about how Pelican Crossing's older citizens provided valuable services to the town as volunteers in schools, hospitals and the library, to mention only a few of their activities. He must remember to tell Liz about it, sure it would amuse her.

*

Liz couldn't wait for the day to be over. Now Julie was back in Pelican Crossing and settled in the house she had rented – Tara had even helped her find a job in a local law firm – Liz was free to see more of Finn. Tonight, they were having dinner at *Crossings*, and Liz had butterflies in her stomach at the thought of the evening ahead. It had been too long since they were alone together. She didn't count the evenings spent snuggled up together on the sofa. Tilly had been in another room and could have appeared at any time.

The apartment was quiet without Tilly's music blaring out. Liz was going to miss her granddaughter. But now she and Julie were living in Pelican Crossing, they'd be sure to meet regularly, Liz reminded herself as she showered and applied her makeup. It was difficult to decide what to wear, and she tried and discarded several outfits before settling on the green dress she had last worn to the yacht club with Mandy and Gary on the night Finn had come over to say hello. How long ago that seemed, and how much had happened since then. She slid her feet into a pair of high heeled sandals which made her feel elegant. She had just finished trying to tame her wild curls and was spraying on her favourite perfume when she heard a knock at the door. He was here!

'Don't you look beautiful!' Finn said, embracing her and kissing her soundly on the lips. 'Maybe we should stay here.'

Liz's heart began to race, a flash of desire shooting through her.

'But we do have a booking at *Crossings*,' he said releasing her gently and dropping a kiss on her forehead.

'We do,' Liz said, trying to fix her hair which had become disarranged.

'Don't,' Finn said, putting up one hand. 'I like it like that. It's more natural. Ready to go?'

'Almost.' Liz picked up her bag and glanced around to make sure she hadn't forgotten anything, then joined Finn, closing the door behind her.

To Liz's surprise, Poppy greeted them when they entered the restaurant. 'Short staffed,' she said with a grimace, 'but Cam's joining me later. Enjoy your meal.' She winked at Liz, who blushed.

Once they had been shown to a table, located in a secluded corner of the restaurant, Finn reached across to take Liz's hands in his. 'You can't know how much I've been looking forward to this. I know you enjoyed Tilly's company, and I appreciate how happy it made you to discover your new family, but I've been desperate to have you to myself again. Selfish, I know.' He squeezed her hands.

Liz felt a warm glow flood her at his words. 'Not selfish. I've been looking forward to it too. I miss Tilly, but…' She smiled, lighting up her whole face.

Finn smiled back, his eyes crinkling with pleasure.

'Now, what shall we order?' Finn picked up a menu, and Liz did the same.

When they had ordered, both choosing the Moreton Bay Bug with Crossings Caesar salad, and Finn ordering a bottle of prosecco, they gazed at each other again. Liz couldn't get enough of seeing Finn sitting there, across from her, his knees touching hers under the table, and it seemed he felt the same about her. Liz was so lost in contemplation of her companion and the evening ahead, encased in a cocoon of happiness, she was startled when the waiter appeared with their wine.

'To us,' Finn said, raising his glass and reminding her of when he'd last said that, and what had followed.

'To us,' she said, her voice almost a whisper.

Then reality intruded. 'What's happening with *The Courier* and the campaign?' she asked. 'It's not long till the end of the financial year.'

'Just over eight weeks.' Finn sighed, the mood broken. 'Nothing has changed at *The Courier*. It's still due to close on June thirtieth, but the campaign is looking good. According to Joe, we're on track to reach our target.'

'That's good, isn't it?' she asked, seeing Finn frown.

'If he's right. I've never seen Joe so enthusiastic about anything, not even last year when we were trying to save the town from that Sydney developer, but…'

'But?'

'It's not his livelyhood at stake here, not only mine, either. I have my staff to consider, young men and women with families and mortgages. What do I say to them when they ask me about their future? I can't lie to them and promise something that at present is pie in the sky, but I don't want to lose them. We'll need them if we want to start up a new paper.' He rubbed his face. 'Sorry, I didn't intend to get into this tonight, to spoil our dinner.'

'No, it's my fault. I did ask. And I understand your dilemma. Have any of them left already?'

'Not yet, but I can tell a few are worried. I don't blame them. I've had some sleepless nights too.'

Liz reached across the table to take his hand. 'I'm so sorry, Finn.' But his worries reminded her of her own concerns about the future of their relationship. 'If… if the campaign doesn't work, will you have to leave Pelican Crossing?' She held her breath.

'No, it won't come to that. Trust me.' Finn shook his head as if to shake away his worries, and grinned, that grin that always took Liz's breath away. 'Let's talk about something more cheerful. Did you know *The Courier* is about to feature your mother in an edition about our elderly residents and the services they provide to the town?'

'I did not. When did this come about?'

'One of my reporters met her when he was interviewing one of the Vietnam vets who lives in *The Haven*. It seems she bent his ear about how they weren't just a lot of old dears but took an active role in the community. Ed was impressed and suggested we make a feature of them.'

Liz laughed. 'Sounds like Mum. I swear she's livelier now than she was when I was growing up.' She frowned, remembering the worry she'd no doubt caused her parents with her teenage pregnancy. 'I bet the Vietnam vet was a new friend of hers, a guy called Stan. I haven't met him yet but she talks about him a lot.'

'Stan Ross. Seems he was a bit of a hero. Ed's writing a follow up article on him too.'

'More reason for a local paper.'

'Absolutely.' Finn was silent for a moment, then, 'What about you?'

'Nothing new.' Liz sighed. 'Apart from Julie moving here, and Tilly moving out of the apartment. Mandy's still ignoring my calls.'

'I saw her and Gary the other night. I took Adele and Sandy to the yacht club for dinner, and they were there. She looked happy.'

'Thanks.' It was good to know things were working out for Mandy with Gary.

They finished their meal with a luscious dessert of chocolate and hazelnut pavlova, then Finn said, 'I think it's time to go, don't you?' and gave Liz a wicked grin which made her legs go weak.

As they left the restaurant, Finn's arm around her shoulders, the prospect of the lovemaking to follow, Liz managed to forget about the demise of the newspaper, the possibility of Finn leaving Pelican Crossing – she had to trust him – and Mandy's stubborn refusal to contact her, and to enjoy the bliss of being with this man who was coming to mean so much to her.

Thirty-nine

The next couple of weeks passed in a flash. Finn spent almost every evening with Liz and his feelings for her deepened. While he hoped she felt the same about him, he was unsure, aware of her ability to hide her feelings, and her fear of being hurt as she had been in the past.

The campaign was still going well. Finn thought of it as Joe's campaign, partly because he was the driving force behind it, and partly because, given his current position at the paper, Finn couldn't be seen to be acting against the interests of his employers. But the end of the financial year was drawing closer, and the deadline was looming large in everyone's minds.

Sadly, he'd lost two of his reporters who had accepted positions interstate, and their leaving had sparked unrest among some of the others. Now it was known the paper was slated for closure, Finn himself had received an approach. To his surprise, it wasn't from another newspaper, but from one of the regional television channels who invited him to send them his CV with the possibility of a position on the production team of their morning news programme. While he and Adele had laughed about the idea of him working in television, he hadn't completely dismissed the possibility, if things in Pelican Crossing fell apart. He hadn't mentioned it to Liz; there was no sense in worrying her unnecessarily.

Today was Saturday and he planned to spend the day with Liz. He knew she was still worrying about Mandy, though she didn't talk much about it, preferring to focus on stories about Tara, Julie and Tilly, all of whom were now getting along famously. Tilly was hugely admiring of her new aunt, and Tara seemed happy to have given up her role as Liz's oldest daughter to Julie.

He'd asked Liz to join him, Adele and Sandy at the Pelican Crossing Primary school annual fete in the hope of taking her mind off her worries. Run by the P&C, the fete was always held the day before Mother's Day, when from 9am till 4pm the school grounds were transformed into a vibrant hub of festivities for parents, students, local business people, and members of the community. In addition to being a reason to celebrate, it was also used as a fundraiser for the school, but this year they had decided to put all funds raised towards the *Save the Courier* campaign.

Sandy was so excited he could barely sit still for breakfast, and Bluey, sensing his master's excitement, was careering around the kitchen getting under everyone's feet. Adele had to give Sandy a stern warning and threaten to forbid him to go to the fete before he settled down to eat his cereal.

Finn was glad to leave the house, promising to meet Adele and Sandy in the school grounds where Sandy was eager to show his grandfather the paintings and craft items his class had on display.

He greeted Liz with a hug and a kiss, relishing the peace of her apartment after the rumpus in his own home.

'Have you time for a coffee?' Liz asked. 'You look frazzled.'

'Thanks, that would be good. Sandy is so excited about the fete, I was glad to leave him and Bluey with Adele. Sometimes I think I'm too old for this lark.'

'I don't believe you,' Liz said, turning on the coffee maker. 'You love the little monkey. The school fete is a big deal. I remember what it was like for Tara and Mandy. And it doesn't get any easier as they get older. Those were good times.' She gazed into space.

'Penny for them?'

'I was thinking about Julie… and Tilly. I've missed so much of their lives. It's hard to imagine what they were like as small children, what Julie was like as a teenager.' She sighed. 'Sorry, I know I should be grateful to have them in my life now, but sometimes…' She shook her head. 'Oh, ignore me. I'm only being fanciful.'

The delicious aroma of coffee filled the kitchen as Liz poured two cups. 'Shall we take them out to the balcony?' she asked.

Finn opened the door, and they sat on the wicker chairs which this morning were catching the sun. From here, he had a good view of the marina where yachts glistened in the sun, and small figures moved around preparing them for the day's sailing. Many of the owners were weekend sailors, while others were visitors to the coast who had moored there to enjoy a pleasant break. A group of pelicans were perched on bollards at the edge of the water hoping for something to eat, and a few seagulls flew overhead, their cries the only sound breaking the stillness of the morning.

'You have a lovely place here,' Finn said.

'So you've said before. I like it but I miss Tilly. She was like a breath of fresh air, reminding me how insular and selfish I'd become. It's easy to get that way when you live alone.'

'She and Julie are settling in well?'

'Very well. Tilly's a different person from she was when she arrived, and Julie seems to be thriving too. She's enjoying the work Tara found for her in the law firm. It's different to what she was doing before, but she says much of the tasks are similar. She's doing a lot of cataloguing and data entry and had to learn a new software system. We're all going out to breakfast tomorrow for Mother's Day.'

'Of course. I'd forgotten.' Finn scratched his head. 'It's why the fete is today, and Sandy did remind me. He's been talking about something special he made for Adele at school. Perhaps we should go out for breakfast, too… or lunch,' he said quickly, seeing Liz's expression.

'Do what you want,' she said, but Finn could tell she didn't mean it. He had no intention of breaking in on her family gathering again.

'It must be time to go,' Liz said.

Finn checked the time. 'You're right. I said we'd see Adele and Sandy there at ten. If we leave now, we should just make it.'

When they arrived at the school grounds, Finn was surprised to see the transformation was complete. The concreted area where the children normally played their ball games and lined up for class was almost completely filled with market stalls selling everything from cakes and jams to plants and second-hand books. The wall of the wet weather shed was being used to display artwork from each of the classes, and the shed itself was host to a variety of musical events which were being announced through a loudspeaker. In the grassy area of what Finn recognised as a football pitch, a number of different carnival rides had been set up, plus a jumping castle and donkey rides. The place was a circus. But everyone seemed to be enjoying themselves.

The area was so crowded with people, parents, children and other members of the community, Finn couldn't see how he was going to be able to find Adele and Sandy. He was gazing around, and Liz was examining a stall containing bric-a-brac, when a small whirlwind came flying towards them.

'Grandy!' Sandy yelled. 'You came!'

'Of course I did. I promised.'

'Come and see what my class did.' Sandy grasped Finn's hand and pulled him in the direction of the shed. Shrugging to Liz and leaving her with a laughing Adele, Finn allowed himself to be led away.

By the time Finn had duly admired the large frieze depicting the ocean and containing cutouts of fish, one of which Sandy proudly pointed out as his work, and had been led past a table of craft items which defied description, Liz and Adele had joined them. Sandy, bored now he had shown off all his work, decided it was time for a donkey ride, and they all made their way through the crowd to the grassy area where the grownups were able to take a seat while Sandy enjoyed his ride.

After this ride, and several of the carnival ones, the scent of sausages and onions cooking on a barbecue made Finn realise he was hungry, and they headed to where the food was being served.

The rest of the afternoon passed uneventfully, with Sandy going on more rides, and Finn and Liz wandering through the stalls where she found a couple of books by authors she admired, and he bought her a pot of herbs to add to the collection on her balcony and a jar of apricot jam for Adele.

By the time Finn and Liz returned to her apartment, they were exhausted.

'I'd forgotten how tiring these events can be,' Liz said, kicking off her shoes and dropping into a chair. 'And to think, when Tara and Mandy were students, Tommy and I used to go back in the evening.'

'You mean it doesn't finish at four?'

'The fete itself does, but there are still the draws for the raffle and the silent auction. These are held in the school hall in the evening, along with drinks. It's quite a party… or used to be.'

'Wow!'

'It's a great money raiser. The campaign should do well out of it.'

'If everyone spent as much as we did.' Finn groaned at the thought of how many dollars he'd shelled out on rides and other things.

'They did, believe me. Hungry?'

'Not really. How about we order a pizza?'

'Sounds good to me.'

*

'You do know how much you mean to me?' Finn said, brushing a lock of hair back from Liz's face. It was later, and he and Liz were lying together in bed, having made passionate love.

'Mmm.'

Finn leant up on one elbow and gazed down at the woman whom he now knew he was beginning to love. *Was it too soon to tell her he loved her?*

'You mean a lot to me too, Finn. But it's all happened so quickly and…'

'I know. Your family.' Finn sat up and leant against the bedhead.

Liz put her head on his shoulder, her hair tickling him and sending ripples of desire through him again. 'It's difficult at the moment, with Mandy… As we said earlier, we both have family obligations. But…'

Finn held his breath.

'I do have feelings for you, strong feelings. You must know that. I don't normally behave like this.'

'I should hope not.' Finn chuckled and dropped a kiss on her forehead.

'Let's get our other things sorted first, then maybe we can think about ourselves.'

'If it's what you want, but you should know that I don't normally behave like this either. You are the first woman I've been… interested in since Adele's mother.'

Afterwards, when he was driving home, Finn relived the conversation, wondering if he'd said too much, too little, if it had been a mistake to even mention Karen who he hadn't thought of for years.

He was really no good at this sort of thing. He hoped Liz understood and would see through his awkwardness.

Forty

Liz awoke with a smile on her face. It had been early morning when Finn had finally left after the weird conversation when she had thought he was going to tell her he loved her. He hadn't said the word but had come close to it. She hugged herself at the notion. Then he'd mentioned his ex, but in a way that indicated she no longer mattered to him. *Had she misunderstood?*

But there was no time to wonder. It was Mother's Day, and she was meeting Joan, Tara, Julie and Tilly at *The Blue Dolphin Café* for breakfast. Mark would be there too. The only person missing would be Mandy. It was the first Mother's Day Mandy wouldn't be joining them for the breakfast which had become somewhat of a tradition in the family… and it hurt. In the back of her mind, Liz held out the hope her youngest daughter would surprise them and suddenly appear, but she knew in her heart it wasn't going to happen.

Dressing in a pair of her smartest jeans and a royal blue and white tunic top, Liz set off to walk to the café, enjoying the fresh breeze in her hair and the sound of seagulls flying overhead. She smiled at the sight of a lone pelican perched on one of the tall lamp posts by the marina. It was difficult to go anywhere in Pelican Crossing without seeing at least one of these magnificent birds. The town was well-named.

As she came in sight of the café, Liz could see her mother was already there. But she wasn't alone. Standing beside her was the man she'd last seen leaving her mother's villa in *The Haven*. She stopped in her tracks. *How could Joan have invited him to their special family*

Mother's Day breakfast? But it was too late to turn back. They'd already seen her. Pasting a smile on her face, Liz joined them.

'Happy Mother's Day,' she said, giving her mother a hug.

'Thanks, darling. This is Stan.' Joan drew him forward. 'I wanted you all to meet him, and this seemed like the perfect opportunity.'

'Hello, Stan.' Liz shook his hand.

The others arrived and in the rush of greetings and introductions, there was no opportunity to say anything more to her mother. She'd talk with her later.

When they were settled at a table, Liz waved to her friend, Poppy, who was seated at another table with Cam, her three daughters, all of their partners and two very small children. Seeing how happy Poppy looked with her family, for a moment, Liz wished Finn could be there with her. Then she dismissed it. He had his own family to celebrate with. They weren't in a recognised relationship. But she couldn't help hoping that maybe next year…

She pulled herself out of her musings in time to hear her mother explain how she and Stan had met, and how he had changed her life. Seeing them together, Liz was forced to revise her opinion. He seemed like a nice man, and by the way he was looking at her mother, he cared deeply for her… and she for him. *Liz couldn't be envious of her mother, could she?* But despite the fact Finn had left her bed in the early hours, it was difficult for her to watch their obvious happiness and not feel a touch of jealousy.

They were all checking out the menus and chatting about what to order when, to Liz's surprise, the waitress arrived with a bunch of small bags tied with pink ribbons and asked who the mothers in the group were. When Joan, Liz and Julie responded, they were each handed one of the bags which, when opened, were revealed to contain three small chocolate truffles.

In the laughter which ensued, they managed to order breakfast, Liz, Tara and Julie choosing eggs benedict, Stan and Mark opting for the big breakfast, and Tilly and Joan deciding on smashed avocado on rye with feta.

Despite Mandy's absence, Liz enjoyed her breakfast, surrounded by her family, thrilled this was her first Mother's Day with Julie and Tilly, the first of what she hoped would be many.

After breakfast, Joan and Stan elected to return to *The Haven*, where they said there was going to be a special Mother's Day event and lunch, while the others decided on a walk along the beach.

The group split into two as they wandered along the edge of the water, Tara and Mark walking ahead, leaving Liz with Julie and Tilly.

'I think it's lovely how Joan has found a man friend,' Julie said. 'Stan seems nice.'

'They play Mahjong together,' Tilly said, 'and like to go for walks. He's a widower and doesn't have any children. That's why she wanted him to meet all of you… she wants to share her family with him.'

'And you know this how?' Liz asked.

Tilly reddened. 'I sometimes ride over to see her after school. She helps me with my homework. Stan does, too. He's a whiz at maths.'

Liz laughed. Stan couldn't be all bad if he was willing to help Joan's teenage great-granddaughter with her homework. She linked arms with Julie. 'Let's catch up with Tara and Mark,' she said. 'I want to ask her if she's spoken to Mandy recently.'

But Tara had nothing to report. In fact, she said Mandy had been particularly difficult to contact for the past couple of weeks. It saddened Liz to think she might have decided to cut off her sister too.

'She's her own worst enemy,' Tara said, grimacing. 'I know my sister, but I've never seen her like this. It's as if she's become a stranger.'

'I hope she's all right.' Liz worried about her, as she did about all three of them. Three! All three of her daughters were now living in Pelican Crossing. How she wished they could all be friends.

They were about to return to the marina end of the beach when they came upon old Agnes and her dog. The spaniel was frolicking in the shallow water, and as usual, Agnes was paddling alongside, her long skirt trailing in the sea.

'Hello, Agnes. Looks as if you're fully recovered.' Liz hadn't seen the old woman since her visit to the medical centre, and she looked much better.

'Yes, thanks. I'd have been fine on my own, but these two young men insisted I needed help.' She peered at Liz. 'I hear you and our local editor have become friends. He's a good man. See you hold on to him.'

Liz stared at her in surprise. If Agnes knew about her and Finn, did the whole town know?

Tara and Julie both laughed.

'You can't keep a secret in Pelican Crossing, Mum,' Tara said. 'Agnes is right. Finn Hunter is a good man. What's going on between the pair of you? Should Julie and I be concerned?'

'Of course not. He's just a friend. He has a lot happening in his life at the moment.'

'Of course… the campaign. What will he do if it doesn't succeed? Will he have to leave Pelican Crossing?'

'I don't know.' It was what was bothering Liz too, when she allowed herself to think about it.

Forty-one

The next two weeks passed in a dream. Liz saw Finn every evening, she spoke to Tara and Julie most days, and Tilly often dropped into her office at the medical centre on her way home from school. Liz had taken to keeping cans of soft drink and a packet of Tim Tams in the small fridge in her office to treat her. Life would be perfect if only she could hear from Mandy, but her youngest daughter remained obdurate and ignored all her attempts to contact her.

The other blot on the landscape was her worry about what might happen if the campaign to save the courier failed. *Would Finn have to leave town?* But each time she mentioned it, he reassured her the campaign was going well and it wasn't likely to happen; he wasn't going anywhere. She had to believe him.

Liz planned to go sailing with Finn on Saturday – he had arranged to hire a boat from Gary's father, Jamie, who ran a fishing charter and boat hire business – but had decided to visit her mother in the morning. Although they'd spoken on the phone, she hadn't seen her since Mother's Day, and she wanted to make sure everything was okay with her, as she'd sounded tired on their last call. Joan assured her she was fine, but Liz knew her mother could make light of any illness and wanted to see for herself.

It was a glorious morning, and there were a few people wandering around when Liz drove into *The Haven*. Stan was one of them and he waved to her. Liz waved back, relieved he wasn't with her mother. Although she'd now accepted he was part of Joan's life, she'd prefer to see her alone.

Liz knocked on her mother's door, then pushed it open. 'Mum!' she called. 'It's only me.'

'Liz! I didn't expect to see you today.'

'We haven't seen each other since Mother's Day, and I didn't want you to feel I was neglecting you. How are you?' She hugged her mother.

'I'm well. What about you?' She held Liz at arm's length. 'You look blooming. Something – or someone – is agreeing with you.' She chuckled.

Liz blushed. 'I've been seeing a bit of Finn Hunter.'

'Ah, yes. Our local editor, though perhaps not for much longer. I've been following the campaign, and it seems it's still short of its goal.'

'There's still time.' But was there? She felt a small niggle of doubt. The end of the financial year was only a few weeks away. They'd need a miracle to achieve the result Finn and Joe were hoping for. But miracles did happen, didn't they? And Finn seemed confident they'd make it. Surely he'd have told her if he had any doubts?

In typical fashion, while they had been talking, Joan had put on the kettle and taken two cups and saucers out of the cupboard. 'I must have known you were coming. I baked some of your favourite cookies yesterday,' she said, opening a cake tin.

Liz opened her mouth to say she'd only just had breakfast but the sight of the gingernut biscuits she'd always loved as a child made her change her mind. She remembered when she was small how she'd loved breaking them on her elbow and, if one broke in three pieces, she'd make a wish.

'Have you heard from Mandy?' Joan asked, when they were seated in her living room, the familiar sound of the grandmother clock chiming each quarter hour.

'No.' Liz sighed. Mandy had been difficult in the past, but this had gone on too long.

'She came to see me.'

'She did? How is she? What did she say? Has she changed her mind about Julie and Tilly?'

'I think she may be rethinking her decision.' Joan took a sip of tea. 'She came to tell me she's pregnant.'

Liz almost dropped her cup. 'She's what?' This was huge. She couldn't believe Mandy had kept the news from her. 'I'm her mother.

She should have told me first.' She knew she sounded pitiful, but she couldn't help it. She was stunned to think Mandy was pregnant and had chosen to tell her grandmother instead of her.

'In different circumstances I expect she would have. I think she's a bit embarrassed by how she behaved and doesn't know how to back down. Typical Mandy.' Joan took another sip of tea and bit into a biscuit.

'How can you just sit there as if this was an everyday occurrence?' Liz asked, incensed at her mother's attitude. 'Your granddaughter – my daughter – is going to have a baby and you… you…'

'Calm down, Lizzie. It's not the end of the world. It's a new beginning. You need to consider it from Mandy's point of view.'

Liz stared at her mother. Joan hadn't called her Lizzie since she was twelve when she told her it was too childish, and she wanted to be called Liz. 'Mandy's point of view… what do you mean?'

'Think about it. Here you are, full of your reunion with Julie and the discovery you already have a granddaughter, and there is Mandy, suddenly about to provide you with the grandchild you've always wanted. It's not surprising she came to me first.'

'But… finding Julie and Tilly has nothing to do with how I feel about Mandy, how I feel about her having a baby.'

'You need to tell her that.'

'How can I? She won't talk to me.'

'Maybe you haven't tried hard enough.'

Liz stared at her mother again. Had she lost her mind? 'I've called and texted. She ignores every attempt I've made.'

'Have you tried going round to see her? She and Gary are living in one of those riverside apartments. I can give you the address.'

'I…' It had never occurred to Liz to go to where Mandy was living… or even to try to talk to her at one of her training sessions. She knew where they were held. Was she at fault too? 'So it's my fault then?' she said bitterly.

'That's not what I'm saying, but someone has to make the first move and it's clearly not going to be Mandy.'

Liz thought for a moment, then, 'Maybe you're right. Let me have her address. I'll go round as soon as I leave here.'

'Good girl.'

For once, Liz didn't object to the term. She was too intent on what she was going to say to her daughter.

'Now, be careful what you say,' Joan said, as if reading Liz's mind. 'Mandy's feeling very vulnerable. I need hardly say this baby wasn't planned. She was in quite a state when she arrived on my doorstep, but I think I managed to calm her and help her realise it was something to be grateful for.'

'Of course it is.' Liz couldn't quite believe it. After yearning for a grandchild for so long, to be soon having two was a small miracle. And it wasn't Tara but Mandy who was going to make her dream come true.

*

As soon as Liz left her mother's, she texted Finn to say she might be delayed. She couldn't think of going sailing after what she'd just heard. She needed to see Mandy to ensure she was well and to find out when the baby was due. She was already planning what she'd knit for the baby. She'd never been one to spend much time knitting when she was pregnant herself, but a grandchild was different. And she couldn't wait to tell her friends at their next lunch. She was sure Rachel and Poppy would be full of advice. She remembered Poppy talking about going baby shopping with Megan, and feeling envious of her. Now she might be able to do the same with Mandy.

She pulled herself up short. First, she had to see Mandy, to restore the trust that had been broken. Then maybe they could regain their old closeness.

Checking the address her mother had given her, Liz recognised it as being in the same development in which Poppy's daughter, Scarlett, lived with her husband, Lachlan. She was surprised. Somehow, she'd imagined Mandy and Gary living in a rundown old fishing shack of which there were several in Pelican Crossing, places which had escaped the gentrification of their neighbours and were considered an eyesore by some, heritage dwellings by others.

It was a pleasant spot, peaceful, close to where old Agnes ran her pelican rescue centre, and not far from where she and Finn had enjoyed their picnic. Liz parked, took a deep breath and rang the bell on the modern home.

Mandy answered, giving Liz a look of astonishment. 'I suppose you'd better come in,' she said grudgingly, stepping aside to allow Liz to enter. There was no pleasant greeting or hug.

As soon as she was inside, Liz, deciding not to beat about the bush, said, 'I spoke to your grandma. She told me you are pregnant.' She heard an indrawn breath and, turning, saw Gary, his eyes wide with surprise. Then he grinned, picked Mandy up and twirled her around.

'We're having a baby! You didn't tell me. Oh, Mandy, this is wonderful news.'

Liz didn't know whether she or Mandy was the more surprised. It seemed she wasn't the only one Mandy hadn't told.

Mandy looked sheepish. 'I'm sorry, Gary. I was afraid to tell you. I didn't know how you'd react. We didn't plan this.'

Liz wished she'd kept her mouth shut. She felt distinctly *de trop*. But she was here now, and it would look silly to leave.

Mandy turned to face Liz. 'I'm sorry I let you find out from Grandma, Mum. I realise I've acted like an idiot, like a spoiled child. Gary's told me a hundred times.' She threw a glance at Gary who nodded. 'I just couldn't get my head around the fact you'd kept something this big secret from Tara and me. Another daughter, and her child. I couldn't face them… or you. And the longer I ignored you, the worse it was. Grandma said I should contact you, said you'd be thrilled about the baby, but I couldn't bring myself to admit I was wrong. I'm sorry,' she repeated. 'Can you forgive me?'

'Come here.' Liz pulled her daughter into a warm hug. 'When you have your own child, you'll realise there's nothing they can do that you can't forgive. Once you've carried that little person inside you for nine months, lived through the sleepless nights, the childhood illnesses, the teenage tantrums, you have a love that can never go away.'

By this time, they were both in tears, and Gary was looking embarrassed.

'I think a celebration is called for,' he said. 'We don't have champagne but there's a bottle of wine in the fridge left over from last weekend. Mandy?'

'Should I, Mum?'

'One small glass won't hurt, and Gary's right, we should celebrate both the baby and our reconciliation.'

'Thanks, Mum. Tara says Julie and Tilly are all right. I think maybe I'd like to meet them.'

Liz felt her heart bloom. It was what she'd been longing to hear. Life couldn't get any better.

Forty-two

Finn was worried. He'd planned a romantic afternoon with Liz. Her text to say she might be delayed had given no reason, and it was now well past the time they were due to leave. He'd tried to call but only reached her voicemail. He was already at the marina, the boat he'd hired ready to go.

'Problem, mate?'

Finn looked up from his phone to see Cam Mitchell staring at him. He didn't know the owner of *Pelican Marine* well, but their paths had crossed the previous year not long after Finn had come to Pelican Crossing. He knew Cam and Liz's friend, Poppy, were a couple. Maybe he could help.

'I'm not sure. I had intended spending the afternoon sailing with Liz, but she's been held up. I may have to cancel the boat I've hired from Jamie Whittaker.'

'Just give me the keys and I'll see he gets them. No worries.'

'It's not that. I don't know what the problem is. She was going to see her mother earlier today. Maybe the old woman's ill.' He indicated his phone. 'Keeps going to voicemail.'

'Want me to give Poppy a call, see if she knows anything?'

'I don't…'

They were interrupted by Jamie's arrival. He was grinning and waving his phone in the air. He stopped abruptly when he saw Finn. 'Thought you'd be out on the water by now.'

'Change of plans,' Finn said, handing him the keys.

'No worries. I'll arrange a refund.' He turned to Cam. 'Great news. I'm going to become a grandfather.'

'Congratulations!' Cam slapped him on the back. 'Gary, I presume?'

'He texted me. Only just found out himself.'

Finn stared at Jamie. Gary Whittaker was the man Liz's daughter, Mandy, was living with. Did this mean…? 'Congratulations,' he said. 'Grandchildren are a blessing. Gary's with Mandy Phillips, isn't he?'

'That's right. They haven't been together long. I didn't expect this. Don't think he did either.' He chuckled. 'This'll make him sit up and take notice. Good thing he set up his dive business. Before that he lacked direction.' He looked at Finn. 'Problem?'

'No, I think you may have solved it.' It suddenly occurred to him Liz's reason for delaying their afternoon together might well have something to do with the news Jamie had received. If her daughter was pregnant, maybe there had been a reconciliation, and of course, Liz would put time with her daughter before her afternoon with Finn. 'Thanks, Jamie, Cam. I'll head home now.'

*

When Finn arrived home, Adele was relaxing with a book, and Sandy was playing with Bluey in the back yard.

'I thought you were seeing Liz,' Adele said.

'Something came up.' Finn didn't want to go into details. He might be completely wrong. He headed to the kitchen, made himself a mug of coffee and took it into his study. Once there, he texted Liz to tell her where he was and suggest they might meet for dinner at the yacht club. Then he opened his laptop to do what he'd been putting off.

Finn was reading the revamped version of his CV which he'd prepared for the television channel when his phone pinged with a reply from Liz.

Sorry about the sailing. Will explain when I see you. Dinner sounds wonderful.

He experienced a sudden lightness as he replied with a time, then went back to his task. He'd hoped to have avoided this step, but unless what Joe called a white knight appeared with an influx of funds, the paper was doomed. The community just hadn't been able to come up with sufficient money to save it, and there was so little time left.

'Grandy, you're back!' Sandy pushed the study door open, Bluey at his heels.

Finn shut down the computer. There was no need to share his worry yet. Maybe there was still hope. 'Hey, champ,' he said. 'What's up?'

'Me and Bluey have been playing in the yard, but we'd like to go to the beach. Bluey likes chasing the waves. Mummy said she was too tired to take us.' He looked up at Finn, his expression matching the spaniel's soulful gaze and making Finn want to laugh.

'Okay. I'll let Mum know, while you find your hat and Bluey's lead.'

Sandy disappeared in a flash.

Finn shook his head, wishing everything in his life could be solved as easily as granting his grandson's wish.

*

There was a chill in the air by the time Finn and Liz arrived at the yacht club, giving him an excuse to put an arm around her shoulders as they walked from the car. Clouds were beginning to build up, a sure sign a storm was approaching. The air was still with a spooky silence and groups of seagulls were flying low over the ocean, heading towards the shore.

Once inside, it was easy to forget the weather outside in the bright lights of the restaurant, but seated at a window table, Finn could see vessels in the marina being buffeted by the wind.

'Sorry about this afternoon,' Liz said. 'It was unavoidable. Mandy…' she took a deep breath, 'Mandy's pregnant.'

'Wow!' Finn didn't want to give away the fact he'd already heard this from Jamie. 'You and she… you're speaking again?'

'We are.' Liz smiled. It was lovely to see her looking so happy. 'She told my mother first, and I went round to see her and Gary. She hadn't even told him. I think she might have been afraid he wouldn't want to be saddled with a baby. But he was thrilled.'

'I'm so pleased for you… and for the young couple. It must have been a shock.'

'For everyone.' Liz laughed. 'I'd never expected Mandy to be the one to produce my first grandchild… though of course, he or she isn't the first. There's Tilly, but I didn't know her as a baby. Mandy never seemed to be the maternal sort, never played with dolls much as a child, always preferred to be active. But I think she'll make a good mother, and Gary's like a dog with two tails. He texted his dad straight away, and his brother. I think they plan to tell Tara and Mark tonight. And… she's agreed to meet Julie and Tilly. I can't quite believe it.'

'That's wonderful.' Finn covered Liz's hand with his.

'Are you ready to order?'

Finn looked up at the waiter who was hovering beside their table. 'Can you give us a few more minutes?' he asked. 'But bring us a bottle of champagne. We have something to celebrate.'

'Thanks.' Liz smiled again, her eyes sparkling with pleasure. 'It really is something special, something I've been hoping would happen, two things, really. Now, we can all be one happy family.'

It wasn't the time to tell her about the offer from the television station. It would keep. He didn't want to spoil the evening with his worries.

But later, when they were lying in each other's arms in her comfortable bed, the storm raging outside, Finn wondered how long he could keep it secret from her.

Forty-three

When Liz opened her eyes on Sunday morning, it was as if the storm had never happened. The sky was clear, the birds were making their usual racket and when she opened the shutters, the sea looked calm.

She rose and showered quickly. There was a lot to do. Before meeting Finn the previous evening, she'd called both Tara and Julie to give them the news and invite them to brunch – she'd already ensured Mandy and Gary would come – and had gone food shopping. While there were plenty of spots in Pelican Crossing where they could have met for breakfast, Liz wanted this special occasion to be held in her apartment. Joan would be there too, and although Liz had told her mother she could bring Stan, to her relief, Joan had refused, saying it would be better if this time, it was family only.

Tuning the radio to a local music programme, Liz sang along as she set the table on the balcony for eight. It would be a crush, but they'd manage to fit. Then she made the tomato and olive damper she loved, chopped the sweet potato and red onion, and grated the carrot for the two salads she planned, ready to add the other ingredients later. She'd bought two ready-made quiches in the delicatessen, knowing they'd be a lot better than any she could make, and it would save her a lot of time.

Finally, everything was ready, and Liz poured herself a glass of champagne and orange juice and leant on the balcony rail to enjoy the view, contemplating how only a few months ago, she could never have predicted this happening.

Everyone was already there when Mandy and Gary arrived. Tilly was more subdued than usual. While excited at the prospect of having a new cousin, she was wary of meeting Mandy who had made such a fuss about her and her mother. Even though Liz assured her it wasn't her fault, she seemed to have difficulty in believing her.

Liz gently drew Julie and Tilly forward to meet Mandy, who was all smiles.

'I'm sorry I was so difficult,' she said. 'I hated that Mum kept such a big secret from us. But I shouldn't have behaved the way I did. Gary told me to get my act together, but it's taken this baby to make me do it. I'm pleased to meet you both.'

'I can't believe I have two new aunts,' Tilly said, forcing Mandy to laugh.

'And I have a new sister and a niece I knew nothing about,' Mandy said. 'Welcome to the family, both of you.'

'I think a drink is in order,' Mark said, picking up the bottle of champagne, while Tara collected the orange juice. 'Can Tilly have a tiny drop too?' he asked Liz who nodded.

Tilly beamed.

'To family reunions,' Joan said, when everyone had a full glass.

'Family reunions,' they all echoed.

Liz was pleased to see everyone getting on famously as the food quickly disappeared. Tilly and Mandy found common ground in a joint interest in exercise with Mandy inviting Tilly to join one of her personal training groups which met outside school hours, while Tara and Julie seemed to be in the process of forming a firm bond.

They were all enjoying coffee when Mark said, 'Bad news about *The Courier*.'

'What?' Liz's ears pricked up.

'I was talking to a mate at the footy yesterday. He said it looks like they're going to come up short of the money they need to keep it going or whatever it was they were trying to do with all the fundraising.'

'No, that can't be right. The fundraising thermometer outside the town hall has been going up.' Her voice rose in alarm. *Surely Finn would have told her if there was a problem?*

'Don't shoot the messenger.' Mark lifted both hands defensively. 'It's what I heard.'

'Well, your source is wrong.' It must be. She and Finn were only at the beginning of their relationship. Everything was going so well. What would happen if the paper couldn't be saved? What would he do? Suddenly, the day which had begun with such promise started to crumble. Tears came to her eyes, which she wiped away with the back of her hand. 'Sorry,' she said. 'I don't know what came over me.'

'Let's all go inside,' Joan said, taking charge and hustling everyone into the apartment's living room. But the celebratory mood had been broken, and the group gradually dispersed till only Liz and her mother were left.

'Finn has never mentioned there was a problem,' Liz said.

'Maybe he didn't want to worry you.'

'But how could he behave as if nothing was wrong, as if the campaign was working, as if they were going to save the paper, if he knew all along it was a lie?'

'Not exactly a lie, Liz. I'm sure he and Joe are still hoping to make it happen. But it's a big ask, to start a new paper if that's what they intend to do. It doesn't happen overnight. It takes a lot of money and effort. The effort has been there but maybe not the money. We're only a small community after all.' She patted Liz's back, making her feel like a child again. But she was no longer a child, and this was something her mother couldn't fix. She pulled away. She needed to talk to Finn to find out if it was true. Then she wasn't sure what she would do.

*

The house was silent when Finn awoke, the kitchen empty when he walked in. He looked around in surprise. Normally, on a Sunday morning, there would be the aroma of coffee, Adele would be preparing breakfast, and Sandy and Bluey would be racing around, getting under everyone's feet.

'Where's Mummy?' Sandy appeared, bleary eyed, Bluey at his heels as usual. He had a guilty expression. 'I'm sorry, Grandy. I know Bluey isn't allowed in my room but…'

'It's okay, champ. I won't tell your mum this time. Don't let it happen again.' But he knew it would, boys would be boys, and a boy and his dog… *Where was Adele?*

He caught sight of the calendar hanging beside the sink. There was a black circle around today's date. How could he have forgotten? It was a year ago today Tim had died, drowned in the ocean trying to save Sandy. A wave of guilt flooded him. He should have remembered. He should have been there for her. He'd been so caught up with Liz and his problems with the paper, he'd completely forgotten the date. What sort of a dad did that make him? He knew where Adele would be. She'd be visiting Tim's grave.

Finn crouched down beside Sandy. 'I think Mummy has gone to visit the cemetery, to talk to your daddy. She'll be feeling sad today. It's a special day to remember him.'

'Oh!' Sandy's eyes filled with tears, and Finn cursed himself for making the little boy feel sad, too.

'Are you hungry, champ?'

'Yes. Bluey is, too.'

'Well, why don't you feed Bluey, and I'll fix us breakfast? Mummy can have hers when she gets back.'

'Okay.' In the way of little children, Sandy's mood lifted immediately. 'Can we have pancakes?'

'We sure can.'

While Sandy poured food into Bluey's bowl, managing to spill most of it on the floor, Finn looked in the pantry, hoping to find the pancake mix he'd seen Adele use. Spying the packet at the back of a shelf, he gave a sigh of relief. He had no idea how to make them from scratch.

Sandy climbed up onto a chair and Bluey, having eaten his fill, lay down on the floor beneath him, while Finn followed the instructions on the box of pancake mix and heated a pan.

Once he had cooked a batch of pancakes, Finn sliced up a banana and took the bottle of maple syrup out of the fridge. He placed them on the table along with a glass of orange juice for Sandy and made himself coffee. Then he sat down beside his grandson.

'Is Daddy in the cemetery or in Heaven?' Sandy asked. He had clearly been thinking about what Finn had said about Adele.

Finn took a deep breath. 'He's in Heaven with Nana and Pop, but because your mum can't visit him there, he has a special place in the cemetery where people can remember him and where your mum can go to speak to him.'

'Can I go there too?'

'If you really want to. We can ask your mum when she gets back.'

'Mmm.' Seemingly satisfied, Sandy cut his pancake into little pieces and began to eat them slowly.

Finn turned a blind eye when he saw Sandy drop a few pieces of pancake to Bluey who immediately gobbled them up.

Now Sandy was occupied, Finn had time to think, and his thoughts turned to Liz. They'd had a lovely time last night at the yacht club… and afterwards, but he felt guilty at keeping his worries about the future from her. He knew it would be a blow if he had to leave Pelican Crossing, and he should have shared the possibility with her. But things were going so well, he didn't want to spoil what they had together unless he had to. Was it selfish of him to want to enjoy their relationship for as long as he could? Was he only setting them both up for heartache if it had to end?

There was no question in his mind what Liz would choose if he had to leave town. He could take his family with him… if Adele and Sandy agreed to go. But all of Liz's family were here, including her newfound daughter and granddaughter and the grandchild Mandy was carrying. No matter how much he thought about it, he knew the relationship wouldn't survive him leaving Pelican Crossing.

The door opened, and Adele walked in, her shoulders drooping, her eyes red with tears.

'Mummy! Did you talk to Daddy? Did you tell him about Bluey?'

Adele stared at Sandy, her eyes wide with astonishment.

'I remembered what day it was. I knew where you'd gone. I told Sandy you'd gone to speak to Tim.'

'Oh!' Adele slid into a chair and closed her eyes.

'Can I get you something? Tea? Coffee?' Finn asked.

'We're having pancakes,' Sandy announced.

'That's nice, darling,' Adele said in a toneless voice. 'Coffee, thanks, Dad. Then I think I'll have a lie-down. I'm not hungry.'

Finn gave her a concerned glance then rose to fetch her a cup of coffee.

'Is Mummy sick?' Sandy asked, when Adele had taken her coffee to her bedroom.

'No, not sick, she's just a little sad,' Finn said.

'Mmm. Did talking to Daddy make her sad?'

'I think so.'

'What will we do today?'

Finn thought quickly. Adele would probably spend most of the day in bed, the visit to the cemetery having sent her back into the pall of grief from which she had gradually been emerging. It would be best if he took Sandy out somewhere so as not to disturb her. It was amazing how much noise one small boy and his dog could generate.

'Why don't we go to the beach?' he said. 'We can have fish and chips for lunch, then watch the pelicans at Pelican Plaza.'

'Yay! Bluey, too?'

'Yes, but you'll have to keep a firm grip on him when we're watching the pelicans.' The area close to the marina which was called Pelican Plaza was a semicircle of stone steps where every day at two o'clock, volunteers fed the pelicans and took the opportunity to educate visitors about the bird colony and keep an eye on the condition of their health. A loose dog could cause havoc.

'I will, Grandy. Promise.'

By the time Finn had cleared up after breakfast and organised Sandy and Bluey, it was mid-morning. The beach was quiet for a Sunday, and the boy and his dog had fun running along the sand, searching for shells and paddling in the water while Finn looked on. Then, after enjoying fish and chips at a bench by the shore, they headed to Pelican Plaza to join the crowd of locals and visitors who were waiting to see the pelican feeding.

They found a seat not too far from the front, and Finn took hold of Bluey's lead. He didn't trust Sandy not to get excited and forget his promise. And Sandy did get excited watching the large pelicans come in to land close to the shore and after coasting the waves for a few moments, hop onto the path and make their ungainly way towards the helpers with their buckets of fish.

The little boy laughed with the rest of the audience as the birds opened their large beaks to catch the fish which were being thrown. But it wasn't all entertainment. Among the volunteers feeding the birds, were a couple of wildlife wardens checking out the creatures. They spotted one which had a fishing line wrapped around one leg and, catching it carefully, managed to untangle it. Once freed, the bird darted off to join its companions in the competition for fish.

As suddenly as it had begun, the entertainment was over. The buckets were empty. One of the volunteers clapped her hands and, as one, and with a great flapping of wings, the pelicans rose into the air and flew off.

As people began to leave, Sandy sat still, mesmerised.

'It's all over, Sandy,' Finn said, as Bluey began to pull on his lead. Fortunately, he'd been very well behaved all through the performance. 'Time to go.'

'Can I have an ice cream?'

'I guess so.' Finn grinned. In Sandy's world, there was nothing that couldn't be cured by an ice cream.

As Finn and Sandy wandered along Main Street eating their ice creams, Finn couldn't help wondering how he would find Adele when they returned home. He hoped she'd managed to have a good rest and was feeling more cheerful, though he wasn't optimistic. The day was a sad reminder of all she'd lost. Only a year ago, she, Tim and Sandy had been a happy family, now she was a single mother living with her dad.

Forty-four

There was no sign of Adele when Finn and Sandy arrived home. Leaving Sandy to play with Bluey, Finn peeked into his daughter's bedroom to see her lying staring into space. 'Hey,' he said gently, 'feel like getting up?'

Adele turned a tearstained face towards him. 'I can't stop thinking about Tim, Dad, about how only a year ago…' She burst into tears.

Feeling helpless, Finn pulled her into his arms, surprised at how frail she felt, like a little bird. Had she lost weight? Why hadn't he noticed? 'I'm so sorry, sweetheart,' he said, stroking her forehead like he remembered doing when she was upset as a child. 'I wish I could make it better. But you have Sandy to think of. Tim wouldn't want you to grieve like this and forget about his boy.'

'You have no idea what Tim would want, Dad. You weren't here!' She burst into a flood of tears again. 'I just want to be left alone.' She turned her head away from him.

Finn backed out of the room, seriously worried about his daughter. Had she been bottling this up all year, only to have it explode today? Did she need more professional help? Suddenly all his own worries faded as his thoughts swirled around his daughter.

'Mummy's still tired,' he said to Sandy when he joined him. 'How about we two men make dinner together, then watch a movie till bedtime?'

'Yay!' This seemed to be Sandy's current favourite term of enthusiasm. 'Can we make pizza?'

'I don't...' Finn began. Pizza dough wasn't one of the skills he'd managed.

'Mummy sometimes makes it with pita bread, and we choose different toppings.'

'Right.' That, he could do.

'And can we watch the *Shaun the Sheep* movie?'

Finn groaned. Sandy had watched it so often, surely he knew it by heart? But Finn guessed that was part of the attraction, especially tonight when the little boy didn't understand why his mother had taken to her bed. 'Of course we can,' he said.

After Sandy had been tucked up in bed, and Finn had checked on Adele to see she had fallen asleep, he poured himself a much-needed glass of whisky and made the call he'd been wanting to make all day.

*

Liz had had a wonderful day with all her family around her. Only the thought Finn hadn't been straight with her was a niggle at the back of her mind. When the phone rang as she was trying unsuccessfully to concentrate on a movie on television, and she saw his number, she gave a sigh of relief.

'Finn, I've been hoping to speak to you.'

'Sorry I've been out of touch. It's been quite a day. It's the anniversary of Tim's death, and Adele isn't coping. I'm worried about her. And I've had to entertain Sandy. How was your day? You were having your family over, weren't you?'

Liz immediately felt a wave of sympathy for Finn. She could picture him, his forehead creased with worry, his hair dishevelled, his lips turned up in a rueful grin. 'We had a good day. Everyone seems happy with the situation, though I guess it will take time for it all to settle down. I'm sorry about Adele. I didn't realise it was the anniversary. It must be difficult for her... and you.'

'It is. On top of everything else...'

'About that.' Despite her sympathy for Adele, Liz decided to voice her concern. 'Mark mentioned something about the funding for the new paper. He said it might not reach the target; it might fail. You didn't tell me.'

There was silence.

Liz held her breath. She could imagine Finn dragging a hand through his hair as he did when he was worried.

'He's right,' Finn said at last. 'I didn't want to worry you. It's still possible we can make it.'

'But you don't think so.' Liz's voice was muted. 'What does that mean for us? Will you have to leave Pelican Crossing?'

Finn sighed loudly. 'I'm hoping it won't come to that, but it is a possibility.'

'What would you do?'

'I've been approached by one of the regional television channels.'

Liz's heart dropped. He was already making plans to leave town, and he hadn't told her.

'Oh!'

'I'm sorry, Liz. I should have been honest with you. I didn't want to spoil what we had together. I suppose it was selfish of me, but…'

'I can't believe you let me believe our relationship was going somewhere when all the time you were planning to leave.'

'No! It wasn't like that. It isn't. Look, I need to see you. We can't do this on the phone. I can't leave when Adele is like this, but tomorrow. Can we meet for lunch?'

'I suppose.' Liz wanted to see him too. She'd be able to tell more from seeing him face-to-face, tell whether or not he was being honest this time.

'*Books and Coffee* at one?'

'I'll be there.' She might need to juggle the lunch breaks at the medical centre, but she'd make sure she was free to meet Finn.

*

Liz's stomach was churning as she walked to *Books and Coffee*. Was this meeting going to mark the end of their relationship?

Pleased she was there first, she smiled hello to Lou when she walked through the bookshop, oblivious today to the display of new releases she normally enjoyed browsing. As she entered the café, Denny greeted her. 'Your usual?' he asked with a grin.

Liz nodded, glad he didn't offer one of his usual quips. She wasn't in the mood for his humour today. 'And I'll have a small quiche with salad, thanks, Denny.'

She had no sooner taken a seat, than Finn appeared, looking flustered.

'Liz.' He leant down to kiss her cheek.

Liz couldn't stem the shudder of yearning that shot through her as it always did at his touch. She swallowed. 'I've ordered,' she said.

He gave her a strange look. 'Okay, I'll put mine in, too.'

When he returned, Finn said, 'I'm glad you were able to meet me. I think I've been all kinds of a fool.' He gave a rueful grin, his lips turning up in the way Liz had come to know and love.

For a moment Liz was tempted to forgive him, to say it didn't matter, nothing mattered. But it did. 'Why didn't you tell me what was going on?' she asked. 'You reassured me, allowed me to hope when all the time…' Her voice broke.

Finn looked shamefaced. 'I'm sorry I wasn't completely honest with you. I didn't want to spoil things. We'd agreed any relationship between us was fraught with difficulty given our family obligations, but things were going so well, I hoped… Then this damned thing with the newspaper.' He shook his head. 'I… we thought we could make the campaign work, raise enough to start again. And we still might. We still have a few weeks. But, you're right, I should have shared my worries. You were caught up with your own family issues, with Julie and Mandy. I didn't want to add to your worries, but it's no excuse for keeping things to myself.'

'No, it's not. I thought we agreed to be honest with each other.' Liz looked down at the table, suddenly noticing how scarred it was. It had been there for a long time.

'Liz, look at me.'

She looked up.

'Do you really think I would deliberately lie to you, after all we've shared, after all the wonderful times we've had together?'

Liz was torn. She wanted to believe him, wanted it so much. 'I don't know,' she said.

Finn dragged a hand through his hair. 'How can I make you believe me?'

Their coffee and meals arrived, but Liz had no appetite. She pushed her plate away and took a sip of coffee. 'I don't know,' she said again. 'Maybe we need to take a break… until we know what's happening. It's clear to me that if the community fails to raise sufficient money to fund a new paper, you'll be leaving Pelican Crossing, Am I right?'

'I guess so.' Finn sighed heavily. 'It's the last thing I want to do. Adele and Sandy need me here, and I believe you and I have something special. But if the paper folds, and we can't fund a new one, there's nothing else for me here. The television offer…' He shook his head again. 'It's not something I ever sought or imagined myself doing, but it seems newspapers are becoming a thing of the past, and I may have to move on.'

'I'm sorry.' Liz was almost in tears. The future she'd envisaged with Finn was disappearing.

'I'm sorry, too. You can't imagine how much.'

'Oh, I think I can.' Liz smiled through her tears. Then she straightened her shoulders, took a deep breath, and wiped her eyes. 'But we need to be sensible about this. If I'm going to be hurt, I'd prefer it happen now, rather than later.' She hated to see how Finn's expression changed, his shoulders drooped. She knew her words hurt him too, but she'd made up her mind. She needed to protect herself, and this was the only way she could do it. She had her family, and Mandy's new baby to look forward to. It would have to be enough.

Forty-five

Finn watched Liz walk off, his heart sinking. He brushed away an incipient tear and looked at the two untouched plates sitting on the table. Neither of them had been hungry and, after what Liz had said, he hadn't felt like eating. What had he done? The sweetest, kindest, most attractive, and genuine woman he'd ever met, the one who he'd thought to spend the rest of his life with, had just left without a backward glance. He knew she was hurting too, but he accepted her decision, agreeing that the longer their relationship continued the greater the hurt would be… for both of them. Knowing this however, didn't make the parting any easier.

With a sigh he rose and began to make his way back to the office. But on the way, he decided to detour past the town hall in the hope that while he and Liz were talking, some miracle had happened. To his disappointment, the funding thermometer was still a fair way from the top.

'It's not looking good, but I haven't given up hope.' Finn turned at the sound of Joe's voice to see his friend, accompanied by his faithful dog. 'I always give Coco a walk around this time,' Joe said, 'It does me good to get out of the office for a bit and stretch my legs. You're looking very despondent.'

'I seems like I'm going to have to accept the television offer… if they really do make it,' Finn said. 'They approached me, but there's no guarantee.'

'Anyone would be lucky to have someone with your skills,' Joe said, 'but don't give up hope. We still have a few weeks till the end of the financial year. Have faith.'

'Easy to say. I can't afford to rely on the hope that the remaining money we need will suddenly appear. The timing couldn't be worse either, Joe. Adele seems to have slipped back into her blanket of grief with the anniversary of Tim's death.'

'Of course, that was yesterday. I'm sorry. But there's something else bothering you. Is everything okay with you and Liz?'

Finn cursed the fact his friend was so perceptive. He kicked the ground, making Coco give a quiet growl of displeasure. 'Sorry, Coco.' He sighed. 'You're right, Joe. Liz and I are finished. I can understand her reasoning. If I'm to be leaving Pelican Crossing, there can be no future for us. It was probably doomed from the start, but…'

'… it doesn't lessen the hurt. I understand.' He patted Finn on the shoulder.

Finn felt ashamed. Here he was seeking sympathy over the loss of a relationship which had only lasted a few months while Joe had lost his wife of over twenty years. 'Thanks, Joe. I should be getting back. I still have a paper to run.'

'Don't give up… on the paper or Liz. I have a good feeling about this, Finn.'

'Thanks.' Finn wished he had his friend's confidence. In his opinion, it was a foregone conclusion that Pelican Crossing would cease to have a newspaper on the thirtieth of June.

*

Liz hurried out of *Books and Coffee*, tears streaming down her cheeks. She couldn't go back to work like this. Taking out her phone, she did something she'd never done before. She texted the receptionist to say she'd been taken ill over lunch and made her way home.

Once inside her apartment, the familiar surroundings provided some comfort. She threw herself onto the bed and gave in to the paroxysm of grief she'd been holding back. She sobbed and sobbed till there were no tears left. She was lying gazing into space, wishing she hadn't been so hasty to end the relationship, while feeling justified that she had, when she was aroused by a knock at the door and a young voice calling, 'Gran, are you home?'

What was Tilly doing here?

'Won't be a minute,' she called, rising quickly and going into the ensuite to sluice her face with cold water before answering the door. She knew she still looked a mess, but she couldn't ignore Tilly.

'What are you doing here, sweetheart?' she asked when she opened the door.

'I popped into the medical centre to see you, and they said you were sick. I came round to see if I could do anything to help you.'

'Oh, you darling girl. I'm feeling much better now.'

Tilly gave her a strange look.

Liz put her hand up to her hair which was all mussed. 'I've been lying down,' she said by way of explanation. 'Come on in.'

Tilly bounced in and dropped her bag in the hallway. 'I can make you some warm milk with honey,' she said. 'It's what Mum makes me when I'm sick.'

'I don't…' Liz began, then stopped. The thought of a mug of warm milk and honey suddenly sounded very comforting. It was what her own mother used to make her when she was sick as a child. 'That would be lovely, Tilly.'

Liz followed Tilly into the kitchen, took a seat at the table and ran her fingers through her hair while Tilly began to heat the milk, chattering all the time about things that happened at school that day. She let the girl's words flow over her, barely paying attention, but at least it took her mind off what had happened at lunchtime.

Taking the mug of warm milk Tilly handed her, Liz took a sip, letting the sweet liquid soothe her. But nothing could take away the despair she felt, knowing she had thrown away her chance of love with a wonderful man.

*

When he arrived home, Finn was relieved to see Adele in the kitchen listening to Sandy read. As usual, Bluey was right there, under Sandy's chair, but for once he was lying still. 'Feeling better? he asked, when

Sandy had finished reading and jumped off his seat, Bluey following him out the door.

'A little.' Adele gave the semblance of a smile. 'I'm sorry I was short with you. You were right what you said about Tim. He'd want me to be there for Sandy. He's all I have left now Tim's gone, him and you, Dad.'

Finn cleared his throat. He wasn't going to make the same mistake with Adele as he had with Liz. No more secrets; she deserved to know score. 'There's something I need to tell you.'

'Ooh, sounds ominous. Why don't I make us a cup of tea and we can take it out into the yard and watch Sandy's antics with Bluey?'

Finn wasn't sure the atmosphere in the yard would be conducive to what he wanted to say, but tea sounded good, so he agreed.

'Right, what's up?' Adele asked, when they were settled in the wicker chairs outside with cups of the herbal tea she preferred.

'It's the newspaper… and the campaign.' Finn put down his cup and ran a hand through his hair. 'We may not reach our goal.'

Adele's eyes widened. 'But I thought it was going well.'

'It was. It is. But it may not be going well enough. It takes a lot of money to start a paper, then there are the salaries while we get it up to speed. Joe's still optimistic, but I have to be prepared for the worst.'

'What would the worst be?' Her eyes clouded.

'I'd need to look for another job, away from here. You and Sandy could come with me if you wanted,' he added quickly, seeing signs of her beginning to panic. 'I know you love it here, but…'

'It's where Tim and I lived together. I don't think I could bear to leave. I want Sandy to grow up here with the beach and the friends he's made at school. I have friends here too, friends Tim and I had.'

'I know, sweetheart.' Finn felt helpless, but how could he stay in Pelican Crossing without a job?

'Where would you go?'

'The regional television channel that approached me. They're based in Townsville.'

'Townsville? That's miles away.'

Finn nodded. It wasn't his ideal solution either. 'I've sent off my CV as a precaution. I hope it doesn't come to that, but…'

'Oh, Dad! It's been so good having you here. You've been such a support to me and Sandy. I don't know how I'd have got through the past year without you. But Townsville? I don't think so.'

Finn was stunned. He'd imagined Adele and Sandy would be happy to go with him to wherever he found work. It was true that apart from her wobble yesterday, she'd improved a lot from how she had been when he arrived in Pelican Crossing, but would she be able to manage without his support if he had to leave?

If the campaign failed and he was forced to accept another position was he not only to lose Liz, but to be separated from his family too?

Forty-six

It had been three weeks since Liz's lunch with Finn and she had cried herself to sleep every night. It didn't make any difference that it had been her decision, the hurt was as great as if it had been him who had ended their relationship. Sometimes, lying awake in the early hours, she wondered if she'd made a mistake, if she should have continued to enjoy his company… and their lovemaking. Then she would remember he was going to leave Pelican Crossing and knew she had made the right decision for her.

Today was the monthly lunch with her friends, and she wasn't looking forward to it. Until finishing with Finn, she had been anticipating their surprise and congratulations at the news of Mandy's pregnancy, but now all she could think of was how their eyes would fill with sympathy when they learned about Finn.

In an attempt to cheer herself up, Liz dressed in a bright pink dress patterned with orange she'd bought at a boutique called *Birds of a Feather* on a shopping expedition to Bellbird Bay. It was much more vibrant than anything else she owned, but she hadn't been able to resist it. She hoped it would divert her friends' attention from the bags under her eyes which even makeup failed to hide.

Today, they were meeting at Rachel's. Since she had no guests staying at the moment, she'd announced it was time she took her turn to play host. Liz was looking forward to telling Rachel about Mandy's pregnancy and their reconciliation, after having shared her problems with her youngest daughter to her earlier.

When Liz arrived, the others were already there and enjoying a glass of wine seated around the large, scrubbed wood table in Rachel's family sized kitchen, her small West Highland Terrier lying in her basket by the doorway.

'Here she is,' Poppy called, when Liz walked in. 'We thought you weren't coming.'

Liz wished she hadn't. She didn't know if she could face the comments which would no doubt ensue when they learned about Finn. It was only now, she regretted her own past actions in commenting, sometimes unkindly, on the misfortunes of others.

'Well, I'm here now,' Liz said, trying to sound upbeat as she accepted a welcome glass of wine from Rachel.

'We were just discussing the *Save the Courier* campaign,' Poppy said. 'With your connection with the newspaper, we were hoping you'd have news on how it's going.'

They all looked at her.

Liz wanted to disappear. She took a gulp of wine. 'Not as well as they'd hoped,' she said. 'Last I heard they were afraid they might not reach their target. But that was a few weeks ago.'

Rachel was the first to speak. 'I thought... you and Finn Hunter...'

'Not anymore, and I don't want to talk about it.' Liz had no intention of going into the details of why she'd decided to end what had been such a promising relationship with the most loving man she'd ever met, and how she regretted it every single day. She was glad no one asked for details, and Poppy immediately started talking about Amber's twins which were due soon.

As the conversation began to revolve around grandchildren, Liz started to relax. 'I have some news on that front,' she said during a gap in the conversation. 'Mandy's pregnant.'

As she'd expected, this prompted a flurry of congratulations and questions, some of which – like if Mandy and Gary were planning to marry – she couldn't answer. But it was pleasant to be the centre of attention for something positive. She hoped the news about her and Finn would soon be forgotten in the excitement of the announcement of the new birth.

Rachel produced lunch, a delicious potato and leek tart with salad, and the discussion turned to other matters. But as she was leaving, both Rachel and Poppy found a moment to whisper to Liz they were there for her if she wanted to talk.

As she drove home, Liz thought how lucky she was to have such good friends. She knew both Rachel and Poppy would listen to her woes without being judgemental, but right now, she had no wish to share her worries with anyone. All she wanted was to feel Finn's arms around her again, but she had only herself to blame. Maybe it would be easier once he'd left town.

*

There were only two weeks to go till the end of June, and Finn knew those of his staff who hadn't already found other positions were actively seeking them. The generous offer from the television company was sitting on his office desk at home, but he still hadn't accepted it, hoping against hope Joe was right. But things didn't look good. The donations had stalled, and the thermometer outside town hall was beginning to look tired. It hadn't moved for days.

It was now a month since Liz had broken up with him and apart from glimpses of her in the distance they'd had no contact. He couldn't believe how much he missed her, not only in bed. He missed her cheerful company, her sweet face, her ready smile. There was a gap in his life nothing else could fill. He'd been happy before they met, surely he could be again, but the ache of emptiness he now felt was almost unbearable. He tried to fill it by spending more time than before with Sandy, and managed to persuade the little boy to swim a few strokes in the ocean. Bluey's constant presence was a big help. Finn also tried to catch up on his reading, but found himself reading and rereading the same passage several times without taking anything in, the image of Liz inserting itself between his eyes and the page.

He was on his way to yet another lunch meeting with Joe, expecting the usual platitudes and false hope. There was no sign of his friend when he entered *The Grand*, so Finn ordered the usual two beers and sipped his while he waited. He had almost decided to send off his acceptance of the television position that afternoon. They wanted him to start in July which didn't give him much time to relocate.

Finn had almost finished his beer and was wondering whether to start on the second one, when Joe rushed in, a wide grin on his face. 'Good news,' he said, slapping Finn on the shoulder. 'We've done it! Forget the beer. We'll have a bottle of champagne,' he said to the barman.

Finn followed Joe across to a corner table in the busy bar. He was full of questions, but Joe didn't speak till both glasses were brimming with the sparking liquid.

'What's happened?' he asked.

'First,' Joe said, taking a gulp of champagne, 'your bosses at the consortium have changed their mind about selling us equipment. They're willing to sell the larger items like the web press and desks, but we'll still need to provide computers, photographic equipment and transport. I think they've realised it would be uneconomical to completely rip out everything in the building.'

'That's all very well, Joe, but we still need money for basic office supplies, staff salaries and rent. I can't imagine, even with your influence, the council would agree to let us have the building rent free.' Finn shook his head. Joe was getting excited about nothing.

'That's only one part of my news. The rest is we've not only met, but exceeded our target.'

Finn stared at his friend. How had that happened? When he passed the town hall only this morning, the thermometer still stood at less than the target amount.

'Hear me out,' Joe said, taking another drink.

This time, Finn followed his example, the bubbles making him sneeze.

'I had almost given up hope,' Joe said, 'when I received a call from the bank. There has been an anonymous donation of $100,000, enough, along with what we have already raised, to provide the starting capital for the new *Courier*. Of course, we can't call it that. Maybe we can have a competition to choose a name.'

Finn almost laughed aloud at Joe's excitement. But he was feeling pretty good himself. It was as if a huge weight had been lifted from his shoulders, and he could face the future with a much lighter heart than before. The first thing he was going to do was to email the regional television channel and regretfully decline their generous offer. No, the first thing would be to tell his remaining staff. This afternoon in the office, there would be a celebration to end all celebrations. Then there was Adele to tell – she'd be delighted he was staying in Pelican Crossing… and Liz…

At the thought of Liz, his heart turned over in excitement. Now he was going to stay, would Liz change her mind? Could they recapture those special moments they'd known or was it too late? Had he ruined everything by failing to tell her about his doubts and fears, by keeping them secret?

Forty-seven

Finn was still feeling euphoric when he arrived home, the cheers of his staff still ringing in his ears. They'd acted as if it had been all due to him, but he'd quickly reminded them it was Joe who'd orchestrated the entire campaign. Then they'd toasted Joe with the champagne Finn had bought on his way back from lunch. He'd included several bottles of the non-alcoholic variety for those who didn't drink and for himself. He'd had more than his usual quota at lunch, though, unlike Joe, he'd stopped at one glass of champagne after his beer.

'You're looking very pleased with yourself.' Adele turned from the stove where she was stirring a pot of what was to become a Bolognese sauce, the spaghetti boiling away nearby.

'I am. It's over, Adele. We can rest easy. The paper is safe.'

'Really?' Her eyes widened in surprise, then she grinned in delight. 'Oh, Dad, I'm so glad. So, no need for you to move. Sandy would have hated you to go. He loves his time with his Grandy.'

'I bought some champagne for us to have with dinner.' He held up a bottle, before placing another in the fridge. He planned to drop in on Liz with it later in the hope she might forgive him.

'Lovely. This is almost ready. Can you fetch Sandy? He's in the yard with Bluey.'

'No problem.' Finn went out to tell Sandy it was time for dinner and to ensure he washed his hands before the meal.

The dinner Adele had prepared was delicious, but Finn felt anything he ate tonight would taste good. He couldn't remember when he had last felt so full of the joys of life. It only needed Liz to forgive him for life to be perfect.

Dinner over, Finn was eager to get away. He'd confided in Adele, and she encouraged him to see Liz as soon as he could. But for Sandy, tonight was no different from any other, and he insisted on Finn reading to him as usual before he went to sleep. The story he'd chosen seemed to go on for ever, but Finn forgot all his impatience when, as Sandy's eyes were closing, the little boy said, 'Love you, Grandy.'

'I love you, too, champ,' Finn said, kissing his grandson on the forehead and tucking his covers more firmly around him.

'I'm off now.' Finn popped his head into the living room where Adele was settled in front of the television watching some romantic movie.

'I won't wait up,' Adele said with a grin, making Finn blush. 'I hope it goes well.'

'So do I,' Finn said to himself. Although he had just eaten, he had an empty feeling in the pit of his stomach. He was as nervous as a teenager on his first date. He had no idea of the reception he might get.

The drive across town was over too soon. Finn lifted the bottle of champagne from the passenger seat and walked up to the apartment building, his heart in his mouth. Stopping outside Liz's door, he took a deep breath and knocked.

*

Liz had had a busy day. The medical centre had been flat out with people arriving for flu vaccinations, as well as the usual run of regular patients. It had been so hectic, Liz had been called upon to provide reception duties and to assist in taking details of those there for vaccinations. Then, when she got home, Tilly was waiting for her to ask for help in talking Julie into letting her have a party for her birthday next month. By the time she'd managed to sit down to eat, her appetite had gone. Instead of the chicken casserole she'd planned, she ended up toasting a couple of slices of bread and topping them with tinned tuna.

She had just poured herself a well-deserved glass of wine and was surfing channels to decide what to watch when there was a knock at the door.

Silently cursing whoever had decided to disturb her during the first time she'd had to herself all day, she went to the door. On the way, she glanced in the hallway mirror and grimaced at her reflection. She hadn't had time to pull a comb through her hair since morning and her makeup had worn off. Whoever was at the door would have to take her as she was. It would serve them right for disturbing her.

She opened the door and stared at the man standing there. She hadn't expected to see Finn Hunter again, and certainly not at her door at this time on a Friday night.

For a moment neither of them spoke.

'I've come to apologise. I have some good news.' He held up a bottle of champagne.

Champagne? What was he thinking? Liz heard footsteps. 'You'd better come in,' she said. She didn't want her neighbours to be privy to whatever he had to say.

Once inside, Finn stood awkwardly in the hallway.

Liz shivered. She couldn't help remembering the previous times he'd been there, times when he'd taken her into his arms and carried her off to bed. Why was he here now? And why the champagne? Had he come to tell her he was finally leaving Pelican Crossing? Did he think it was a cause for celebration? She had no intention of drinking to his future, to a future which didn't include her.

'I…' he said, hesitatingly. 'I got good news today. It's over, Liz. The paper is safe. I won't be leaving.'

Liz felt her world turn upside down. Finn hadn't come to tell her he was leaving; against all odds he and Joe had managed to save the paper.

'Are you all right?'

She heard his voice as if it was coming from the end of a long tunnel.

'Liz, are you all right?' he asked again.

'Yes, thanks.' Her legs felt weak. 'I just need to sit down.'

Finn helped her into the living room and onto the sofa. He took a seat opposite. It was as if they were strangers instead of two people who had enjoyed so many intimate moments together.

'So you reached your target,' Liz said when she felt able to speak again, annoyed with her weakness, annoyed, too, at her dishevelled appearance. She was at a distinct disadvantage. Finn looked as attractive as ever. It would be so easy to throw herself into his arms, to forget how he'd tried to mislead her.

'We did. An anonymous donor, Joe said. I thought… I hoped… we could let bygones be bygones and go back to where we were before…' He seemed to recognise the expression in her eyes, the indication he and Liz were not on the same page. 'I know I stuffed up,' he said, 'but it was for the best of reasons. I didn't want to end what we had. It's been hell for me these past weeks, Liz, catching glimpses of you in the distance, wanting to speak to you, to hold you, but knowing what you'd said. Is it too late for us, Liz? Please say it's not.'

'I can't do that, Finn, not easily. It's been hard for me too, but I've tried to accept we can't have a relationship. Now you turn up at my door with a bottle of champagne…' she glanced at the offering with disgust, '… telling me everything's changed and expect me to say all is forgiven and fall into your arms.'

She saw from his expression it was exactly what he had thought… or hoped.

'I'm sorry, Finn. I can't do it.'

Finn looked crushed, the lips she loved so much tightening into a thin line as if stifling a strong emotion. 'Will you at least think about it?' he asked.

Speechless, Liz nodded.

Finn rose and left, the front door slamming behind him.

Liz sat there, staring into space. What had she done? Had she just thrown away her last chance at love for the second time?

Forty-eight

When Liz walked into the living room next morning, the bottle of champagne was still there, sitting on the coffee table where Finn had placed it, a stark reminder of the previous evening. She was glad it was Saturday, and she didn't need to go to work today. She didn't think she could have faced everyone, put a smile on her face and acted as if nothing had happened. She'd lain awake most of the night alternately castigating herself for being a fool and congratulating herself on maintaining her position.

Her phone pinged with a text, reminding her of her promise to go baby shopping with Mandy. It was something she'd longed for, but today it was the last thing she felt like doing. She forced herself to drink a cup of coffee and took two bites of toast, before throwing the rest in the bin. Then, dressing in a pair of her favourite black pants and a pink and white shirt, and shrugging on a black jacket patterned with bright pink flamingos – another purchase from the boutique, *Birds of a Feather*, in Bellbird Bay, she set off.

Luckily for Liz, Mandy didn't notice her mother's sombre mood, her exuberance making up for both of them as they drove across town to *Purdies* where Mandy was determined to buy as much as she could for her baby.

As they moved around the store, Liz found her mood rise as Mandy's excitement grew.

'I never thought I'd be so excited to be pregnant, Mum,' she said, when they stopped for lunch. 'And I haven't even had any morning sickness… not yet anyway. We've decided we like the names Lisa for a girl and Jesse for a boy. What do you think?'

'Lisa… is that…' Liz's eyes moistened.

'Sort of after you, and Jesse would be a nod to Gary's dad, Jamie. I thought you'd be pleased.'

'Oh, my darling. How lovely of you.' Liz gave Mandy a hug. To think that only a few weeks ago, she'd almost given up hope of Mandy speaking to her again, and now here they were. 'What do you want to do after lunch?'

'I think I'm ready to go home. We should be able to get most of the smaller things in the car and they'll send the rest. Gary will have fun putting the cot and change table together.' She laughed.

Liz would be pleased to go home too. They'd had a busy morning, but at least it had taken her mind off Finn and the previous evening. She'd dumped the champagne in the bin, not wanting to be reminded of it every time she opened the fridge.

Back home, having helped Mandy carry the packages of toys and small baby garments into their apartment and hugged her goodbye, Liz found herself at a loose end, unable to settle to anything. Taking her hat off the peg by the door, she went out of the apartment and made her way down to the marina, intending to go for a walk along the beach.

She was about to step onto the sand when she heard her name being called. Looking round, she saw Rachel with her two granddaughters.

'Hello, Rach,' she said. 'Looks like you're doing grandma duty today.'

'It won't be long before you are too. I'm just about to hand these two back to Jess. Here she is now,' she said, as a tall blonde woman came hurrying along the path.

'Thanks, Mum,' she said. 'Sorry I'm late. Can't stop.' She hugged Rachel, clasped the two girls by their hands and rushed off in the direction of the car park, leaving Liz and Rachel staring after her.

'They have their dance class this afternoon,' Rachel said, 'and Jess is always running late. Are you busy or have you time for a coffee? After spending a few hours with the two terrors, I need one.'

Liz suddenly realised coffee and the chance to chat with Rachel was exactly what she needed.

A few minutes later, they were seated in *The Blue Dolphin Café* with steaming cups of cappuccino and a plate of ginger scones with jam and cream which Rachel had insisted on ordering, despite Liz's protests.

The coffee was good, and when, to be polite, Liz accepted one of the scones, she discovered she was hungry after all. She hadn't had any breakfast and had only picked at the salad she'd ordered with Mandy.

'Now, what's up?' Rachel asked. 'And don't say "Nothing". I can tell when you're upset.'

Liz picked up her spoon and stirred her coffee, reluctant to say anything. But this was Rachel, who she'd confided in before. She knew anything she told her would go no further. 'Finn came round last night,' she said.

'What did he want?'

'He wanted to tell me the paper has been saved. He won't be leaving. He even brought champagne, thinking I'd welcome him with open arms.'

'I'm guessing you didn't?'

'How could I, Rach… after what he did?'

Rachel looked at Liz intently. 'What did he actually do, Liz? He tried to protect you from the fact he *might* be leaving town. That seems to me like a kind thing to do.'

'He kept me in the dark, Rach, treated me as if I was a fool.'

'And now you're punishing him for his mistake… and punishing yourself too, I suspect.' She raised one eyebrow.

'I don't see it that way.'

'Forgive me for saying this, but you're acting a tad like your daughter. I can see where Mandy gets her pig-headedness.'

'I'm nothing like Mandy.' But was she? Joan had often told Liz how like her Mandy was… and it wasn't in looks, as both Tara and she took after their father. 'Anyway, I gave him short shrift.'

'You didn't give the poor man a chance?'

'He caught me unawares. I've been trying to put him out of my mind, to forget what we had together, then he suddenly appeared out of the blue with the news he wasn't leaving after all. What was I supposed to do?'

'Maybe listen to him, give him another chance?' Rachel's voice was gentle, but Liz could hear the disapproval in her tone.

'I did say I'd think about it.' Liz knew she must sound difficult. Maybe she *was* like Mandy.

'And have you?'

'I've thought of nothing else… except when I was helping Mandy choose baby things this morning. She didn't allow me a moment to think about anything apart from the baby. If it's a girl they plan to call her Lisa,' Liz said, hoping to divert Rachel's attention.

'That's lovely, Liz, but it doesn't change the fact you may have made a huge mistake. Grandchildren are wonderful. I love mine to bits. And I know how much you enjoy Tilly and are looking forward to the new baby. But they're no substitute for the companionship of a good man, and, to put it bluntly, they won't keep you warm in bed at night.'

Liz stared at her friend, her eyes wide with disbelief. She'd never heard her speak like this before.

But Rachel hadn't finished. 'I know for a time there, our lunch group were all single, though I always suspected that, even without Mandy's interference, you had a secret yearning to meet someone. Then Poppy surprised us all by getting together with Cam. Seeing them so happy must have reignited your desire to find love too. I know I felt a twinge of envy seeing them together. You met Finn, and everything seemed perfect – at least from where I stood. Then it was over, and you didn't want to talk about it, but were obviously miserable. Now he's giving you another chance and you're throwing it back in his face. Men are just as vulnerable as we are. It must have taken a lot of courage to come round to see you like he did. How do you think he is feeling today?'

Liz flinched. She hadn't given any thought to Finn's feelings. She'd been too caught up in her own. Rachel was right. She was being selfish. But it didn't change things… or did it?

*

Finn hadn't slept. He'd tossed and turned as he remembered the reception he'd received from Liz. He hadn't exactly expected her to fall into his arms – although it would have been wonderful if she had – but he had at least hoped for a conversation. Instead, she'd sounded almost bitter. True, he'd caught her unawares, but she'd looked as lovely as ever, her slightly mussed appearance setting him on fire with longing. Now what was he to do? She'd agreed to think about things, but he had the impression she'd only agreed to get him to leave.

'I heard you come in last night. It was still early. What happened with Liz?' Adele asked when he walked into the kitchen.

Finn could see Sandy and Bluey outside in the yard. They must already have had their breakfasts. 'Don't ask,' he said, filling a mug with coffee and taking a long gulp.

'Breakfast? I made scrambled eggs for Sandy and me. I can make more.'

'Thanks, Adele, but I'm not hungry. I'll make a slice of toast and vegemite. I think I'll go into the office this morning. There's a lot to organise now we know we can continue to run a newspaper. I need to talk with Joe about what we need to order, and figure out how the finances will work. We won't be able to start right away but hopefully there won't be too lengthy a delay.' If his relationship with Liz was dead, he'd plough his energy into the new paper.

'I'm guessing it didn't go well with Liz last night, huh? You sound grumpy this morning.'

'Grumpy? Me? Never.' Finn gave a wry grin. He knew he should be on top of the world today, but getting the cold shoulder from Liz last night had sapped all his energy, leaving him filled with regret. The enthusiasm he'd felt at Joe's announcement had disappeared, to be replaced by an empty sensation.

'Hmm. Will you be back for lunch?'

'I doubt it. Don't worry about me. I'll get something in town.'

'Well, try to come back in a better mood. I know you must be disappointed about Liz, but it's not the end of the world. I bet she comes round when she's had time to think things through. You do sometimes go at things like a bull at a gate. We women need time to mull things over.'

'Hmm.' Finn drained his coffee, and taking a bite of toast, stuck the rest in his mouth and made his way to his car.

*

Finn decided to swing by the mayor's office first, pretty sure he'd find Joe there. He was right. His friend was at his desk, Coco lying at his feet. The dog rose when Finn walked in, but after sniffing Finn's feet, returned to her spot under Joe's chair.

'Welcome,' Joe said. 'I was hoping to catch up with you today. We have a lot to do if we're to be ready by July first.'

'You're not wrong, but July first? That's a bit of a stretch. I was thinking more like August or September.'

'Mmm.' Joe rubbed his chin. 'You could be right. You'd be in a better position than me to judge. But we need to be prepared, let the town know *The Courier* – or its replacement – will be in their mailboxes before too long. Tell me what needs to be done.'

Finn scratched his head. 'I was about to go into the office to do exactly that today. I need to check what pieces of equipment the consortium intend to remove, then make a list and budget for what we're going to need to purchase. It may take some time to have everything delivered, then we need to set up the equipment, hire staff to replace those who've already left, and…' He dragged a hand through his hair. This wasn't going to be easy, but it could be fun. At least it might take his mind off Liz Phillips.

Forty-nine

Since speaking with Rachel, Liz hadn't been able to get her friend's words out of her head. She flinched every time she remembered her saying how like Mandy she was, with her stubborn refusal to change her mind about Finn. Her comments about grandchildren had shocked her too. She'd never imagined Rachel felt that way. She always seemed so content with her life. It just showed, Liz thought, how you never really knew anyone, not even your closest friends.

But she had to admit Rachel was right about one thing. No matter how many grandchildren she had, they couldn't take the place of Finn in her bed. She shuddered at the memory of his arms around her, their lips meeting, their… She gave herself a shake. She'd made her decision. So, why did it seem so hard, as if she was punishing herself. Today was Sunday, an entire day to reflect on how she'd spoken to Finn. She needed something to take her mind off him. She picked up her phone.

Fifteen minutes later, she threw her phone down in disgust. All three of her children had made plans for the day, plans which didn't include her. To be fair, Julie had offered to cancel the trip she and Tilly had arranged with a friend from school and her mother, but Liz couldn't allow her to do that. So she was stuck with her own company, and her own thoughts, none of which were very edifying.

Deciding on her usual form of solace, Liz set off for the beach. But today, the feeling of sand between her toes and the sound of the waves didn't have their customary comforting effect. It was almost a relief when she saw Agnes coming towards her with her dog.

'Hello, Liz. On your own today? Where's that lovely granddaughter of yours?'

'Busy. They're all busy, Agnes.' Liz couldn't keep the note of bitterness out of her voice.

The two women had stopped to talk, the dog continuing to play in the water. There was no one else in sight.

Agnes peered at Liz from under the brim of her floppy straw hat. 'You sound as if you need to talk to someone.'

'No, I...' How could she confide in Agnes? But the old woman had been around for a long time. She was known for her wisdom. She might take care of pelicans these days, but she hadn't always done that. Liz seemed to recall hearing she'd once been a social worker and it was a small step from caring for people to caring for animals. 'How long have you got?' she asked.

'All the time in the world. My birds won't miss me till a lot later. Lady and I are at your disposal.' She peered at Liz again. 'Why don't we find somewhere to sit?'

Liz followed Agnes to one of the benches the council had provided on the edge of the beach, where, much to her surprise, she poured out her troubles to the old woman, finishing with, 'I don't know what to do,' as her eyes filled with tears.

'Oh, I think you do, my dear. You love this man?'

Liz nodded, brushing away the tears and feeling slightly foolish for breaking down like this.

'Then it seems to me you have nothing to lose but your pride. And your friend is right, pride won't keep you warm at night. I may not have married and had a family, but it doesn't mean I didn't have chances. To my shame, I put other things before my own happiness. I'd hate to see you make the same mistake.'

It was Liz's turn to peer at Agnes, to try to picture the young, attractive woman she'd once been. Then what the old woman had said struck her. She was right. It was pride that was keeping her from accepting Finn's olive branch, for refusing to acknowledge she'd been wrong.

'Thank you, Agnes.' Liz threw her arms around the old woman and hugged her.

'Now, now, no need for that,' Agnes said but she was smiling. 'I only told you what you already knew. There's not a relationship in the world that doesn't begin with a few bumps on the road. Finn's a good man. I saw that in him when I had my little accident. Don't let pride get in the way of true love. Now, off you go and talk to your young man before *he* changes his mind.' Then, calling to her dog, Agnes walked away.

Left to herself, Liz thought about what Agnes had said. Could it be so simple? *Pride*, thought Liz. Is that what it was? Could she pocket her pride and apologise to Finn? She tried to put herself in his place, thinking how worried he must have been for his livelihood and an uncertain future.

What if Agnes was right and the opportunity to make amends was lost?

Turning, Liz made her way back along the beach, oblivious to the beauty of the ocean which normally drew her attention.

When she arrived home, her stomach was churning at the prospect of facing Finn again. She threw off the jeans and tee-shirt she'd worn to the beach and stepped into the shower. As the water cascaded over her, Liz remembered Finn's last words to her and hers to him. She'd promised to think about it. Maybe he'd be glad to see her, but what if he wasn't? What if he'd had second thoughts? She couldn't blame him after the way she'd treated him.

Dressing in a pair of smart jeans and a floral shirt, Liz took particular care with her makeup and managed to tame her hair into a neat style. Before leaving the apartment, she did one last thing. She took the bottle of champagne out of the bin and placed it in the fridge. Then, her heart thumping madly, her legs weak, she headed for her car.

All the way to the house where Finn lived with his daughter, Liz practiced what she was going to say. She hoped Adele and Sandy were out and she could catch Finn by himself. Both his daughter and grandson had been kind to her, but she had no desire to make them privy to her asking for forgiveness, or, horror of horrors, to witness Finn rejecting her.

At last she was there. As she got out of the car, she could hear the sound of children's voices coming from the yard. Her heart dropped – no chance of catching Finn on his own. It sounded as if there was a party going on. She almost got back in the car and drove off. But she didn't. Taking a deep breath, her heart in her mouth, Liz made her way to the door and knocked.

'Liz!' Adele's eyes widened when she opened the door, Sandy's small dog behind her. 'Bluey, stay!' she said firmly. 'Sorry, Sandy has a few friends round. It's like a circus here today. Are you looking for Finn?'

'Ye…es.'

'I'm sorry, he's not here.'

Liz's heart sank.

'He's spent the weekend at the newspaper office getting everything arranged for the changeover. You can catch him there.'

'Oh, I don't think…' Liz didn't want to disturb Finn if he was busy at work.

'No, do. He'll be pleased to see you, and I'm sure he needs a break. Sorry, I need to get back,' she said, as the sound of children's voices grew louder in the background. 'I look forward to seeing you again soon.'

Liz made her way back to the car, puzzling over Adele's last comment. Was she only being polite, or did she know something about Finn's feelings? There was only one way to find out. Sliding into the driver's seat, she turned on the engine and drove to the newspaper office.

This part of town was deserted on a Sunday afternoon, and Liz felt very noticeable as she parked and got out of the car. Peering through the window of the *Courier* building, there was no one to be seen, and Liz wondered if Adele had been mistaken or if Finn had already left. Her heart in her mouth she knocked on the glass door. At first there was no response, then she saw a tall figure coming towards her.

Finn opened the door, and they stood gazing at each other.

Liz's heart sank; she began to shake. Maybe this had been a mistake. Then he smiled and said, 'You'd better come in.'

Liz followed him through the large room filled with desks and computers to a small glass-walled office at the back of the room. The desk held a large computer and was covered with papers and files. The floor was almost completely hidden by boxes.

'Excuse the mess,' Finn said, dragging a hand through his hair. 'Take a seat.' He cleared a bundle of files off a chair and perched on the edge of the desk. 'I didn't expect to see you here today.'

He looked so attractive, his glasses perched on top of his head, his blue chambray shirt sleeves rolled up to the elbows showing his sinewy arms, his jeans stretched tightly across his thighs, that for a moment Liz was lost for words. 'Adele told me you were here,' she said.

'Ah!' He waited.

Liz knew it was up to her to explain herself. She took yet another deep breath. 'I'm sorry,' she said. 'I let my pride get in the way. Oh, Finn, I've missed you so much, I was a fool. I should have accepted your explanation when you told me you only wanted to keep what we had together for as long as you could. Can you forgive me?'

Without a moment's hesitation, Finn slid off the desk. He pulled Liz up from the chair and into his arms. When their lips met, it was as if she'd come home.

'When they finally disentangled, Liz said, 'I have that bottle of champagne in my fridge.'

'I thought you might have thrown it out.'

'I did, but I retrieved it before I left, when I decided to speak with you, to beg your forgiveness.'

Finn chuckled. 'What are we waiting for?'

'Don't you have work to do?'

'It'll keep.'

Once outside, Finn said, 'We can take your car. You can drop me off in the morning.'

Lizz gazed at him in surprise. He'd never stayed overnight before.

'This time, I don't intend to allow you to have second thoughts, and I can't wait to wake up next to you.'

Liz couldn't keep the grin off her face. Everything was going to be all right.

Fifty

The next two weeks passed in a flash and suddenly it seemed, it was July first, and *The Crossing Courier* was no more. First thing in the morning, a fleet of vans arrived to remove everything which belonged to the consortium, apart from the larger items they'd agreed Joe and Finn could purchase.

Liz and Tilly arrived as the vans were leaving and just as a couple of workmen were removing the sign. It was a teacher-free day for Tilly, and she'd begged to come along. Liz didn't have the heart to refuse and had picked her up on the way.

It was sad to see the newspaper they all loved disappearing, and there was quite a gathering of community members in the street outside. But despite the sadness, there was an air of excitement when another van appeared, and the new sign was unloaded.

It had been Tilly's idea, one afternoon when she had met Liz with Finn on the beach. They had been discussing Tilly's birthday, and the girl expressed her desire to get an Amazon Echo Pop from Liz. When Liz said she'd never heard of it, Tilly started to explain how she'd use the smart speaker to play music and listen to audiobooks in her bedroom. Then she had stopped in her tracks and said, 'That's what you should call the newspaper.' And *The Crossing Echo* was born.

'Glad you could make it,' Finn came out to greet them, and welcome Liz with a hug and a kiss, despite the fact it wasn't long since he'd left her, after they'd enjoyed breakfast together. 'Come on in. We're about to start.'

Inside the almost empty building were gathered the staff of the old *Courier*, along with Joe and various local dignitaries, council members and local business proprietors, all there to farewell the old paper and celebrate the new one.

'To *The Crossing Echo*,' Joe said, holding up a glass of champagne, after waiters from *Crossings*, provided by Poppy, mingled with the crowd offering glasses to everyone.

'To *The Crossing Echo*,' everyone yelled, then they broke into a loud cheer. Someone began to sing *For he's a jolly good fellow*, and everyone joined in, to Joe's obvious embarrassment.

'And thanks to young Tilly for our new name,' Finn said, gesturing to where she was standing.

Everyone turned to look at Tilly, and it was her turn to blush.

When they were all enjoying the magnificent spread Poppy and her staff had provided, Tilly whispered to Liz, 'I'm so glad Mum and I came to Pelican Crossing, Gran. Life here is so much more exciting. I have a new family and I got to name the new newspaper.'

Liz hugged her granddaughter, a warm glow engulfing her. She was glad Julie and Tilly had moved here too. Their arrival had changed her life. Then she looked across the room to where Finn was standing beside Joe. Their eyes met. Finn Hunter had changed her life too, in so many ways. Her thoughts went to the previous night.

'I love you, Liz Phillips. I never imagined I'd find someone like you, never dreamt coming to Pelican Crossing would be such a new beginning for me,' Finn said, as they were lying in bed, her head on his chest, their legs entwined, having made beautiful love.

'I love you too,' Liz said. 'You have made my life complete. No more secrets.'

'No more secrets,' he agreed, before pulling her back into his arms and kissing her.

The End

If you've enjoyed Liz and Finn's story, a way you can say thank you to me is to leave a review on Amazon and/or Goodreads. A few words will suffice, no need for a lengthy review. It will mean a lot to me and help other readers find my books.

I've been thrilled with the reaction of readers and reviewers to the first book in this series, The Restaurant in Pelican Crossing. It's always a challenge to start a new series and I'm delighted readers have taken Pelican Crossing and its characters to their hearts.

The third book in the series, *A New Dawn in Pelican Crossing* is Gill's story.

A perfect romance to make your heart soar with hope and happiness.

Divorce lawyer *Gill Dickson* thinks she has seen it all, until she finds herself in the midst of her own acrimonious divorce and estranged from her daughter. Her one certainty is that the last thing she wants in her life is another man.

Pelican Crossing mayor *Joe Harris* has buried himself in his work after his wife's death, finding solace with the companionship of his faithful dog, Coco. But when Joe needs Gill's legal expertise for a family matter, he is unexpectedly drawn to her.

Can Joe break through Gill's emotional barriers and earn her trust? And can these two lonely souls find the happiness they deserve in each other?

Set in the small Queensland coastal town of Pelican Crossing, this heartwarming romance will keep you captivated until the very end.

You can order it here: https://mybook.to/NewDawninPC

From the Author

Dear Reader,

First, I'd like to thank you for choosing to read *Secrets in Pelican Crossing.* I hope you've enjoyed visiting Pelican Crossing as much as I've enjoyed creating it.

I'm really enjoying starting this new series in another fictional town in Queensland and populating it with characters who I hope you will come to love. As book one in my new series, I'm hoping you will fall in love with the characters as much as you did with those in Bellbird Bay. Like all my other books, although it is part of a series, it can be read as a standalone.

If you'd like to stay up to date with my new releases and special offers you can sign up to my reader's group.

You can sign up here

https://subscribe.maggiechristensenauthor.com/readersgroup

I'll never share your email address, and you can unsubscribe at any time. You can also contact me via Facebook, Twitter or by email. I love hearing from my readers and will always reply.

Thanks again.

MaggieC

Acknowledgements

As always, this book could not have been written without the help and advice of a number of people.

Firstly, my husband Jim for listening to my plotlines without complaint, for his patience and insights as I discuss my characters and storyline with him, for his patience and help with difficult passages and advice on my male dialogue, and for being there when I need him.

John Hudspith, editor extraordinaire for his ideas, suggestions, encouragement and attention to detail, and for helping me make this book better.

Jane Dixon-Smith for her patience and for working her magic on my beautiful cover and interior.

My thanks also to early readers of this book – Helen, Maggie and Louise for their helpful comments and advice. I'm also indebted to Karina from The Benevolent Society and Tiffany from The Queensland Department of Child Safety for their assistance in ensuring I had my facts straight regarding adoptions.

And to all of my readers, reviewers and bloggers. Your support and comments make it all worthwhile.

About the Author

After a career in education, Maggie Christensen began writing contemporary women's fiction portraying mature women facing life-changing situations, and historical fiction set in her native Scotland. Her travels inspire her writing, be it her trips to visit family in Scotland, in Oregon, USA or her home on Queensland's beautiful Sunshine Coast. Maggie writes of mature heroines coming to terms with changes in their lives and the heroes worthy of them. Maggie has been called *the queen of mature age fiction* and her writing has been described by one reviewer as *like a nice warm cup of tea. It is warm, nourishing, comforting and embracing.*

From the small town in Scotland where she grew up, Maggie was lured to Australia by the call to 'Come and teach in the sun'. Once there, she worked as a primary school teacher, university lecturer and in educational management. Now living with her husband of over thirty years on Queensland's Sunshine Coast, she loves walking on the deserted beach in the early mornings and having coffee by the river on weekends. Her days are spent surrounded by books, either reading or writing them – her idea of heaven!

Maggie can be found on Facebook, Twitter, Goodreads, Instagram, Bookbub or on her website.

https://www.facebook.com/maggiechristensenauthor
https://twitter.com/MaggieChriste33
https://www.goodreads.com/author/show/8120020.Maggie_Christensen
https://www.instagram.com/maggiechriste33/
https://www.bookbub.com/profile/maggie-christensen
https://maggiechristensenauthor.com/

www.ingramcontent.com/pod-product-compliance
Lightning Source LLC
Chambersburg PA
CBHW020006140726
47904CB00018B/1927